Tatting and Mandolinata

More Handheld Classics

Tatting and Mandolinata

A Novel and Fourteen Short Stories

By *Faith Compton Mackenzie*

With an introduction by Kate Macdonald

Handheld Classic 39

This edition published in 2024 by Handheld Press
16 Peachfield Road, Malvern WR14 4AP, United Kingdom.
www.handheldpress.co.uk

ISBN 978-1-912766-84-0

1 2 3 4 5 6 7 8 9 0

Series design by Nadja Robinson and typeset in Adobe Caslon Pro and Open Sans.

Printed and bound in Great Britain by Short Run Press, Exeter.

Contents

Acknowledgements

Many thanks to Lisa Dowdeswell of the Society of Authors for her help in clarifying the administration of Faith Compton Mackenzie's estate. Thanks also to Hilary Ely who gave expert research assistance with the *Times Literary Supplement* archives, and to Nic Bottomley who gave sensible advice about the book cover.

Note on this edition

The text for this edition was scanned from the first editions of 1931 and 1957 and proofread. Typographical errors have been silently corrected, and some spellings have been modernised. Some words from the stories in *Mandolinata*, routinely used in the 1920s and 1930s that are now offensive to modern readers, have been removed where their excision would not affect the meaning or effect of the text.

Kate Macdonald is a literary historian and a publisher. She has written previous introductions for Handheld Press, which she runs, for *My Life and I* (2023) by Betty Bendell, *The Gap in the Curtain* (1932) by John Buchan, *The Runagates Club* (1928) by John Buchan, *The Voluble Topsy, 1927–1947* by A P Herbert, *Personal Pleasures* (1935) by Rose Macaulay, *Business as Usual* (1933) by Jane Oliver and Ann Stafford and (with Luke Seaber) *England is My Village* by John Llewelyn Rhys.

Introduction

BY KATE MACDONALD

Faith eclipsed

Faith Compton Mackenzie has not been well-served by biographers. The outline below has been assembled from her memoirs, from advertisements, from her husband Compton Mackenzie's exhaustive accounts of his life and from Andro Linklater's 1987 biography *Compton Mackenzie. A Life*, which did not mention Faith's two novels. For most of her life Faith was not known as a novelist. As Mrs Compton Mackenzie, later Lady Mackenzie, she gained public attention from 1931 for her biographies, for a limited edition of her short stories and for her three memoirs. Her two novels, written in her late seventies, did not receive much critical acclaim. Any surviving copies of *Tatting* might be languishing unrecognised on the handicraft shelves in second-hand bookshops rather than in Fiction, since tatting is a craft like lacemaking.

Another strong reason for Faith's eclipse as a writer was her husband. Sir Edward Montague Compton Mackenzie was one of the most prolific British writers of the twentieth century. He published over one hundred books, including over forty novels, copious volumes of history and a colossal ten-volume or 'octave' work of memoir. He embraced the media age enthusiastically, finding the television as receptive to his performing skills as was the stage. Mackenzie wrote on an epic scale and kept vast amounts of the paperwork of his life. His biographer notes with stunned horror that the Harry Ransom Center at the University of Texas at Austin, which houses the Mackenzie papers, holds what 'appears to be the entire contents of his postbag from about the age of thirty onwards, together with copies of many of his own letters, typescripts of novels, tax returns, visiting cards, bills and press notices. There are also some of his mother's and first wife's personal papers, among them the latter's diary covering the entire period of their marriage'. Linklater estimates that reading every word of this immense hoard during the Center's opening hours would take at least two years (Linklater xiii).

The presence of Faith's diaries among her husband's papers explains in practical terms why her memory has largely disappeared beneath the volume of Compton Mackenzie's paper remains. She also left no will. She may have assumed that making a will was not necessary: Monty would take care of her estate, such as it was. She may never have considered that she had a *literary* estate. Her confidence in her status as a writer may not have been high, as her eleven books – certainly an achievement – may have looked insignificant when measured against the mountain of volumes that her husband produced.

After her death Faith's diaries were no longer accessible to anyone who might have wanted to write her biography. (Her husband's memoirs do not mention that anyone had asked.) Faith's papers went to Texas as if by right, as if they had no separate existence from him, or that there was any need for such material to remain in Britain. Even the family of Faith's youngest brother, to whom she was always close, had no knowledge of where her papers might be. The administrators of the Sir Compton Mackenzie estate had no instructions or information about Faith's literary estate, although after consultation they agreed that they should take her works into their care. Thus are the records of women writers eclipsed.

Faith and Monty

Faith Nona Stone was born in 1878 at Eton in Berkshire, the ninth in a family of ten children. Her parents were the Reverend Edward Stone, an Eton Classics master and later the headmaster of Stonehouse School in Kent, and his wife Elizabeth 'Lily' Vidal. While her five elder sisters all married into the Church or entered religious communities, Faith chose a diametrically opposite path. She began acting professionally from 1901 under the stage name of Faith Reynolds, becoming successful enough to make frequent tours in the USA.

Her younger brother Christopher Stone, later to become a pioneer in promoting recorded music on radio and the first BBC DJ, had become friends with another Oxford undergraduate, the dazzling and polymathic Edward Montague Compton Mackenzie. Monty was the eldest son of the distinguished English actor-manager of the same name, and the only one of his five children to not make his career on the stage. Christopher and Monty later rented Lady Ham together, a country house outside Burford in Oxfordshire. Faith, Christopher's favourite sister, was a frequent visitor there and to Christopher's London flat, where she and Monty fell in love. In November 1905 she and Monty were married in secret at a Pimlico church. One of the witnesses was a street sweeper who had been brought in by the verger in the absence of anyone more suitable being provided by the preoccupied bride and groom (FCM Dare 179).

> In choosing the stage I had unconsciously laid a pretty good foundation for the peculiar structure of my future life. I was proof against surprises. I knew from the first that I didn't want a nice conventional marriage, and I was justifiably sure that I had avoided this. (FCM Dare 188).

Faith was five years older than Monty, and Monty was a dynamic and authoritative young man, accustomed to having his own way in all things. At the time of their marriage he was reading for the Bar, and was already an accomplished actor, and a playwright and a poet as well. Faith's engagement ring (designed by Monty) arrived from the jeweller the day after the wedding, and they kept the marriage secret for ten days, until their parents had been told. Predictably, none were pleased, though were soon reconciled.

Faith's future life was spent entirely in Monty's wake. His enthusiasms, and what she called his 'earthquake tendency' (FCM

Dare 5) decided where she would live and how she would spend her time. She was quite aware of the sometimes devastating effects of his energetic support for a cause or a neglected object, but for her the results were worth it.

> How many corpses or sickly infants has Monty revived with his life-giving enthusiasm, and abandoned as soon as they could stand alone! It is the creative instinct, and the most unhappy manifestations of this aspect of his genius are the gardens he has made and deserted, mostly island gardens swept by storms, pestered by rabbits, coming to life almost by a series of miracles, growing to beauty and richness under his watchful and affectionate eye. They grow; they are achieved. Then he leaves them without a backward glance. He has created something, and moves on …
>
> I was prepared for almost any possibility in my marriage; neglect, abandonment, even divorce. With such a torch beside me, how could I guess which way its flame would sweep? (FCM Dare, 197)

Two years after their marriage Faith and Monty moved to Cornwall, initially to stay with Monty's friend the Reverend Sandys Wason, because Monty had decided that he wanted to explore his inclination for ordination more seriously and wanted to train as a lay preacher. In early 1908 he was licensed as a lay preacher in the Anglican Church, becoming locally famous for his enthralling sermons. He became a popular Sunday School teacher as well, since he was always a showman. Faith, on the other hand, was without occupation, since her entire focus was on her husband, now concerned with his own projects.

Faith provided Monty with 'the elegance and wit of an older woman. She understood his needs and adored him, and as his wife offered the sense of permanence he had lacked' (Linklater 83). This did not extend to creating a house for him: Faith never learned to cook and refused to consider it, though she did find that she had to do the household chores at the Cornish vicarage since she did not get on with the servants. She found the combative and possessive atmosphere generated by local ladies competing to serve Reverend Wason very wearying (Linklater 92). In her first memoir, *As Much As I Dare* (1938), Faith is clearly rehearsing events from the Cornish years of twenty years earlier that would re-emerge, some of them almost verbatim from her memoir, in *Tatting*, twenty years later.

If Faith had had children they might have given her a different focus for her devotion, but her only child, a son, was stillborn in 1909. 'Monty didn't want children; she was persuaded not to try again (due to her premature labour), but she explored adopting a child later in life twice, and never forgot her son' (Linklater 96).

Monty's career as a playwright and a novelist had taken off like a rocket by 1912, but his health was precarious, and constant international travel played havoc with his sciatica and his nerves. In 1913 Faith and Monty travelled to Italy in search of a home in a warmer climate. The author Norman Douglas, whom they had met once at a dinner in New York, had praised Capri, so they went to stay there for a weekend. They instantly began looking for a house, bought some land, and Capri became Faith's home, in a series of houses, until 1927. Many of the stories in *Mandolinata*, and Monty's novels *Vestal Fire* (1927) and *Extraordinary Women* (1928) are based on people and events from their Caprese lives.

During the First World War Monty served as an officer in the Royal Marines at Gallipoli and then was appointed to run British counter-espionage operations in Athens. Faith tried volunteering with canteen work in London but found that she was not helpful in that role, and retreated back to Capri, to live out the war among her friends in an international and flamboyant community of rich ex-patriate residents, many of them homosexual and/or artists. She re-encountered Norman Douglas, who would become the most important of her friends from Capri. He was 'the first in a distinguished line of homosexuals of both sexes to discover in her a strength of character and sharpness of wit which owed nothing to her husband. In the summer of 1916 she typed his novel *South Wind*.' (Linklater 164). Throughout the war and the early 1920s Faith became close to many leading artists and writers of the day, including Rebecca West, Romaine Brooks and, briefly, D H Lawrence.

During the war, perhaps inevitably, given Monty's enforced absence for several consecutive years, Faith had an affair with a much younger man, Nini Caracciolo, on Capri. She later wrote: 'when a Northern woman loses her head over a Latin she seldom finds it again' (FCM Sibyl 73). One of the rare sightings of Faith in modern literature is in Giuseppe Aprea's collection *L'Aria blu – Lettere da Capri mai scritte, mai spedite* (*The blue air – Letters from Capri, never written, never sent*) (La Conchiglia Press 2008). This recounts the imaginary letters from famous writers and other artists who lived on Capri, in which Faith features prominently, including her invented farewell note to Monty about her affair with Nini.

When Monty discovered the affair he asked Faith not to meet Nini that night. Nini, who had waited patiently for Faith outdoors in a rainstorm, developed pneumonia and died some days later. Both the Mackenzies attended his funeral, but their marriage was effectively over, since Monty would not tolerate such a public betrayal. (Monty's own infidelities, pre-dating and continuing during their marriage, of course did not count.) He could not decide to leave Faith, since he depended on her for her nursing (he was frequently debilitated by psychosomatic illnesses) and for her superb piano playing which he required as a stimulus while he was writing his novels. On the other hand, he was conflicted 'between the wish to behave well and the need to punish her'.

> [Their friend] Axel Munthe ... advised [Monty] neither to abandon his wife nor to overlook her infidelity, but to follow a third course. "Why don't you both admit that marriage in the conventional sense is no longer possible? Why don't you give freedom to each of you to live his or

her own life and yet agree to live together in friendship as man and wife?"

[...] Once this solution had been arrived at, the continuous emotional pain, registered by his sciatica, gradually became more sporadic ... For the rest of Faith's life the public appearance of their marriage was of a civilised friendship. They often shared the same house, and went to the same parties. Monty continued to trust her judgement and liked her to participate in each of his new adventures. He wrote to her regularly; when he could he paid the enormous bills which she ran up, and he never forgot their wedding anniversary. The observance of their bargain presented little difficulty to one so accustomed to private self-discipline and public performance, but Faith was less experienced in these matters. It was also true that during their marriage she had given herself up more completely to him than he to her. There were, in consequence, flaws on her side of the bargain ... Once in his presence her spirits soared at any attention and wilted at each rebuff until, irritated by the intensity of her feelings, he contrived an excuse to send her away again. A quarter of a century was to pass before she was emotionally independent of him. (Linklater 175–76)

In 1928 Monty imported Christina MacSween, a young Scottish teacher from a crofting family from Lewis in the Outer Hebrides, into his household to act as his secretary and as a kind of companion-housekeeper for Faith. Twenty years younger than Monty, Chrissie soon became his devoted and docile mistress (Linklater 244). Faith was good-natured towards her, but 'it was not an easy position for Chrissie. Faith had a snobbish streak and never disguised her feelings of social superiority. She was equally sensitive to slights upon her status as wife. In her presence the fiction had to be maintained that Chrissie was an employee; her employer was always referred to as "Mr Mackenzie", and Faith was assumed to run the household' (Linklater 245).

After leaving Capri in the mid 1920s Monty embarked on a career of buying or leasing small islands – Herm and Jethou in the Channel Isles, Eilean Aigas in the River Beauly north of Inverness, and Barra in the Outer Hebrides – living on them, creating gardens for Faith to develop, and then growing bored (or financially embarrassed) and moving on to his next enthusiasm, all the while producing book after book to keep the income flowing to maintain his increasingly numerous extended household. Faith supported Monty in the longest-lasting of his enthusiasms, his campaigning for Scottish Nationalism, but she did not share his political views.

Faith maintained an old relationship with a Russian singer and actor, Nikolai 'Bion' or 'Bim' Nadegin (now spelled Nadezhin), whom she had first met in Capri in 1918, when he had become 'first Faith's lover and in course of time the most loyal of all her companions' (Linklater 182). In 1938 Nadegin was helping Faith paint Peace Close, the small house in the Somerset village of Kingweston that Monty had bought for Faith to live in while he and Chrissie remained in Barra. Four years later Peace Close had to be sold, and Faith moved back to Barra. Later she tried to relive her Capri memories by spending several months at a time in Majorca, where she heard with pleasure the news of Monty's knighthood in January 1952. A few years later she moved back to London, never travelling again. She died in 1960.

Chrissie would become Monty's second wife in 1962, but she died from cancer in October 1963. Monty married Chrissie's younger sister Lily in March 1965; thirty-five years younger than him, she had been his protegée for some years. Monty died on 30 November 1972.

Faith and work

Faith's music was her first independent creative outlet. She was already an accomplished pianist (her elder sister Lucy had been a violinist in the Shinner Quartet, the first professional women's string ensemble) and her competence and stamina as a musician became essential for Monty's early career as a novelist. Until he accidentally acquired a gramophone in the early 1920s (the Aeolian organ he had ordered could not be supplied), Monty relied on Faith to play 'the piano until late at night while he wrote' (Linklater 206). The gramophone, whose technology had been much improved since Monty had last bothered to listen to one in 1910, impressed them both: for sound fidelity, for its convenience and for the opportunity to explore music they had not yet heard in concert. Faith began to write music and radio reviews for London newspapers and magazines. Monty decided to found a magazine for record reviews, and the first issue of *Gramophone* appeared in 1923, with Monty as its first editor. Christopher later took on the editorial work and Faith was a regular columnist: her first pen-name for this was F Sharp. By the 1930s her endorsement of a patent course teaching piano technique was appearing regularly in magazine advertisements. In 1950 the conversion of her *Gramophone* shares into an annuity gave Faith her first regular independent income, making her old age free from financial anxiety (Linklater 316).

Surrounded as she was by artists, novelists and authors, it was inevitable that Faith would herself begin to explore these arts. She had begun to sculpt after the war, and also began writing short stories. Several of these were published in the *New Statesman*, where they demonstrate 'the dominant postwar sense of unsettledness, restlessness, flight, worriedness, and longing for a different home' in modernist writing by Englishwomen between the wars (Abu-Manneh 2011, 126). A limited subscription edition of fourteen of Faith's stories, *Mandolinata*, was published by Cope and Fenwick in 1931, and was dedicated to her husband.

The *Times Literary Supplement* reviewer was pleased with the individual stories ('agreeable entertainment'; Anon 1931, 512), but not as a collection, which they found boring. In 1938 the stories were republished in an enlarged edition called *The Angle of Error*. The novelist Marjorie Grant Cook enjoyed this collection as a 'handful of lively tales with their well-devised surprises and touches of gay humour' (Grant 1938, 505).

Faith also began to write biography and memoir. Monty had suggested that she write a biography of the seventeenth-century Queen Christina of Sweden, possibly thinking that researching the life of an imperious and unconventional woman from Italian archival sources would appeal to Faith's restless intellect. *The Sibyl of the North* (1931) was dedicated to Axel Munthe, and was eventually filmed, the royalties from the paperback edition giving Faith an unexpected small income of her own in later years. Faith demonstrated a rather advanced attitude for the period by queering Christina, describing her as having 'the point of view of the homosexual male in regard to women. There were certain ladies distinguished for their beauty or wit whom she admired almost beyond the bounds of what is compatible with admiration' (FCM Sibyl 21). It is remarkable that Faith felt free to make the suggestion that Christina was lesbian, and to cite 'the point of view of the homosexual male'. Faith also noted Christina's masculine upbringing, her choice to take her coronation oath as King of Sweden, her lifelong refusal to marry her extremely eligible cousin Gustavus, and her preference for masculine cross-dressing for most of her adult life. G M Gathorne-Hardy praised *The Sybil of the North* as an 'extremely readable … remarkably complete and highly intelligent study' (Gathorne-Hardy 1931).

Faith's next biography, *The Cardinal's Niece* (1935), about Marie Mancini, the first love of the Sun King, Louis XIV, and the other nieces and nephew of Cardinal Mazarin, shows her fascination in tracing the fortunes of a lively family of privileged seventeenth-century siblings on the make. There is a sympathetic fellow-feeling, possibly from her own experiences as a touring actress, in her descriptions of the hair-raising adventures of the Mazarinettes, Marie, Philippe, Hortense, Olympe and Marie-Ann, across France and Italy, in and out of prison, palaces and political peril. It was reviewed appreciatively in the *Times Literary Supplement*: 'attractively written. She makes her heroine live' (Falls 1935).

Written at the same time as the biographies were Faith's own memoirs. *As Much As I Dare* (1938), *More Than I Should* (1940) and *Always Afternoon* (1943) made her name as a friend and acquaintance of the Western world, since large numbers of culturally important figures seem to have passed through her ambit. *As Much As I Dare* has a breezier, more mannered tone compared to the two later volumes, adhering to a linear account of Faith's childhood, youth, family life, early career and the first ten years of her marriage. Anthony Powell admired it with appreciation in *The Spectator*: 'an accomplished piece of showmanship ... Mrs Mackenzie is tolerant, adventurous and sometimes very funny indeed' (29 April 1938, 32). Orlo Williams particularly praised the first section, on her early childhood, which is 'the real achievement by which this book attains art' (Williams 1938).

Wiliams evidently enjoyed the memoir enough to request its sequel, *More Than I Should* for review, praising this for 'her remarkable capacity for appreciation, neither parading nor complaining' in a hectic life in Monty's wake (Williams 1940). Graham Greene, on the other hand, reviewed *More Than I Should* with evident distaste as 'gossip ... trivial, exaggerated, a little vulgar' (Greene 1954).

Always Afternoon, her last volume of memoir, is a scrapbag of memories and photographs, ending with a deliberate return to Faith as a baby at Eton, where her first memoir began. Her then home was noted by a reviewer as the heart of the memoir. 'No part of the book has the author's particular quality than that which describes the finding, the furnishing, the gardening, the inhabiting and the sad disposal of Peace Close, the Somersetshire cottage – the whole blend of joy and sorrow compressed into a couple of years' (Graves 1943).

Naturally Faith left out of her memoirs the material that could not be published. Information in the Linklater biography suggests that Faith deliberately set a veil to obscure the infidelities, hints of lesbian coteries, the marital separation, Chrissie's true role. Also glossed over were her own extravagances that Monty financed, heroically, it has to be said.

In 1942 Faith and Compton Mackenzie published their only known collaboration, *Calvary*, two short essays in a fundraising volume for the Lord Mayor of London's Air Raid Distress Fund for John Lane The Bodley Head. Both Mackenzies wrote an essay each about the lives of ordinary people tossed into catastrophe by war, to support the vivid and sometimes disturbing illustrations by 'Peregrine', a Central European artist. Faith's contribution was to imagine an Italian tenor drowned at sea by a Nazi torpedo and buried with dignity under Catholic rites on the island of Barra where his body was found (Eyles 1942).

In 1943 Faith published her biographical account *Napoleon at the Briars* about Napoleon's last years on St Helena, which was brought out by Jonathan Cape in a limited edition. It is a more fictionalised biography than Faith had hitherto attempted, and was dedicated to Bryher, the English writer and wealthy literary philanthropist who sent Faith regular cheques to the end of her life and funded her travels abroad from the 1940s (Linklater 299). In 1944 it appears that Faith may have been working with Mass Observation on a project to write a book on rural villages, although the resulting book was eventually published without her involvement (Sarsby 1998, note 27).

In 1950 Faith published her last biography, of her great-uncle the Eton schoolmaster and poet William Cory, which was reviewed in lengthy appreciations in *The Spectator* and in the *Times Literary Supplement*. These reviews were the longest notices she would receive for any of her books, due to the Etonian loyalties of the reviewers. In 1954 and 1957 Faith published her only novels: *The Crooked Wall* and *Tatting*.

I want to discuss the stories of *Mandolinata* before the novels. They predate *Tatting* by some twenty years and have a sharper edge, dealing with risky (for the 1920s) subjects like the desirability of birth control, embracing one's sexuality, the abandonment of an unsuitable marriage, and the easy acceptance of homosexuality as a fact of life. All those stories are set in the present day, whereas they are bracketed by *Tatting*, which was written twenty years later but is set twenty years earlier, in the Edwardian period.

Mandolinata

Faith noted in her second memoir that in the winter of 1925 she had been writing short stories in the style of Chekov and Katherine Mansfield (FCM Should 176).

> I had been writing nostalgic short stories about Italy since I left Capri, and sent them to high-brow weeklies and monthlies. Desmond MacCarthy not only accepted the first for the *New Statesman*, but took the trouble to send a letter of criticism, so that the story, when it appeared, was up to the Miscellany standard. It was called 'The Suit', and was founded on an episode in the life of Nadegine [sic]. (FCM Should 203)

In the 1920s Faith made a new friend, the editor and bibliophile Colin Summerford who also joined the circle around Compton Mackenzie's own household. Colin was keen to set up a new publishing house, Cope and Fenwick, and wanted to publish a collection of Faith's stories as its first offering. *Mandolinata* was to be published as a *de luxe* edition, an ambitious first project for a new firm that proved to be commercially sound.

> Colin brought a dummy of *Mandolinata*, the size of which alarmed me. Were my stories worth this handsome Tuscan red linen binding and all this hand-made paper? And would anyone want to pay a guinea for a signed copy? 'Cheques are coming in already,' he said. (FCM Should 233).

Mandolinata contains fourteen short stories, one with two parts. The first five stories are set in Capri and Rome, and the remaining stories are set in England or France. All the stories seem post-war in mood and aesthetic detail, and remarkably modern in the freedom with which they explore themes of sexuality and poverty, but the war is barely mentioned. It is likely that having experienced the First World War only briefly during her month or so of canteen volunteering, and then living unthreatened on Capri in moderate comfort for the war's duration, with no personal losses, Faith chose to avoid writing about the experience of war. Instead, her characters react to shocking and powerful events at a social and a sexual level. Most importantly, they are all deeply concerned with the economics of living, a pressure of which Faith would have been well aware.

'Mandolinata' is a perturbing story based on an event Faith witnessed and returned to in two of her memoirs. 'The huge Hungarian, Oscar, whom Louis Golding had brought to see me one day ... a temperamental tragedy, always threatening suicide and getting laughed at, but finally doing it, outside the cemetery gate, "to save trouble". I write a short story for him after he died' (FCM Should 177). This story is about desperation and boredom, and a shocking lack of community interest in why a man should constantly threaten to kill himself. Yet he is a visitor, someone with no stake in Caprese society; he is tolerated and treated affectionately, but his performative suicidal desire becomes merely a background noise.

In 'La Bonne Mine' the inexorable force that takes the young Prussian boy Gluck to his death is wholly outside his control. He too is a visitor who lingers to enjoy the sybaritic living of Capri and the pleasures of falling in love with two young women. But he is unable to refuse the Fatherland's summons to a war far away, and he is forgotten, almost immediately, by the girls he had loved. Yet these young women have their own stories: they did not ask to be fallen in love with, and they have poverty to overcome. Grazia and Mafalda bravely lead the life of the class they were born into but they are sliding inexorably down the social ladder.

The two stories of 'Variations on a Theme' are about inexperienced women encountering sexual love for the first time. One gives in, rapturously, while the other holds out against relentless pressure. Faith's ability to write about women's desires and how they regard sexual attraction is unusually direct. The women in her stories are semi-protected by fear and by chaperonage. But fear can be overcome by persistent wooing, and a chaperone who can be eluded is no good to anyone.

In 'The Suit' and 'The Wedding Present' Nadegin features as a large Russian baritone called Boris, a generous man who gives away what he cannot really afford, to the delight, oddly expressed, of the men who receive it. Faith's eye for the poverty of struggling artists draws a parallel with the native poverty of the actual poor of Capri and of Whitechapel.

In contrast, in 'The Writing Case' the easy wealth of a comfortable middle-class English family conceals a savage survival instinct. What can a family do when a child refuses to do the decent thing, the thing they have been trained for by class and culture, and by which civilised standards are maintained? The ferocious intensity with which the child Anna refuses to give up the present she wants above all others is almost supernatural, recalling the equally young and rebellious Viola in Helen de Guerry Simpson's 'Young Magic', published in her first collection *The Baseless Fabric* (1925), and whom Faith knew (FCM Should 268).

In 'With Custody of the Child' and 'Queer Lady' Faith introduces ladies of the *demi-monde*. The former is a story of modern divorce as experienced by a neglected little boy in a comfortable middle-class English home. The absent mother is damned by the manner of her departure, and by the confusion and distress this causes as the little boy's world collapses.

'Queer Lady' is a feminine version of the Edwardian boy-meets-dazzling-woman story that both Kenneth Grahame and John Buchan used in their stories 'The Finding of the Princess' (1895) and 'Afternoon' (1896) respectively. While in the male authors' stories the Princess is clearly a desirable young lady of the right class and background, Faith's Princess is a kept woman whose very existence is an affront to the little girl's nurse.

'Children of God' is a truly remarkable torrent of scorn on a self-satisfied middle-class vicar. His indulgence of his own desires ensures that his wife is continually pregnant, and his unnecessarily growing family cannot be supported adequately on his meagre stipend. Faith's first memoir, *As Much As I Dare*, indicates that this story is a clear criticism of her father for her own mother's ten pregnancies that she barely survived. Like the oldest son of the story Faith's elder brother, also called Guy, also went to Canada to farm, and articulates an anger in this story that feels personal. Faith returned to the subject in *Tatting*, writing about 'impoverished rectors and vicars with immense unwieldy families, bright boys and girls worthy of first-class education struggling for scholarships or exhibitions' (56).

The final story in *Mandolinata* is, unexpectedly, filled with the joy of a passion fulfilled. After so much ambivalence in the earlier stories about tormenting passions, in 'Cushions' the fuss-free delight of being in love permeates the existence of Roxy, a young lady travelling alone by ship (first class) from South Africa to London to meet her fiancé. Roxy is nobody's fool. After she has disembarked she realises that she will be marrying not just Gregory but also Gregory's Aunt Marion and Cousin Ruth, with whom Gregory had grown up. Faith lacerates the aesthetic values of the Bloomsbury set with the metaphor of cushions, which Roxy buys for her own comfort since comfort is absent from the painfully Jacobean cottage that Gregory (and Aunt Marion and Ruth) have furnished for her. One small act of rebellion leads most satisfyingly to another.

As a collection *Mandolinata* is beguiling and very modern, with a distinct mood in the stories: they are sympathetic to human happiness, and their characters do not wish to cause embarrassment. Yet they also reject sophistication and pretence. Honesty brings about happiness; good manners are defined by doing as you would be done by. But honesty is not always the right approach for other people's happiness: children can be brutally honest since this is all they know. Adults have other, conflicting responsibilities, which may simply have to be endured.

The Crooked Wall, and *Tatting*

Faith's first novel, *The Crooked Wall*, is set in the 1870s in London. Bertha Pringle and Judith Jasmin are best friends at a girls' boarding school run by two not very competent spinsters whose own emotional dramas flavour the school atmosphere. An unpopular girl causes social ructions in the school's life, and then there is a sudden and tragic death. Judith is the only child of a rich and careless man, and the progress of her love affairs, her marriage, and her melodramatic life form the remainder of the novel, watched by Bertha with perturbation and pity as the plot unwinds towards an explanation of that tragic death at school.

The Crooked Wall is absorbing and very readable with memorable plot developments, but there is something not quite right about its narrative historicity. It was reviewed as 'a period piece with an oddly haunting effect; its characters move as it were behind glass, in an elegant world which has a flavour of ghostliness' (Sturch 1954). This sense of artificiality can be seen in Faith's depiction of her characters' emotions and the modernity of some of the plot points, which seem out of step with the Victorian setting. Very pleasingly for Faith and her publisher Jonathan Cape the novel was selected as a Book Society Choice. This publicity brought about further reviews: an excoriation by Sean O'Faolain in *The Observer* and a tactful nod by Kingsley Amis in *The Spectator*. Other reviews were much kinder. C V Wedgwood cited Faith's 'steady craftsmanship' and praised her for writing in a style worthy of 'the best of the late Victorian novelists'. The *Sunday Times* called the novel 'intelligently written, smoothly professional' and the *National and English Review* focused, interestingly, on the 'intricate plot surprisingly rich in violence and a gallery of lively characters' (all quotes from the dustwrapper for *Tatting*).

Those warm praises must have given Faith the encouragement to write another novel. In 1957 *Tatting* was reviewed in the *Times Literary Supplement* by Siriol Hart as 'bizarre and deceptively simple, like a sampler worked by a very sophisticated Sunday sempstress ... the feeling of mischief is alive in every sentence' (Hart 1957). In the novel Faith returned to the early years of her marriage to write about an eccentric Irish artist invading an Anglo-Catholic ménage in Cornwall. Without reading her diaries it is impossible to know why she did this, but the incongruity of the situation and the outsize personalities involved clearly called out to be written down. Perhaps after forty years she felt it was safe to do so, as most of the originals for her characters were now dead.

Many of the details of the plot are documented in Faith's memoirs. Faith and Monty had become friends with a starving Irish artist in London before they left for Cornwall, Althea Gyles (1868–1949), who had been active as an artist and poet on the fringes of the *Yellow Book*, the Celtic Twilight and the Fellowship of the Golden Dawn from the 1890s. She was a friend of Yeats, of Wilde and of Aubrey Beardsley, and had had 'an ostentatious affair' (Gould 2004) in Paris with Beardsley's patron Leonard Smithers, also a publisher and a pornographer (a detail applied to Ariadne's life also). Like Ariadne, Althea nearly starved to death in London through poverty. Like Ariadne, Althea was passionately loyal to the memory of Oscar Wilde and of Beardsley. As a personality she must have been quite extraordinary, even for Faith who was well accustomed to the excesses of London and New York theatre. Faith invents (or embroiders) a sympathetic and striking back story for Ariadne that colours the novel with authentic tones of the Irish *fin de siècle* deriving directly from Althea's life.

Father St John was modelled on Monty's friend the Reverend Sandys Wason, with whom Monty and Faith lived at first as paying guests, though they later took a cottage in the parish. Wason was an eccentric priest with firm ideas about his independence from the Anglican church, whom 'Monty had met years ago when as a young priest he had appeared at Lady Ham, wearing a cassock, a Romish hat and buckle shoes, and carrying a large turbot as an offering to Mrs Compton' (FCM Dare 198). (In the novel Laura refers to this episode from Guy's life.) In his parish of Cury and Gunwalloe on the Lizard in south Cornwall Wason worked hard to create 'centres of Catholic worship that rivalled even Rome's' (Butler-Gallie 11). These efforts included two very long Latin Masses each Sunday. This approach to proselytising undoubtedly appealed to Monty's sense of spectacle and performance.

Apart from Laura and Guy who are Faith and Monty from the life, and Mrs Mallory, who is Monty's formidable mother, many of the other characters in *Tatting* could have been recalled from Faith's diaries at the time. The atmosphere is captured with rich flavours, with an imperturbable parish tolerating the inexplicable behaviour of their very High Church priest and the raging paranoia of the 'church fowl' Miss Want, who simply wants to interfere.

Tatting's matter-of-fact presentation of English rural eccentricity is similar to that in the short stories of Sylvia Townsend Warner and the novels of David Garnett and T F Powys. Stella Gibbons' *Cold Comfort Farm* might also be recalled. Faith's unadorned narration is an arresting contrast to the incongruity of the characters' actions, and the challenges to social norms of the period. Miss Want is shot at, poison pen letters arrive at the rectory, and a local farmer and rival preacher is discovered lying face down in his field while ladies are walking by: these alarming events are received with equanimity. Ariadne's dramatic destitution, Miss Want's stumping determination to manage the parish, and Father St John's inclination to vanish into hiding whenever a tiresome woman appears: these create a blackly comic effect. This is a character-driven novel intended to amuse and to prickle at the same time, with Laura's innocent affection and Guy's mischievousness soothing the jealous passions of others: a very strange episode drawn from Faith's own strange and remarkable life.

Faith distributed signed copies of *Tatting* to friends, and began to write a book about the English colony at Bagni di Lucca. After Nadegin's death in 1959 Faith was no longer able to cope with life on her own, and moved from her London flat into a flat in the sub-basement of Monty and Chrissie's London home, and finally to a nursing home in Brunswick Gardens. Monty records that even in the nursing home Faith was thinking about writing more. She had put the Italian book project aside and was beginning to plan a book about Majorca (Mackenzie 122). But her health deteriorated all through 1959 and 1960, putting an end to her authorship. She died on 9th July 1960, aged eighty-two.

References

Anon, 'Fiction', *Times Literary Supplement*, 25 July 1931, 511–13.

Bashir Abu-Manneh, *Fiction of the New Statesman 1913–1939* (University of Delaware Press 2011).

Fergus Butler-Gallie, *A Field Guide to the English Clergy* (OneWorld 2018).

Leonora Eyles, 'War and the Common Man', *Times Literary Supplement*, 27 June 1942, 315.

C Falls 'Marie Mancini', *Times Literary Supplement*, 7 February 1935, 69.

G M Gathorne-Hardy, 'Christina of Sweden', *Times Literary Supplement*, 25 June 1931, 497.

Warwick Gould, 'Gyles, Margaret Alethea (1868–1949)' *Oxford Dictionary of National Biography*, 23 September 2004.

Marjorie Grant, 'New Novels', *Times Literary Supplement*, 30 July 1938, 505.

P P Graves et al, 'A Critic of the Victorians' *Times Literary Supplement*, 5 June 1943, 268.

Graham Greene, 'Escape', *The Spectator* 165: 5858 (4 October 1954), 16.

Siriol Hart, 'Domestic Drama', *Times Literary Supplement*, 22 March 1957, 123.

Andro Linklater, *Compton Mackenzie. A Life* (Chatto & Windus, 1987).

Compton Mackenzie, *My Life and Times. Octave Ten 1953–1963* (Chatto & Windus, 1971)

Faith Compton Mackenzie, *As Much As I Dare. The autobiography of Faith Compton Mackenzie* (Collins 1938).

Faith Compton Mackenzie, *More Than I Should* (Collins, 1940).

Faith Compton Mackenzie, *The Sibyl of the North. The Tale of Christina Queen of Sweden* (Cassell 1931).

Jacqueline Sarsby, 'Exmoor Village Revisited: Mass-Observation's "Anthropology of Ourselves", the "Feel-Good Factor" in Wartime Colour Photography and the Photograph as Art or Social Document', in *Rural History* 9:1 (1998), 99–115, 114.

Elizabeth L Sturch, 'Ladies First', *Times Literary Supplement* (29 January 1954, 69).

Orlo Williams, 'Memoirs of a Novelist's Wife', *Times Literary Supplement*, 2 April 1938, 230.

Orlo Williams, 'The Restless Years', *Times Literary Supplement*, 28 September 1940, 498.

Works by Faith Compton Mackenzie

Mandolinata (Cope and Fenwick, 1931)

The Sibyl of the North. The Tale of Christina Queen of Sweden (Cassell, 1931)

The Cardinal's Niece. The story of Marie Mancini (Martin Secker, 1935)

The Angle of Error. Seventeen stories (Martin Secker, 1938)

As Much As I Dare. The autobiography of Faith Compton Mackenzie (Collins, 1938)

More Than I Should (Collins, 1940)

[with Compton Mackenzie] *Calvary* (John Lane The Bodley Head, 1943)

Always Afternoon (Collins, 1943)

Napoleon at the Briars (Jonathan Cape, 1943)

William Cory. A biography (Constable, 1950)

The Crooked Wall. A Victorian story of love (Cape, 1954)

Tatting. A novel (Cape, 1957)

Tatting

Chapter One

'How good of you! Please take some money out of my purse which is lying about somewhere. You can get everything at the dairy opposite. I deal there. But I haven't an account. I always pay, to save bills. I hate bills. Don't you?'

There was no need to answer or to look for the purse. It lay on its side at the end of the chimneypiece yawning hungrily. Laura Mallory had never seen a larger or more conspicuously empty purse.

At the other end of the fireplace was a rose, complete but brown with age. It must have lain there a long time, for it was surrounded and covered by a fine dust. There was nothing else on the chimneypiece.

Laura stood in front of the purse to mask its emptiness, shut it with a snap and went to the door.

'That's all right. I shan't be long.'

She bought milk, eggs, brown bread and a pot of honey.

'Haven't you come from the artist lady at Number 7?'

Laura gave a second's thought before replying.

'You mean Miss Berden? Yes I have.'

'You might tell her that she owes us six shillings. I'll give you the bill, to remind her.'

'She has asked me to pay it, and I will pay for this too.'

'Very good, Madam.' His manner changed. He opened the door for her. Laura went out with a sigh.

Poor Ariadne! So brilliant, so tired and so ill, and without a halfpenny in her purse. Those blazing feverish eyes, that cavernous mouth, lacking teeth that she could not afford, that wild faded hair, and those fine artistic hands. Oh, it was terrible to think of her lying there helpless in that squalid Chelsea room neglected by the famous friends who had admired and praised her work in the nineties, when she was young. She had known them all; to her Oscar Wilde was poor Oscar, and when he died she had wept. 'No one ever lived who was so kind.' The small residue of that fascinating company now hardly remembered the existence of the child of promise, Ariadne. If one was not in Paris, one was not. How could they understand an artist living in England?

It was fantastic and absurd, she declared, but it had happened. And here she was translated from the Rue du Bac almost unconsciously to Chelsea. The reason for it floated in the air, enveloped in a cloud of surmise and hypothesis.

In fact it was quite simple. The offer of a regular job as art critic in a highbrow paper had brought her over, propelled by the urgent good wishes of her Paris friends, almost too urgent, she had sometimes thought since. The job evaporated almost at once and with it all her energy. She remained where she was, in the room she had rented at the top of an old house in a Chelsea street, letting the dust gather week by week between a charwoman's visits, lying in her camp-bed most of the day, her pencil beside her, or poised for inspiration. Some evenings she would wrap herself in a long dark cape and dine in Soho, chattering cleverly in a high brittle voice, her thin blood warmed by plenty of *vin ordinaire*, which in those days was included in the menu.

Or she would go to a house on the Regent's Canal, and drink strong coffee made straight into the cups, in a room that might have been a salon once, with noble windows, slim columns and walls enriched by vast rococo mirrors in which lustre chandeliers pendant from a moulded ceiling were reflected.

It was in this curiously romantic room that Laura and her husband Guy met Ariadne Berden. The early summer evening was turquoise blue through the open windows: the chandeliers, unlit, were prismatic in the light of a six-candle sconce on the chimneypiece. In the delicate shadow sat Ariadne and Clare Dobson, the owner of the mirrors, drinking coffee while a small silver kettle steamed sweetly but did not boil. Freshly ground coffee in a red enamelled box awaited the newcomers.

Mrs Dobson was in an interesting condition. If it was interesting to her, she kept it, as one is reserved about a hobby, not secret, for that was now impossible, but undiscussed. She remained what she must always have been, compact in mind and body, her stature not great, her intellect not formidable, but well nurtured by fastidious taste. Somewhere between thirty-five and forty, she had lately married a seafaring man ten years her junior, who loved her exceedingly (the child would lie in a cradle shaped like the King of Rome's, gazing at rainbow crystals and sparkling lights).

That summer evening Ariadne was wearing a gloomy black lace hat which hung like a half-open umbrella over her pallid face. Its effect was as striking as it was meant to be, but when the Mallorys had recovered from its mystery, it was removed. It was impossible to carry on the most languid conversation beneath it, and as soon as Guy Mallory appeared among the mirrors and columns, she knew that this was no time for languor. She must sparkle. Off came the hat.

The introduction had been carefully planned. Clare had prepared Ariadne for a dazzling personality. He had great beauty, was extremely young, extremely witty, extremely fascinating. And Ariadne had interrupted:

'Didn't you say he was married too? Can you see her through the dazzle?'

Clare half shut her eyes at this.

'Can't you see her?' had laughed Ariadne.

'Yes. But only just. She is there, very much so, and is likely to remain. She came here alone once, and yes — then outside the dazzle, she shone too, but faintly as though she were far away. I think she is too deeply in love to be much use to anyone else. But she can be amusing too. She has humour of course, or he wouldn't be able to stand her. Perhaps that is what she is for. To be stood by him and to understand him. She can look beautiful too, but not always.'

Ariadne looking back for a moment to Paris, remembered that someone had said just that about herself — and she had liked it. To look always beautiful. That was rather monotonous, and he who had said it had murmured, 'You sweet darling dirty tramp,' and kissed her. This digression in Ariadne's thoughts was clearly etched in her face. Clare observed it as she did most of her friend's emotional vibrations. She had been long enough her friend to assess her virtues and her vices. She was also rather bitterly conscious that there were few friends left for Ariadne beside herself. She had known the Paris milieu, had thought it rotten, and Ariadne's *amour* with the person who had found her not always beautiful was one of the darkest shadows on their friendship. She would be in sympathy always with love, but Ariadne, after treating reasonable admirers with prudish contempt, had fallen into the arms of an abominable creature of high intelligence, no morals, and the vivid imagination which was perhaps what she had been waiting for. He had the worst of reputations even among the Paris set. Ariadne lost caste, and when the affair ended after more than a year of heady intoxication, and with a certain amount of inspired work, she collapsed.

The dilemma was clearly recognised as a possible infliction on her fellow artists, who hastened her removal to London, and the job that had been arranged for her. By then Clare was established in London, had married, and knew that she must help Ariadne, whether her job lasted or not. She was not surprised when it failed. Ariadne, after feeble protest, allowed her to pay for the Chelsea room and the charwoman until something turned up.

This was the situation when Clare, always thoughtful and practical, asked Laura to a quiet little lunch, 'just you and me'. She had added, referring to the first and only note she had had from Laura:

What a beautiful name yours is! Almost beautiful enough.

This was quite lost on Laura who had thought it must have something to do with Guy. That was her present state of mind.

The lunch was quite simply designed to fascinate Laura with the story of Ariadne. It was romantic enough. Flight from an aristocratic impoverished home in Ireland to become an artist, making a stir in Dublin, and then in the fantastic world of Paris in the 'nineties, her friendship with the famous, and no divulging of the disastrous *amour* but stress on delicate health, poverty and genius.

Laura was enchanted by the prospect of seeing such a paragon, and Guy was glad to accept the invitation because he liked Clare Dobson and enjoyed her salon and its mirrors, though he was not particularly interested in Paris symbolists.

If, on the face of it, there might be a suspicion that Clare Dobson was shunning responsibility for Ariadne's welfare, it was in a sense desperation that led her to draw Laura into the net. Here was the sailor husband on his way home, and the many duties and delights that awaited them both. The Ariadne preoccupation would have to be modified on his account. She knew too well that he was not enthusiastic about Ariadne. Why should he be? He did not see what exactly she signified, except that she was definitely opposed to him in every way.

When the Mallorys walked away from that meeting the evening was misted lavender with a half moon high in the sky. They went silently until they had crossed the canal, and Guy began:

'Very queer.'

'What is?'

'That woman. She may be a genius. I know Clare Dobson thinks she is. But *she* is evidently under the spell.'

'Under the spell! Is that what it is?'

'That what it is'?', then 'Did *you* feel it?'

'Something happened to me. There's a fascination. She's not at all beautiful really.'

'Was once, perhaps. She's a physical ruin. Must be quite thirty-five if not forty.'

Laura shivered, and he went on: 'I liked her best in that floppy hat. Her eyes certainly did glow under it. Then she flung it off and showed us that scarecrow haggard face, long pointed nose — much too long, and mouth, much too small, and her voice — rushing up the scale. Her hair was probably quite a good red once,' he added without pity.

'It seemed to me rather like an aureole,' she suggested tentatively.

'Aureole be damned. She was playing up — for my benefit I suppose.'

'I don't see why — for yours —. Anyway it got me too,' she added hastily, seeing a faint shadow cloud Guy's vivid face. Sometimes she liked to tease him a little, but only a little. 'I don't see why' she hoped was the lightest of badinage. But of course it *was* for his benefit, so obviously that she had ventured the silly challenge, with perhaps a slight hope that she also had been expected to benefit. She had not a trace of humility in her character. Only Guy could produce in her such mildness. He, with all his sensitiveness to other people's moods, her own especially, and always being so unquestionably the centre of any company he was in, sometimes at some jesting criticism, would shut himself in his shell with a snap. He would not be teased or laughed at. Though he was by nature a practical joker, it seemed to her impossible that anyone should play a practical joke on him.

Surely it was never done! Laughter with him rang to the roof. Laughter at him was never heard; not by him, at any rate.

The shadow passed on this occasion. He hummed lightly, looked up at the sky and suggested walking all the way home. Home was then a flat at the slummy end of Chelsea Embankment, close to what was once Cremorne. A dingy grey stucco building, originally a private house, was inhabited by a distinguished woman painter on the ground floor who had one evening rushed up the dark stairs in a rage at the sound of the Mallorys' piano being noisily played by a musical friend of Guy's. She had stopped short on the landing below when Laura appeared at the top of the stairs, holding a lighted candlestick in her hand. The painter was so taken aback by the apparition that she stood still, staring, and then withdrew with a muttered apology. Laura was quite conscious that she looked her best by the light of one candle (who does not?), but that was disappointingly her only meeting with the great painter, who was evidently shocked but not inspired. She painted landscapes —

Above the painter and under the Mallorys lived a literary couple. They were unobtrusively friendly, and had an unusual opportunity of being both, when Guy, stricken with scarlet fever and diphtheria was carried downstairs like a sack to a fever hospital, leaving Laura in sudden and startling loneliness, forbidden to communicate with anyone at all until matters were arranged by the family as to her fate.

She had stood looking out at the Turner view, which was one of the privileges of Number 28, through tears for which a sleepless night with Guy choking in her arms until daylight was partly responsible. The doctor came early and saw the rash; the ambulance did not arrive till evening and it was in a sunset that she was lost when there was a gentle knock at the door. The literary neighbour had heard something and seen the ambulance. She realised the solitary night which Laura must spend, and asked her to come down to dinner.

Laura explained that she was not allowed to see anyone.

'I am dangerous. I have not had scarlet fever.'

This provoked no remark except, 'Please come down in ten minutes. Everything will be ready by then.'

This was an order to be obeyed, and the comfort of those two good people on such a sad night she knew she would never forget. When Guy came back from hospital after six weeks, with an official order that he was not to be allowed to play with other children's toys, one of the dubious problems of their marriage had arranged itself. The day after he was taken away Laura moved to the Mallory home in Kensington. This was an opportunity for a reluctant mother-in-law to study the wife Guy had married without warning. She already had no doubt that it might have been worse, judging by the looks and manners of Laura, and the fact that her family was well enough known to her and approved of. Still that was not enough to satisfy her as to Laura's behaviour in having dared to marry Guy without leave.

An amicable relationship was established quite simply and unexpectedly on the first evening at the high red house in Pulham Square. Mrs Mallory insisted upon her 'taking' dinner in bed, where she should stay until the doctor declared her free of infection. A finely presented tray of what could only be adequately described as viands lay before Laura, with Mrs Mallory standing eagerly beside her.

'A very light dinner. You must not eat anything heavy in bed. Just a little chicken, potatoes and sweet corn.'

'Sweet corn? Is that what it is!'

Mrs Mallory was amazed that Laura did not know it.

'We get it in tins from America. Guy is very fond of it.'

If there was faint reproach in this remark, Laura shyly admitted that they seldom ate properly in the flat.

'We lead a restaurant life at present, except when we have dined with you. It is certainly delicious, this sweet corn.'

'And I never gave it to you! We will have it next time you come here together. It is much better on the cob, but very difficult to get and to eat gracefully. We ate a great deal of it in Virginia.'

Mrs Mallory was a Virginian by birth.

'Drink your wine. It will do you good. Then when you are safe from infection you will go every day with fruit and flowers to the hospital, in the brougham. It is rather a long way, and you must not tire yourself.'

Laura remembered how Guy had borrowed his mother's brougham for the wedding, and Mrs Mallory met her look with a smile.

'That was just like Guy, the rogue. I thought it was a lunch party.'

'In a way it was,' Laura murmured. 'We had lunch afterwards in Soho with his best man. We drank champagne with the proprietor.'

A wistful look stole across Mrs Mallory's face.

'Ah. Champagne ... We must all have some when Guy comes back.' Laura felt that Mrs Mallory was not exactly resentful but hurt that the proprietor of a Soho restaurant should have been allowed to provide champagne for such an occasion, and not herself.

Sweet corn might, therefore, be said to have laid the foundation of a friendship between two highly strung women, who could easily have fallen out from the beginning and never made friends at all. This first encounter alone was a serious one, but it turned out to be effortless, and neither was trying to overwhelm or propitiate. Mrs Mallory had no illusions. Her worldly wisdom matched her glowing faith in ultimate good.

Laura was soon perfectly happy taking daily parcels to the

hospital, getting baked letters from Guy, talking about Guy and being shown endless photographs of Guy from babyhood. Some of them were in his mother's arms, revealing to her how beautiful Mrs Mallory had been twenty-four years ago, and how solemn was her baby. Once there was a small boy in a cotta.

'Is that Guy too? Did he sing in a choir?

'Not exactly. He helped at the altar sometimes.'

'It is a wonderful picture of a boy, but I should never have recognised it as Guy.'

Mrs Mallory took it from her and after a glance at it put it away. She then produced Guy aged about five in a toy Lancer's uniform.

'This is the saddest of all,' Laura exclaimed.

'I gave him the uniform to cheer him up because I had to go away. He always hated that. It was a mistake of his nurse's to have him photographed in it before I left, because he was in the depths of depression and would not smile or look cheerful or proud of his uniform.'

Laura nearly cried at this; a more forlorn expression she had never seen on any face.

'He was a very sensitive little boy,' was all his mother said, and Laura knew that she meant more than she said.

✕

It was as a poet that Laura had married Guy. She did not begin to wonder how they would live. When he came back from hospital he would write more poems, and as there was some money on both sides — more on his — she did not worry much, though they each had nothing but their family allowances to live on. And at any rate, she thought, she had escaped the possibility of marrying into the church, which her sisters had automatically and happily done. She had decided at an early age that this was what she could never do. She had even 'gone on the stage' to avoid the possibility, shocking a good many friends and relations but not her immediate family. Her father had actually encouraged her. He was a clergyman, but had great sympathy for her ambition though he did not realise it was chiefly an escape. It was unusual then for daughters of clergymen to become actresses. Legally stage people liked to consider themselves still rogues and vagabonds, but Mr Mildmay, her father, did not accept such distinctions, being no mean performer on the amateur stage himself. At the university he had been specially applauded in comic women's parts. The ADC in those days did not invite actresses to take part in their performances.

Laura desired to see the world, to avoid church work that would as obviously be her fate as the curate who would inevitably fall in love with her. She had realised this at sixteen, had known enough of it all to realise that unless she took unusual steps she was doomed to a useful life, which she was convinced was not for her. She would never be useful. From both her parents she inherited gaiety of spirit. It had not been entirely quenched in them by lives devoted to good works. Yet she remembered the time when she was discontented and dreading the life that seemed to be inevitable, her mother had said:

'My dear, you are like that tree.'

'What tree?'

'The plane tree. Look at it.'

The great plane tree, the pride of the Rectory garden, was flinging its splendid branches here and there, swelling and surging in graceful abandon to a strong laughing wind.

They had watched it together from the old nursery window, fascinated by its vagaries.

'How lovely it is!'

'So are you, and that is why I say that you must resist the idea which I know you have of being an actress. It is out of the question, you know, as I am sure father will always agree. Because you have been able to play parts well as an amateur, is no reason why you should have any success on the stage. The tree though it flings about quite madly, is deeply rooted as you are and can't get away. Nor can you. At least — I know myself,' she had suddenly changed her tone. 'I never wanted the stage. Naturally that never occurred to me. But I was as gay as you are when a girl, and did not at all want the serious life that was my destiny. I'm thankful for it now, because I know what I might have been ...'

'Mother, darling, what might you have been?' Laura was laughing now.

'Never mind!' She laughed too. 'All I want to say is that you are lovely and your loveliness is not for the stage.'

Her mother died when she was seventeen and a year later she went on the stage. Because she did she met Guy before the stage had time to change her much.

Their marriage was another shock for everyone. It was secret because they both disliked weddings, and she could not see herself as a bride. Guy had been eating dinners throughout the brief courtship, and her natural assumption was that he would be called to the Bar if he did anything but write poetry.

And now, the hospital era well behind them, they reached their Chelsea flat after the long walk from Clare Dobson's house.

There were a few letters in the letterbox. Guy lit another pipe and settled into the most comfortable chair. His legs had begun to hurt a little.

'Nothing to do with scarlet fever,' he assured her. 'I always had cramps as a boy.'

She gave him his letters. There was one rather insignificant looking small business-shaped envelope with a crest on the flap.

'This is from Cornwall.'

'I've noticed a good many like that lately. What does it mean?'

'Almost anything,' he laughed.

'Why a crest on such a mean little envelope?'

'Just a fad.'

Then he read the letter, which was obviously very short.

'How would you like to go and live in Cornwall?'

'I should like it very much, I'm sure.'

'This letter is from Father St John. I've told you something about him, haven't I?'

'I think so. Isn't he the priest who arrived at your country home wearing buckle shoes and carrying a whole turbot in a fish basket as a present to your mother?'

'That's the chap. It was his first visit, and he wasn't very sure about the food. Read his letter.'

Dear Guy All right, one pound a week each. No luxuries or comforts full till autumn yours ever.

'That looks as if we were going to stay with him.'

'How quick you are! Does it sound all right?'

'Pretty good. Can we afford it?'

'*Never* ask that. It doesn't enter into it at all. Remember that. It *never* does. The only question is, whether you would like it.'

'Would *you*? That's another question already answered, judging by this letter.'

'Naturally.'

'Supposing I said I wouldn't like it. What would you do?'

'That doesn't enter into it either. Because you *will* like it.'

'Because I must, perhaps.'

'Put it that way if you like. It's all the same ...'

'You know best. And why are we going?'

'Because I want to get out of London and be quiet and think. I've got something on my mind that I want to get settled. I won't bother you with it now.'

'Yes, you will. Is it the Church?'

'Well, yes, it is an idea. I've always had it at the back of my mind.'

'And now it's *on* it. I know so little about you really, and I'm not much good at this sort of thing. But I can always be agreeable about it, I hope.'

'That's very nice of you. You won't mind going to church rather often?'

'I'm quite ready for that. There will be no novelty in it.'

'You'll probably find that there is at Helzephron.'

'All the better for me. That would help a lot.'

'Perhaps too much novelty. We shall see.'

'Helzephron is a promising name. And I can't be bored, with you about. I used to get bored with the inevitability of religious practices, if you know what I mean.'

'That is a little bit pompously put for you. I guess that you are alluding to Protestant church-going generally.'

'Yes, but I enjoyed High Anglican goings-on at St Mary Magdalene, Paddington, in early days.'

'What on earth were you doing there?'

'Staying with people I liked. I never missed High Mass all the time I was with them.'

'We might have met. Though I preferred St Alban's, Holborn, I was often at St Mary Magdalene's.'

'But on the other side of the aisle. Women were segregated then, you remember.'

'Indeed I do. An excellent discipline.'

'I generally sat on the inner edge of a row, not to see or lure the gentlemen opposite but because one could get a good view in the procession of a priest who looked like a young Savonarola. Once I heard him preach — and that was a pity.'

'You enjoyed the ceremonial part of it all, I expect.'

'I was enthralled. Who wouldn't be? It was St Mary's that lured me out of the Protestant church, but unfortunately into the wilderness. Not long afterwards I found myself in the Little Church Around the Corner in New York. It was there one could be married at any time of day or night without a licence.'

'Really? And — er — was one?'

'No, but was invited once, after midnight.'

'Your past is full of mystery. At Helzephron you will get no excitements of either kind. No midnight nuptials and no processions and probably only a harmonium, if that.'

'And when do we go?'

'Father St John has his cousin and family there for the summer.'

'Ah. So there's breathing space,' she mused.

'You're thinking of Ariadne.'

'Partly, perhaps. She has asked me to visit her next week. Clare Dobson warned me that she might be in bed. She is always collapsing and has to rest.'

'Don't let her become a liability, anyway,' said Guy, and began to think of other things.

✕

That first visit of Laura's to Ariadne had been exciting enough. There was so much talk of Paris and the tragedy of not being there, and the misery of being in England and the stories of the famous people she had known, that Laura forgot the prospect of Cornwall, and it was not till she called on her a few days later that she revealed the prospect of their departure, and the future had become slightly obscured.

Ariadne was horrified.

'A clergyman! But that is fearful. Surely you never expected anything like that from him, of all people. Anything but that. Didn't he tell you he was religious before you married him?'

Laura admitted that there hadn't been time to know

everything about him. 'We were only engaged for a fortnight.'

'But you were married in church. Didn't he show any signs then?'

'No. He tried to put the ring on twice before he should. That's all I remember. It's not so much a question of his being religious. I expected it. But I don't look forward to that sort of life. In fact I thought I had avoided it. I don't feel I'm fit for a parson's wife.'

'I shouldn't think you were.' That was the end for the moment. Ariadne looked suddenly tired.

The walk to Ariadne was only too easy for Laura. Not so easy for Guy, whose leg seemed always stricken when a visit was in view.

'A bone in me leg?' Laura would remember her nurse's excuse to avoid unnecessary effort.

'Call it that if you like.'

But he had been once. He was too deeply depressed by artistic squalor to go again. A fisherman's cottage — a shieling — yes, that indeed, in a dim frowst, and a strong reek of peat, shag, sweat and dripping dogs — he could spend hours happily in such an atmosphere. But this arid dusty discomfort, unreasonable and helpless, filled him with gloom. He saw no excuse for living like that. He sat on a slippery Windsor chair watching Ariadne pour weak tea into cracked china cups. Then his eyes had wandered to the chimneypiece, to the decayed rose, and his spirits fell. Symbolism — and how dusty! Silence enwrapped him. Laura saw the signs. He must never come again.

He had no objection to Ariadne at the flat. After all, she had to eat occasionally, and she was better as a guest than as a hostess. As long as she did not get excited and shrill she talked with great charm and understanding. Art was only lightly touched upon. Life was safer, and she warmed to general conversation that was never banal or tedious. The afternoon would often draw on into dusk, and Clare Dobson was sometimes there, to lead Ariadne into reminiscences of Paris and sometimes of childhood, less often of the Dublin era, at which she seemed to shy like a wild pony. Was there a mystery there or only boredom? Could Ariadne ever have enjoyed starvation for the sake of her art, for which in those days she was apparently ready to die? That was what Laura was asking herself after Ariadne had spent the last evening with them before their move to Cornwall.

'What do you think about it?' she asked Guy.

He looked out of the window. His slanting eyes narrowed. Then:

'It's quite true about the starvation.'

'How do you know?'

'I know a good deal more which you can read in this letter from Dublin.'

'Who wrote it?'

'An old friend. I asked him if he knew anything about her.'

'Why?'

'Why? Because I was interested. I am interested in her and her relation to us. She is either a fraud or genuine. I like to know. Of course she is not a fraud. You must read the letter. Then you will know all you need to know.'

A letter from Dublin

Dear Guy,

Your surprising letter comes well to me. I am just in the mood to write the story of Ariadne Berden, short though it may be from me, but you will find other sources no doubt. The good is that my father knew her, and he is still about and gives it at first hand.

She belonged to people in the West, a proud lot, known to neighbours far and wide as the Royal Family, not, mind you, because there was any boast of descent from Kings of Eire or any such cheap nonsense. It was, so I understand, simply that they kept inviolate the grand manner.

For them, you will laugh to hear, the present Royal Family was merely 'these Guelphs', to be dismissed as medieval ghosts of no importance whatever.

At the age of eighteen she escaped from home, cursed, when he found her gone, by a fox-hunting, mean-hearted father who had never unscrewed the top of his flask with any man, said the neighbours. His sisters, Melanie and Eulalie the old maids, and Grizelda, the youngest, were mouldering together with the estate — the slow progressive dilapidation of which was the liveliest and, I should think, the most absorbing activity in the domain.

The aunts, Eulalie and Melanie, denounced the truant girl, drew the cobwebs closer and forgot her. Their brother stormed and raved but made no effort to get her back. She had disgraced the family and there was an end. Aunt Grizelda who years ago had mourned a young husband, held her tongue. She took no steps. Her small independent income was essential to the needs of the enclosed family. Renegades could hope for nothing. This was made plain enough, when Ariadne's note was found in the hall:

> I am going away and will never come back. I am called.
> Ariadne.

Naturally the old man suspected the worst, not having the wits to know that his daughter had been spending all her days in a studio attic doing something more than look out of the window. When she had gone, the attic studio was given for the first time a grand clearance of 'Ariadne's rubbish', followed by a bonfire. The aunts were not allowed to see the holocaust superintended by the master. He had never heard the word symbolic. Ariadne's vagaries were damned unpleasant, he thought, and conveyed as much to his sisters who knew even less than he did and accepted his verdict, I presume without suffering frustrated curiosity at all.

Ariadne took the best of her work with her, and began at the art school straight away. She also took some good trinkets and her quarter's dress allowance, and, would you believe it, the dear simple lady engaged a poor woman to escort her to and from the school at half a crown a day, thinking it not proper for a female of quality to be seen out alone. This didn't last long, nor did the trinkets, and she soon had as much escort as she needed among the other students. The art school hailed her as a genius and she soon got noticed by Dublin society. I don't know how long this lasted. Not long, I fancy. My father knew her only when she had rid herself of all except her passion for art. She would die for it. This was the CALL, and she would answer it with her life, if necessary. She would starve for it. And she did. Funds were low and she was proud.

She rented a small half-furnished room and troubled no one. She lived for weeks on cocoa and bread alone, spending a penny a day. Being already of a delicate constitution, she wilted. She sank into the state when dreams become realities without pen being put to paper or brush to canvas.

She would go to the school, full of fervent inspiration. Then, faced by the tools that threatened hard work, she would find an excuse for abandoning them. Some urgent task unfinished at home … smiling gently she would fade away into her dreams that led to nothing. In her case there was no need for drugs; hunger and longing were enough.

The word went round, of course. The girl from the West was starving herself to death. Something should be done. It was known that she and her father were equally obdurate. There was no help there. A kind creature who was not artist or poet, offered her a room in his home and engaged her as companion to his delicate wife, this latter to save her pride. Surprisingly she accepted the offer, knowing that he would pay her fees at the school. But her pride was not saved, because she had not quite understood what being a companion involved. However decent the delicate wife was, and she was, I believe, an admirable lady, the position would not for long please one who had never known servitude and was anxious to die for her art.

She went back to cocoa and bread and the half-empty room, and her abstract fantasies, some of which, I believe, later on made a stir. But I have never seen them.

Then came a great poet to rescue her with a fine offer from a business friend. To draw advertisements … 'Not so tiring as artistic creation, and would bring in a good sum meanwhile,' he was suggesting when she withered him with elaborate thanks and showed him the door, assuring him that she would rather die than degrade her art to that extent. So the situation remained the same … She would rather die.

This great man was convinced that she had talent of a high order, but no sense. No inheritance of hard brain work — no inheritance, so far as he knew, of brains at all. Dying for your art's foolish, if you accomplish nothing before dying. To reach a mystical state by cocoa and bread and dreams was emptiness. He himself had a long family history of scholars and workers behind him; he knew that even so art was difficult and long. He continued to interest himself in her welfare until she fell in love with a drunken scoundrel and lost whatever prestige she had by foolish behaviour which wasn't really surprising in such an innocent virtuous girl who knew no better and got lost in the unexpected.

My father tells me of the portentous change that came over her and the effort made by certain good mystics who had befriended her, to help her when she seemed forsaken by everyone. This is the end of my story, for she left Dublin after being distressfully ill and cared for by those same mystics (and let me now confess that my father was one of them) and I understand, landed not long afterwards in Paris where they tell me she picked up again with that miserable scoundrel, but that doesn't come into my story, and I'm glad of it. I know nothing more of her.

When will I be seeing you again? My compliments to your fortunate wife.

Yours ever,
Terence

Chapter Two

The Cornish Riviera Express made its usual grand exit from Paddington Station on a fine day in late August 1909. The novelty of this wonderful romantic train still excited the traveller in search of sunburnt mirth; the word Riviera alone was magical in those days, and to do it all in about six hours was luxury beyond dreams.

Solitary on the platform, her eyes on the retreating train, stood Mrs Mallory, Senior. Unexpectedly she had arrived at the very moment when Guy and Laura were getting into their reserved third-class seats, fortunately with only a little hand luggage. The large trunks had been stored in the van, and there was a sense of freedom in the disposal of them, for they were very large and heavy and had already given more trouble than was bearable in transit from the flat to the station. Books and music bulked them even more than boots and shoes. They had left the flat to be inhabited by Laura's brother John, though Guy was convinced that he would at once make a pig-sty of it. Laura thought it would not matter if he did. It could always be cleared up, and after all, John was a nice person to think was there even if he was untidy. This was Laura's point of view, revealing to him clearly the happy-go-lucky side of her character. However, the prospect before them — and they were on their way to the station when this revelation of Laura's tendency took place — was so entrancing and the disposing of luggage so engrossing to Guy that all was forgotten until they settled down into their seats. Then Mrs Mallory appeared at the door of the compartment, followed by a porter carrying a large elegant basket.

'Just a few little oddments for the journey, my dears, on the top, and an offering to Father St John with my kind regards, underneath. Nothing perishable.'

They had both leapt out and greeted her while the porter rearranged the light luggage on the rack. There was not much time.

'I had to come, my dear children, and am sorry to be a little late. But you must get back quickly. The train is going to start. Just a kiss. Ah, wait! There is a bottle of champagne for you to drink when you arrive. You will be very tired I am sure. Don't forget it.'

'Dear Mother, you think of everything! We certainly shan't.'

She kissed them both and seemed to walk away. But as the train glided out she watched it sadly and wondered …

'What does it mean? Is it madness, this idea? Or is it exactly what I want? Will they have proper food? What sort of a household is it? How can I tell? They know almost as little about that as I do. One can only pray,' she decided, as she climbed into her brougham for home. 'I shall miss them. Yes, now I realise that he is gone, and it will never be the same again. Cornwall is a very long way off. I shall miss him. He is no longer mine, but she, I must admit fairly, does not seem possessive. At any rate if she were, it would be fatal for her. I was possessive, and he soon showed me that a possessive mother would be what he called a blight. He was alluding to another mother, but he meant it for me. A warning. That is his way. Not to hurt me but to warn. He has such delicacy always with me. Perhaps with everyone … I am not sure about that. Nor was it quite delicate perhaps to marry as he did without warning. It's no good arguing with myself about him. And then this priest, Father St John. A man of great charm, there was no doubt. Socially congenial, surely unorthodox; even a rebel, one might say, and from some points of view — notorious. But undoubtedly sincere and a true Christian in his convictions. But was this the right atmosphere for Guy to choose for meditation on sacred matters? Nothing better could happen than Guy in the Church. He would be a great influence. Whatever he does he will be that, it's true enough. A great actor? Easily, but that's almost a commonplace on both sides of the family. A great scholar? He promised that at school and college. A great Judge? Good heavens! He might be anything — useless to prophesy … That will be enough for the present.' She laughed at herself as she stepped out of the brougham and cheerfully dismissed the coachman.

✳

In the train Laura was not in the mood to read papers. She was soon as deep in thought as Guy's mother had been. He was reading, with every now and then an eye cocked at the landscape they were passing through, not to miss anything worth seeing, and determined not to be engrossed by it until half-way through Somerset, the prelude to Dorset, the western county which had most attracted him since childhood.

'Dorset has the worst train service of them all so it will probably be the last to be spoiled. Most people rush through it to get to Devon and even probably to Cornwall, but I don't know about that yet. Dorset is the loveliest of counties. We may live there one day. I wouldn't wonder.'

'Nor would I,' Laura agreed. She wouldn't wonder at anything, she had decided some time ago.

She gazed at the pattern of hills slashed green, gold and umber in the magical afternoon light. 'It looks peaceful.'

'Yes, but there's as much history buried under those gentle hills as anywhere in Britain. And the great Roman road (comparatively modern) goes right through it as far as Cornwall starting from the Norfolk coast. That makes you think.'

'It certainly does.'

There was enough to make her think, past, present and future. 'Anyway, it's lovely country.'

They fell into silence. Laura's thoughts wandered while she gazed more at Guy than the landscape in which he was engrossed. What lay beneath the surface of the fair pattern, so brightly displayed, so elusive, of his character? Why, for instance, that secret inquiry in Dublin, that unrevealed desire to probe the legend of Ariadne after discussing it openly with her. And the dramatic production of the Terence letter out of the blue? Not vastly important, of course, but eminently practical and surprising because of that, characteristic after all, perhaps, of the incalculable being now to be ever her beloved problem.

Her mind went revolving — revolving through the maze of her new life. She went back to the beginning of it, while he was still lost in contemplation of the landscape.

✕

And how had it all begun?

Guy had first appeared concretely in John's shady room at Oxford in their last term. Before that, he had been merely a tormenting fact in the background of all her projects for her brother John. There was scarcely a plan that was not frustrated by Guy Mallory. To begin with, they had borrowed between them enough to buy a house in the Cotswolds, to which they were to retire when they came down from Oxford. She remembered how her holiday at home was shattered because John was tied to the Cotswold house all through the Easter vacation, preparing it for Guy's occupation. He never went near it all the time. But he might have done so, at any moment. John had to be there in any case. Guy was staying in Wiltshire with the family of a girl he admired. There was not the least likelihood of his moving from there till he went up for his last term. But in the Cotswolds John stayed obstinately, in a half-empty house by himself, with an occasional visit from his disapproving family.

Why should John have been allowed to borrow enough to buy (with mortgages) a house at his age? His elder brothers had never thought of such a thing when they were undergraduates. The whole idea was inconceivably mad and almost improper. This was the family. Laura did not share those sentiments for she had no objection to the idea of a Cotswold house, if she were ever able to stay there, with John only. She was jealous of the influence that Mallory had upon her favourite brother, resented deeply this personality consuming apparently the whole of John's existence.

There was something vampire-like about it. She pondered over the large photograph of Guy that hung in John's deserted bedroom. Under a high Byronic forehead glowed large almond-shaped eyes. The cheekbones were high, the face wide but tapering to a cleft chin. Above this chin a small vain mouth, a Cupid's bow. Hair brushed back smoothly and ears pointed like a faun's. This young man was obviously an egotist and a cold-blooded sensualist. He might be a poet. He might even be, as John declared with heat, a genius. But why should John give up a dance at the home of the girl he loved best because Guy might turn up from Wiltshire?

'But my dear John, even if he does, your house-keeper is there to look after him. Why on earth —?'

'Couldn't possibly risk it. She might do everything all wrong. Besides, I want to be there if he comes.'

But he didn't.

There had been a telegram, 'Arriving Thursday.' Vast preparations were made. Super tinned things from Oxford in case Mrs Dane made a mess of the cooking. His favourite Burton beer ordered. Flowers in all the rooms from the garden. Fires everywhere for fear of damp. And then another wire.

'Not coming.'

At this, John came and spent a night at home. He blushed when Laura scoffed and said, 'I told you so.'

'Of course there's a very sound reason. He may come later.'

'This Guy of yours is a myth. I believe you invented him.'

'I wish you could meet him. He is really a wonderful person. There is no one like him.'

'I still don't believe in him. And anyway I think you're possessed.'

'You don't understand,' was all he said at that.

So Laura did not go to the Cotswold cottage, though John begged her to spend a week-end. She wouldn't risk meeting Guy. The idea of him was frightening.

So term began, and the cottage was deserted, and Laura went up to Oxford for Eights Week. And there, among the shadows of John's room, she met Guy.

There were about half a dozen young men drinking iced coffee and eating strawberries and cream when she arrived. She knew Guy was expected. She felt nervous and defiant and had violent toothache. She knew as soon as she entered that he was not there. A quick glance at each pleasant young man presented to her assured her that this was not the paragon.

John was watching the door out of the corner of his eye.

'Toothache, poor girl? Then you mustn't eat an ice.' He gave her some tea abstractedly. Someone sat down at the piano and began to play Chopin.

Then the door opened, and Guy was there …

The piano stopped, the shady room was illumined. Was it the vivid green tie that Guy was wearing?

When she had shaken hands she retired to the window and looked out at the meadows and at the hideous gargoyle grinning into the room. She was dazzled by that brilliant creature who was like a flash of lightning in a dull sky. She knew at once it was no use expecting John to resist the fascination of him. She disliked him more because of his power; she pitied that poor girl he was making love to. While she looked out she listened to his talk. He was, of course, holding the stage and being amusing. There were bursts of laughter.

Then suddenly he was standing beside her.

'A glass of port's the best thing for toothache. John, you must have a bottle somewhere? Give some to your sister.'

His eyes were as brilliant as his tie (only they were sapphire blue). The small vain mouth surprisingly stretched into a wide rather sad smile. Was there mockery in his glance? But she drank the port when he gave it to her, his left hand raised in a priestly gesture.

'Better already,' he smiled after watching her intently as she drank. He took the glass from her and held it until she said 'Yes' with a faint unwilling smile.

'Now I must leave you all. A train to meet.'

He forced his way through protesting undergraduates and was gone.

The shadows thickened and her tooth began to throb. The party was obviously over.

The charm began to work not long after the first meeting, at a Ladies v Gentlemen cricket match not far from Oxford. After tea when the match was finished she was not surprised when he walked her up and down at the other end of the field, not because, she thought, he was attracted by her, but because he would have known that at least one of the lady cricketers finishing their tea against a distant wall might be mad with envy at the sight.

This was, in fact, so, but Laura should not have been suspected of connivance, for she was quite sure that the principal envious young lady was indeed the lady of the moment, and she had no ambition to alter the situation.

But it had altered — decidedly. In London she got into the habit of lunching with her brother John, who was now sharing rooms with Guy. She still carefully avoided meeting Guy, until one midday she was told that Mr John had been unexpectedly called away. She therefore left the house only to be recalled by the landlady, who said that Mr Mallory was in, and would be glad if she would come up for a moment. The door being held open invitingly, she could hardly refuse. The door was open ... she went up nervously. He took her to lunch in Soho, and later in the day, to the Canterbury Music Hall. A fine test for a well-brought-up girl. They were married in a month.

Chapter Three

For some weeks Father St John had been anticipating the arrival of Guy Mallory and his wife with mixed but usually fairly sanguine emotions. He knew enough of Guy to realise that wherever he went, he would leave a light yet indelible footstep. His wife was unlikely to be a nice mousy little woman who would at once undertake the housekeeping in a humble spirit. That was more than one could expect — or perhaps endure. Women were inclined at the slightest encouragement to take possession of the house and everyone in it, which involved no peace or comfort, but an embittered resentment. This he had known once and, suddenly realising the threat of spiritual annihilation, had sacked the housekeeper and advertised for deaf and dumb servants, without success. He could only hope that Guy's wife would not be a disturbing *femme fatale* in their midst. He had a dim horror of such infestations, so remote from his own experience. However, he had enough faith in Guy's good taste to risk housing them both indefinitely. After all, he mused in an optimistic mood, he usually found a way out of whatever predicament threatened him. He looked back, for instance, at his reception by this parish three years ago after his induction, when he startled a large spurious congregation which had gathered to hear a good hearty Matins at eleven o'clock and something fresh in the way of a sermon. A liberal Asperges had driven them from the church. There was even a threat of a summons for assault by a prominent chapel member who had played truant from curiosity and occupied the most conspicuous seat on the aisle, down which the Vicar passed with half-closed eyes, flicking Holy Water in the faces of his congregation with what was afterwards described as a large painter's brush. The chapel member, possibly by accident, got it full in the eyes. Father St

John smiled to himself when he remembered this. A surprise he had known it would be, but it was also a demonstration, a warning of what to expect. The result was, naturally, that in three years the congregation had shrunk to less than a dozen. There had been indignant episcopal visitations during which occasionally the distinguished visitant would be invited before retiring to bed to play two-handed bridge with the culprit, which he usually enjoyed. Mr Kensit had brawled frequently, and his top-hat was once kicked down the aisle by a fervent young Anglo-Catholic. There had, in fact, been plenty of excitement. And now, here he was, encompassed by a small band of followers who loved him for his charm, his eccentricity and his white-hot child-like faith that warmed their hearts. Puzzled and exasperated they frequently were, these simple villagers by the dear Father's antics in church. The Latin Mass recited at top speed left John Bonython, for instance, in a dither.

'I can't keep harking like a fox,' he grumbled to his wife who pulled him up sharply (she was always doing that) for muddling his genuflections. 'How can I tell what it's all about?'

Mrs Bonython, not quite sure herself, crushed him with a frowning silence. She had a small proud head and dark passionate eyes, was one of those who would go to the stake for their beliefs (if necessary). Commonsense leavened her emotional character; she had been one of the first to appreciate the quality of the Vicar. John, her husband, was no fool, but he was slower than she, contented in the background. They kept the village shop and sometimes gave teas to trippers in the summer.

There was one member of the congregation who knew very well what it was all about, and that was Miss Josephine Want, who had chosen to follow Father St John from his last parish, with no encouragement from him. She was an old hand at

High Anglican ritual, and kept her beady eyes on the Vicar's vagaries at the altar with a surge of indignation, excitement and love. There was some confusion in her worship.

'If he does that again, I swear I won't come any more!' she would mutter.

It was hard to differentiate the Vicar from the ritual of the Mass — in spite of his disgusting rudeness to her on every possible occasion. Yes, disgusting!

'Miss Want, you are forbidden the vicarage,' was a constant threat flung at her after Mass.

'Don't be silly, Father. You know perfectly well that I am coming to breakfast.'

'Very well, very well. For the last time.'

He would rush ahead of her from the church to the vicarage. She always stayed on her knees until she saw that he had finished in the vestry. He would sit in stubborn oblivion of her presence while they consumed boiled eggs and coffee in the vicarage. (And what good coffee it was! Made by himself, of course.) Breakfast over, she would go resolutely into the study and light her cigarette (she was a great smoker), while the Vicar sat busily at his desk, doing nothing, his back turned, inviting her by his attitude and curt replies to get out and leave him in peace.

At last she would go and get her bicycle (which she always left at the vicarage before Mass, a hostage) and call loudly:

'Rex! Rex! Come along, old man. Poor old man!'

Her sheepdog lay in the church porch during Mass, and, denied entry into the vicarage, wandered about the back premises while his mistress was at breakfast, yelping frequently and without confidence at the firmly shut kitchen door. He was a handsome dog of the collie breed, cruelly suspected by neighbouring farmers of sheep maiming, without, said Miss Want, an ounce of evidence. Nevertheless, she had sometimes been summoned to her front door after dark by a heavy attack on the knocker to be confronted by a rough figure carrying a lantern and a gun, who with loud oaths declared that Rex must die and that he was there to shoot him. Then Rex would become a hero carrying his feathery tail more proudly than usual after his owner had routed the intruder and produced an extra bone for supper, with a great many tearful caresses to which he responded with long sweeps of his tongue across her face. These nocturnal visits were generally regarded as a practical joke, which the personality of Miss Want most unfortunately invited. And next day the village would have a good laugh.

And now, off they would go, Miss Want and her faithful dog, she pushing her bike vigorously up the short sloping drive, her ankles encased in liver-coloured spats, her wild eyes, in a face which reminded one of a half-ripe blackberry, roving to right and left, her ears strained for the crunch of gravel behind her. Pursuit? No, it would only be Jude the house-boy, and he would do it on purpose to annoy — the wretched creature! Well, she didn't care. She wasn't a soldier's daughter for nothing. Reverses were part of the game. Stimulating! She wasn't going to give in. Never! 'Up guards and at 'em.'

With a hop, skip and a jump, she was on her bike, with Rex barking idiotically, bounding beside her.

※

The prospect of the Mallorys' visit could not long be kept from Miss Want, since their first appearance in public would certainly be in the church. The Vicar never explained his visitors to Miss Want or to anyone else. There were plenty of queer, sometimes frumpish souls seeking truth whom he did not feel it necessary even to introduce to Miss Want, avid as she always was to investigate arrivals. Indeed, part of his pleasure was to keep Miss Want guessing. This was, in fact, one of his favourite diversions — innocent at least, and quite devoid of sin. Sometimes he allowed a veil of mystery to spread itself over specially dull people, so that Miss Want would come peering into the vicarage to take them for a jolly cliff walk and so relieve the Vicar of intolerable boredom and responsibility. In this way she sometimes proved useful to him, which she would not admit. She liked to regard it as her social duty to pay calls and be friendly, as the only lady in the village.

'Nonsense, Miss Want. It is the duty of the priest to call on the villagers. It is no part of your duty as a dweller in the village. By all means take some of my visitors for walks. You know all the best routes, but do not consider it a social or Christian duty to meddle in the parish.'

The last was said with one of his bitter-sweet smiles that she knew so well, and left one nowhere. Of course it was only his joke. He could not possibly accuse her of 'meddling'. A kind interest in their affairs was encouraging for them, poor souls. She was convinced that they loved her. She delighted in the thought that she was a Lady Bountiful of the old regime — in a small way, she had to admit, with cheap sweets for the children and damaged blouses for their mothers. She would have liked to do more, but — LSD, she sometimes hinted, with a chiselled grin, was not what it used to be. She liked to help.

'A finger in every pie,' chanted the Vicar with another of his thwarting smiles, so that one could not take offence at his levity. But what he would keep close from Miss Want was the motive of this threatened invasion — the plan — the plan — the motive — the reason of it — And he would blench in sudden panic. Why? Why? he would exclaim as his mind rushed madly into a cloud of apprehension. Why allow himself to get agitated about it for a moment? Guy was a delightful creature to have about the place, a companion, unmatched, after his own heart. He had hailed the prospect of this visit and its object with enthusiasm. Guy would have been better alone, but there! He was married and that had been known and understood from the beginning. Why? he demanded of himself, while fingers with their hard bitten nails clutched at his disordered hair (his habit when distressed), why did his heart sink when he passed the spare room door and caught a glimpse of Mrs Jolly and a village girl in brisk action with brush and broom redding up after his cousin Thelma's occupation — the huge double mattress that she had bought, airing on the bed? Surely this last was an unnecessary extravagance by Thelma, who had been only too lavish in her decorations of the upper floor, almost completely renewed, except that his small bedroom facing north had been forgotten in the excitement. This he had not regretted. He was afraid of luxury and blamed the comfortable home of his youth for the deplorable idleness which he had always been too lazy to fight. The frugal cell with the punctilio of daily Mass held for him a reassurance, an affirmation — something to grasp at in unfortunate moments.

Lavish was the word for Thelma! A family characteristic, not altogether to be deplored, especially when results were seen at the vicarage. Quite unexpectedly she had allowed her boys to spend their holidays running wild about the beaches and towans while she devoted herself to supervising improvements in the house which she found in what she called a ghastly condition. He had not agreed with her, assured her that he had been quite satisfied with it for three years. Dust had accumulated, he admitted, for lack of proper service, but he enjoyed it.

'That is absurd,' said Thelma, 'and only shows how much you yourself need a spring cleaning, inside and out.'

'Concentrate, then, please, upon the upper floor, and leave downstairs as it is, so that I can live in peace'.

'You mean, of course, the house, not yourself.'

'Of course,' replied her cousin shortly. 'What else should I mean? Get on with it, and don't try to spring clean me or touch my little room.'

And so it came about. For a month workmen were busy with ladders, paint and papers, creating havoc on the landing, while the Vicar enjoyed the peace of his own domain downstairs in daylight, and crept peacefully through the disorder to his own untouched little bedroom at night. No, it was not altogether to be deplored, he decided when the upper floor was finished and shining with creamy paint and quiet wallpapers, the cranky boards covered with such good linoleum, said the village, awed by that and the bathroom — most of all by the bathroom, to be shown with pride to people who had most of them never seen such a thing before. Nothing but cold baths as yet, for the hot water system was at a rudimentary stage, and likely to remain there, thought the Vicar, when he contemplated the array of estimates and demands which had been assembling for months in his business drawer. (This was Thelma's idea, to have a business drawer, a real novelty.) There was nothing in it but these documents which he examined as seldom as possible, adding one now and then with averted eyes. He hoped they would settle themselves, somehow or other, in due course.

Meanwhile, here it all was, ready for the Mallorys. Thelma and family vanished; peace reigning more or less and — good heavens! The Mallorys were imminent — in three days they would be here.

He packed a small holdall and called to Jude.

'Get my bicycle ready. I am leaving in half an hour.'

'Leaving, Father? How's that?'

'Going into Retreat. Truro. Shall be back in three days. Tell Mrs Jolly. She must look after Mr and Mrs Mallory till I come back — the same evening.'

'The same evening as what, Father?'

'Don't be impertinent. You know quite what I mean, you tiresome boy. As Mrs Jolly is out I can't stop to give orders, but she will know what to do. To tell Mr and Mrs Mallory to make themselves comfortable, and that I shall be back the same evening in time for supper.'

'Your tyres belong to be blown, and you've lost your mudguard, Father.'

'I never had one ...'

'Yes, you did, Father. I mind tying it on for you after you had that scramble in the ditch at Chegwidden.'

'Tying it on! How could you do that? Nonsense. Stop talking and get the bicycle ready at once. And find my crystal rosary.'

'I found it this morning all scat under your bed. It's on your dressing-table. Will you take it with you?'

'Not like that, of course. Have it mended before I come back — if you can,' he added with a sudden misgiving.

'I can and all.'

'No. Better not touch it. Too complicated. I shall send it to London.'

Jude picked up the bicycle pump, whistling.

'That boy needs discipline,' the Vicar complained to himself. 'So do we all,' he added, trying to embrace the whole Church of England in this generalisation, but finally concentrating it on himself as he stood before his dressing-table and sadly surveyed the broken rosary.

'Not *all* scat after all.' He put it in his pocket. 'Safer there. And still usable at a pinch.'

Mrs Jolly received the news from Jude of the Vicar's departure with a sniff.

'Hm. Another vagary.'

Being already under notice she was not really interested.

✕

The cab was waiting for Guy and Laura at the station, but it was not capable of carrying more than light luggage, and it promised to be a long tedious business engaging transport for the rest. They had left the Riviera express at Gwinear Road, and this was a minor station with few amenities, the best of which were achieved by Guy, who soon charmed the station into an eager bustle so that the big luggage would without doubt arrive that very night at the vicarage, five miles though it was with rain threatening.

They entered the cab which was by this time surrounded by an interested little crowd. The cab was stuffy as all cabs were, but it was only necessary to open both windows by their shabby leather straps, when they reached open country, to breathe the richly scented autumn evening air. They were thrilled by the lonely haunted road, with every now and then a weather-grey signpost pointing vaguely to a fabulous destination. At last they reached the vicarage. It was twilight. The house was white, square and mid-Victorian. A garden facing them sloped down into a dell which suggested fairies. Pink amaryllis with purple-brown stalks grew round the house, the air was bitter sweet and there was a plague of daddy-long-legs. But where was the Vicar?

Mrs Jolly appeared, followed by Jude in his best blue jersey and his black hair well brushed.

'Well, I never did—!' Mrs Jolly had exclaimed when he joined her in the kitchen before the arrival.

'No more didn't I,' he replied, tweaking at her Sunday frills.

Then the crackle of wheels brought them both out on the porch.

✕

Guy was the first to appear from the cab. He shot a quick glance into the dim interior over the heads of Mrs Jolly and Jude. The Vicar? As nothing transpired Guy helped Laura to alight with her large handbag, and Jude, his face flushed with excitement, hastened to take it from her. The cab was cleared like lightning, the luggage upstairs in a twinkling. This was no ordinary arrival, as Jude had already anticipated. Mrs Jolly soberly carried the tea-tray into the study where the guests were already established in apparent comfort. The question of the Vicar's absence was left to explain itself, as Mrs Jolly, with a severe glance at Guy, produced a paper which she handed to him.

'The Father was to be here in time for supper tonight, but this paper was handed in at the kitchen door by a man on a bicycle two hours ago.'

A flimsy paper torn from a notebook:

Unavoidably delayed. Hope to be back tomorrow with luck. Don't wait for me try Looe Pool for a walk if fine. Primitive and lovely. Excalibur!

'The Father can never be depended on,' Mrs Jolly ventured. Guy hastened to turn the implied criticism with a cheerful announcement of a visit to Looe Pool tomorrow. Mrs Jolly retired with a glance at Laura who also showed plainly with a smile that she had not expected to have the note handed to her, nor was she put out by the news.

The whole of next day was a delight to both. They left the vicarage early, taking a basket of hard-boiled eggs and Cornish pasties gladly packed by Mrs Jolly who was anxious to get rid of them and put the house to rights after their unpacking operations which had seriously upset the evening since the arrival of the big luggage. The sight of it was enough to send Mrs Jolly straight to bed, while Jude was about until after midnight carrying books upstairs under the direction of Guy. Laura puzzled for a time over the disposal of their wardrobe, which seemed to her unnecessarily abundant for a country visit now that it had to be her duty to separate and arrange it.

Lightheartedly they had both made decisions on what they would need, and flung in afterthoughts at the last minute. Now here they all were and where would they go? Guy's suits and shirts were easy to deal with and in fact everything of his was soon in order. She hung up her own dresses and suits in a fairly convenient cupboard, then decided to leave the rest to the morning. She shut down the ravaged trunks when Guy dismissed Jude, the books half unpacked down below, and they went to bed. Jude retired to a small study by the front door which had become his bedroom.

Next morning they set out in a rosy mist for their walk to Looe Pool. Rain was in the air, but it was only a threat. On their way they found a sandy cove, and a small church facing the towans, with nothing between it and the sea but a great rock which must have protected it for hundreds of years; it looked very ancient. Steps led up to the church, yellow mesembryanthemums trailed to the beach. They found the church locked. Notices on a battered board were not informative, but Guy knew that this was the other cure of Father St John's.

A cheap varnished pitch pine pew lay on its back, rain-washed, beside the porch.

'That looks rather depressing.'

'It would look worse inside,' was all Guy said about it.

Laura sensed an enigma at the back of this remark, but did not try to penetrate further. Plenty of time …

They reached the Pool, lying tranquilly behind the bar of sand that had divided it from the sea for generations (the work, it was firmly believed locally, of demons who still stopped at nothing). In case of flooding the Lord of the Manor granted a permit to the privileged inhabitants of his domain occasionally to break the bar, by digging a small channel in the bank, and letting the pent-up river pour forth its waters and meet the disturbed and angry sea with a resounding impact heard and seen for miles. Today it was silent. A few elegant birds swept through the grey limpid air. ('Terns,' said Guy.)

There was mystery about. Not a sign of humanity anywhere.

'Lunch now.' Guy broke the spell. He was not keen on spells. The legend of Excalibur he preferred to place in the Vale of Avalon. In any case, a display of sentimental ecstasies must always be avoided in everyday life. He was not quite convinced as yet that Laura was of the same mind as he was. So far, she had shown restraint under provocation — too much perhaps, he mused, looking at her profile which he admired more than he admitted. Her reaction, however, to this dangerous situation, was to unpack Mrs Jolly's basket and give him his lunch on a grassy knoll.

While they sat there, the peace did hold them entranced. They ate in silence, drank the Cornish cider Mrs Jolly had thought of. Then he whispered, 'Did you hear anything?'

She held her breath and shook her head.

'I heard something. Can it be the Echo?'

'What echo?'

'A double echo across the water which no one can explain, and of course no one wants to. It's a rich mystery. Let's listen.'

There was a sound, and as they heard it something appeared in the distance, outlined against the sea.

'What can that be?'

'I think,' said Laura, 'that it's human and might be a woman led by a dog.'

'The dog was the echo then.'

'Or perhaps the woman?'

'She won't come this way.'

As he said this the figure stopped and stared with hand raised to forehead — hesitated, and then went on its way.

'I don't think it's a native. It might, of course, have come out of the sea. A draggled look. Anything could happen here. Or perhaps a visitor if there is such a thing at this time of year.'

'Let us pack up. It will soon rain.'

They were back at the vicarage before the rain, which came down in drenching plumps. A fire was blazing in the study and Mrs Jolly was fussing about whether the Father would be back tonight, and whether she should get the joint in or prepare eggs when he did arrive.

'There's no knowing about anything here. No order at all,' she grumbled, half excusing herself for indecision and half accusing the Vicar of bad manners.

The joint was decided upon. A late supper if necessary would hurt no one. Mrs Jolly began to realise that the Mallorys would not fuss. They sat down calmly before the fire with books, ready for the Vicar or not the Vicar. What did it matter? Mrs Jolly retired with a faint fleck of foam at the corner of her mouth, which had already been observed yesterday in the excitement of their arrival.

'They take it easy anyway,' she muttered. 'Why doesn't she go up and tidy their room? It's in a nice mess … I shan't go and turn down the bed. Just to show her.'

But she did. She went straight up before she prepared the joint and removed a quantity of books and a pile of feminine garments from the bed to chairs. It was meant for a demonstration of disapproval. Only she did not realise that it would not be noticed at all. The turned down bed was taken for granted.

So they sat calmly, expecting the Father, and at between nine and ten he appeared. He was not wet, the rain had ceased, but a spine of mud was streaking his back. He greeted them with:

'Hullo, Guy, do you play bridge?' Then he shook Laura's hand with a shy glance soon averted. Laura understood his apprehension and took an instant liking to the old friend of Guy's boyhood.

They played two-handed bridge, each with a wooden screen to hold his dummy hand, until supper was announced by Jude. 'My rubber,' said the Vicar. 'Have a drink. Nothing but altar wine in the house.'

Jude brought in glasses and they drank success to the Lay-readership. It was the Vicar's toast, a faintly benevolent smile lighting his pale face.

This was rather sudden for the Mallorys. Since they had arrived they had been so lost in the mad fairyland atmosphere of Helzephron that the object of their visit had been almost forgotten. They drank, and dinner was ready at the right moment. They moved on to their first meal together. Talk between the two men was mostly reminiscent. Laura had developed the art of being amused and not interrupting; her lively expression was, thought her husband, always, on such occasions, a useful accessory to talk. She tacitly agreed with him and, being of a lazy disposition, was content to enjoy good company.

The pudding course was an exquisite créme caramel, which happened to be a favourite of Guy's, and so delicious was its creaminess that he suggested it was a pity Mrs Jolly was under notice.

'Don't believe it, my dear. It's her show piece, taught by me. And I am responsible for the garlic cloves stuck into the joint. Her cooking is atrocious when she is let loose. Muck, my dear.'

Such plain speaking roused an unexpectedly hearty laugh from Laura.

'You cook, then? You like cooking?' She was enchanted when he nodded gravely at her.

'Will you teach me?' She was eager. The very atmosphere of the house was changed in this surprising revelation.

'I can tell you how to make a good French dressing, if you don't know it already.'

'I know nothing,' she declared, determined to make this flash of light into the rather dim domestic future become a firm reality.

'I don't believe that,' he said with politeness. 'Is it true, Guy?'

'Only lack of experience. She can do most things if she likes.'

This confident statement from Guy, though pleasant to hear, reminded her of a school report, too familiar to be quite comfortable.

'I should like to learn anything you can teach me, Father,' she said humbly, without coyness.

'Are you interested in sweets?' asked the Vicar.

'What kind of sweets?'

'Chocolates, confectionery — that sort of thing.'

'I never thought of it.'

'There's someone here who makes sweets and sells them. I don't think she can cook anything else. I know she would be delighted to teach you.'

'Don't lead me away now,' was her unspoken demand. 'I don't want to learn sweets from a confectioner. I want to learn cooking from you.' Aloud she said:

'And who is she?'

'She is a lady who comes to church and has a dog.'

'Could we have seen her by Looe Pool?'

'Probably. She has a habit of wandering about the countryside. For no particular reason. Did she see you?'

'She peered at us from afar, and walked on.'

'That's her. She will be calling on you tomorrow, I expect. She never loses any time. She was one of the church fowls at my last parish, and has a lot of energy for good works, but I discourage this as much as possible. There is really no need for them. The people can look after themselves perfectly well and are quite beyond help.'

'That sounds rather desperate.'

'Perhaps I should qualify that last opinion. I mean, of course, that they don't really need the sort of help that she can give them. The same applies to me. I don't attempt anything but prayer and an occasional visit, boring always for both parties, but must be done. Miss Want is not bored with visiting. She adores it.'

'Is Miss Want the woman we saw yesterday?'

'Must be. Josephine Want, daughter of what she herself describes as a peppery colonel. She has only brothers, and tells me she was once a tomboy, whatever that may mean. Now she occupies herself with religion, long bicycle rides and making sweets in the quiet of her home for charities. I have never tasted them so cannot recommend —' he turned towards Laura. 'An enamel basin appears to be the primary implement in her *batterie de cuisine*. She is really a good soul, but must never be allowed to think so. She gets above herself, and to tell the truth can be a terrific bore. A cigarette for you, lady?'

This gesture from the Vicar was significant. It implied perhaps a reassurance that in his opinion Laura could never be a 'terrific bore'. The fat Sullivan proffered from the battered silver case might be taken as a pledge of camaraderie. At any rate she chose to take it that way. She need not waste time trying to understand Father St John. She was convinced that there would be no difficulty in their relationship. It would surely be amusing and peculiar — just what she liked. She was not good at understanding the average man. And this was usually reciprocated. Here was a dreamer, but not too dreamy, a poet, but not taking himself too seriously. (She knew that he was famous in his undergraduate days for nonsense verse.) The relationship was already established. No church fowl, he was confident. No expectation of religious fervour, she was assured.

The worst problem host and female guest had faced in the prospect of this encounter would seem to be already solved.

Both saw the light and Guy, sensing it, knew a great easing of the mind which he had hoped for though without absolute assurance, seeing how the remote eccentricity of the Father might be too much for her. True, he had not bothered himself greatly when the plan was made. He had managed to convince himself that Laura would surely appreciate the quality of such a man as Father St John obviously was.

And this had certainly happened. Everything so far had gone with a swing. The Lay-readership was Guy's with no ado. He had served at Mass on his first Lay Reader Sunday. Laura had watched with wonder her husband in an occupation she had never envisaged. His ease and his reverence brought tears to her eyes. She realised, however, that she could not yet bring herself to genuflect nor make the sign of the Cross. Despite her experiences at St Mary Magdalene's, Paddington, where the ceremonies had so deeply moved her, she would still resist the outward signs that seemed to come naturally here to this small congregation, but could never come easily to her unless, or until, she became a Roman Catholic. There in the front row was Miss Want, who had already called, as the Vicar had predicted, in fact the day following their sight of her at Looe Pool. She had heard rumours of the arrival, naturally. Even Father St John could not prevent that. Her excuse, however, was not a formal call but the return of a borrowed garden tool. As soon as she had been introduced to the Mallorys by the Vicar she was left alone with them. Her restless eyes flashed from one to the other. 'What on earth are they here for?' rushed through her mind, while she tried to lead them into some sort of clue to the mystery. Nothing but talk about the charm of Cornwall as far as their explorations had gone. General small talk of a maddening futility, she declared to herself. Deliberate, she concluded, and decided to come down to what she called brass tacks. At the same time, she dived into the large homespun bag that lay beside her and set upon a confused tangle of discoloured cotton, which at first they thought must be a form of cat's cradle for general amusement. It was nothing of the sort. It punctuated the conversation with sweeping gestures from weatherbeaten hands as she ventured, blinking nervously:

'Are you spending the winter here?'

She glanced at the hired piano, the sight of which had taken her breath away, as she entered. It had been installed that morning, from Truro. It was for Laura to play.

The answer was noncommittal. They were not sure how long. Perhaps. It depended. Where did Miss Want live? diverted the sluggish stream of conversation. Guy was playing the Vicar's game of mystification; drat the man! Who was he, anyway? She gave her reply direct to Laura, who so far had been engrossed by the tangle of Miss Want's agitated handwork.

'I live in a nice little thatched cottage three miles from here. A small hamlet, part of the Vicar's parish. Chollow, they call it. It means cowshed I believe. Some of the villagers drive over to Mass at Helzephron, or walk to the little old church by the sea when Father St John celebrates Mass there. But most of the inhabitants are, like the majority of folk round here, chapel. We do what we can to counteract this,' she added, a fanatic spasm twisting her already gnarled features, 'The only hope is the children. Father St John is trying very hard with them. So am I.' She bridled. 'They like treats in a small way, but parents are suspicious, very ...'

Laura's gaze, moving from the fascination of Miss Want's activity, rested upon her husband's face and surprised there a change of expression that held her spellbound. It was not fanaticism — no indeed — it was a glow from within that lit his countenance.

'I am sure you are right,' was all he said. The glow subsided and the conversation took another turn until the Vicar entered, and frowningly asked if they had had tea.

Whatever Miss Want had been doing with her cat's cradle, she bundled it all into her homespun bag and pretended to regard this query as her dismissal. It was probably intended for it, but Laura was not yet experienced enough in the Vicar's theory of management of Miss Want. She politely asked her to stay, as the teacups could already be heard in the hall. Miss Want was dazzled by Laura's courage in dealing thus with the Father. She at once foresaw an amelioration of her position at the vicarage. If Mrs Mallory was friendly, visits could become almost normal, instead of a discordant jangle of disagreements, dismissals and repudiations. There might even be a pleasant weekend at the vicarage, a rainy night spent comfortably in the lesser spare bedroom! As she sped on her bicycle through the twilight, still rose-flecked in the west, she blessed the Mallorys. Their assurance before she left them that they were there possibly for the winter delighted her. She had even gathered, in the general conversation at tea, the prospect of Lay-readership for Mallory. In fact it was all very promising, and Mrs Mallory had even seemed attracted by the idea of making sweets. It might mean a nice new set of rubber forms for fondants and chocolates. Her own were in a nasty state. Practically worn out. After all, luck may be changing!

They were rather unique people, she decided. Rather unique was a favourite phrase of hers. She had thus described the Father on early acquaintance, but he soon proved to be quite, and remained so. Someone had once remarked that Father St John was unique. She had capped it with 'Oh, quite.' It could never stand alone.

They were both good-looking, the Mallorys, he rather flamboyantly, in her opinion. No better dressed than the golfing visitors, but they didn't look like golfing visitors, exactly. Those were the plague of Father St John, swarming into church for no reason except to look amused at the Mass and the celebrant, and sometimes even to walk out if they felt it strongly. The golf links were only too near the little church in the cove, and Sunday was the favourite day for golf. This had sometimes led to trouble when overloud conversation upon the nearest green brought the Vicar himself on the spot, sometimes even in his robes, to rail at Sabbath breakers who could only stare at the unusual sight and continue their game. Nothing, not even a cloudburst, could stop that.

These difficulties seriously interfered with Miss Want's social life. She liked meeting the golf visitors. They were a change after a long spell of clergy and villagers. Some golfers, especially the ladies, were quite, so to speak, her own kind, and sometimes she was flattered by their obvious surprise at finding her living in such an outlandish place. She was quite unconscious that she was a comic figure, in the same category as the Vicar himself, who could only be treated by them as a joke. Of this last fact she was aware, and it embarrassed her relationship with the visitors who found him an amusing topic and could not resist Miss Want's angry looks when they were discussing him. So that was really no good to her, and with a surge of exultation she drove her bicycle ahead with vigour at the thought of the Mallorys safely housed at the vicarage for the winter. Poor Miss Want!

Chapter Four

The winter, a panorama of drifting rain, wild gales, soft air, sparkling blue days and grey raging seas, rolled out its infinite variety over Helzephron. The vicarage vibrations had noticeably quickened since the arrival of Mallory. There was, however, no sign of routine as yet, beyond the already daily Mass. Laura soon decided that it was useless, even if she had wanted, which she didn't, to make a pretence of routine, when every day began and ended a separate and completely self-contained unit, sometimes irrelevant, nearly always surprising, and generally entertaining. Laura knew enough about vicarages to realise that this was far removed from the home that she had dreaded to face, the well-ordered household with family prayers night and morning, breakfast at eight, herbaceous borders and, with luck, ponies in the paddock.

A trace of conventionality revealed itself in her when one morning a strange man came to the front door, and emptied a sack on the step, with the remark:

'A good fine one!'

He was going the rounds with the fox he had shot, collecting money from grateful householders for deliverance from this pest.

'Good heavens! A shot fox!' She was actually horrified. And why? Since she was a small child she had been anti-hunt. As a member of the Band of Mercy (*not* Hope) she had even written little pieces for their weekly magazine, actually printed, some of them, railing childishly against cruelty to wild animals. Yet, alone in that silly prejudice, she had early been impressed into the convention that it was a heinous offence to shoot a fox. It was against the Law — it was not done.

But it was done in the Duchy.

The fox lay there dirty and draggled from his journey in the sack. He was dead. He had been well shot. He had ended a happy life with probably never a sound of hunting horn. She had read of the 'treeing of a fox' and even seen a picture of one with a gay crowd enjoying itself and the hounds ecstatically leaping at their prey. She knew that a live fox was sometimes flung to the hounds for their amusement. If foxes had to go, and of course they were a nuisance, this was surely the right way of it and the people were honestly served by the deed. The Duchy was right.

The Duchy was no doubt right, and as time moved on through that first winter at Helzephron, she revealed with shy wild charm her eccentricity, her indifference to criticism.

Yes, the Duchy was surely right, even in the matter of a hunt ball to which the Mallorys were surprisingly invited. It was a little ball not too remote from Helzephron, yet still just in Cornwall. They had left the Vicar smiling an oblique *au revoir* as they drove off in a cab to the station. They put up at a small hotel. Laura dressed in a dark little room, with a bedroom candlestick on the bed to temper the light from a glaring passage lamp on her dressing-table which blinded her. By a curious coincidence Mr Lloyd George had only just launched his National Insurance scheme on an astonished and outraged society. Loud was the hunt ball in detestation of this meddlesome Welshman. Only Guy was anti-social enough to applaud the little statesman's action. But Guy was a Liberal from his first breath, and the fact that nearly all the guests were unknown to him did not worry him. The ladies dared to be enchanted by such, to them, novel views from this elegant young stranger. Their men were not so pleased and the atmosphere became more electrified than was usual at a small hunt ball. Laura found some good dancers and had no objection to Lloyd George or to Tory umbrage. It was, she thought, a jolly little country dance.

Return to Helzephron after three days' of social activities was surprisingly like coming home. Though the Vicar was out when they arrived, there were ample reminders of his existence in the study, the floor was scattered with enormous sheets of seemingly blank super foolscap. On his writing-table were signs of a desperate struggle with a heavily loaded goose quill.

'What has he been up to?' Laura picked up a sheet from the floor on which was scrawled the one word 'Keren-Happuch'.

'Ah, here you are.' The Father entered at this moment holding a slim pastoral staff. 'Forgive the mess. I got caught in a nonsense verse, and then was called to visit a sick parishioner. Jude is taking him the soup we were to have tonight. Not much good, I'm afraid. Mrs Jolly's dish-water. But it won't hurt him, and they like the idea. Have you seen your post? Quite a pile, and I've got something that might interest you.'

Guy always eager, vanished into the hall.

'Shall I pick up some of your papers?' Laura asked.

'No, no, pray don't trouble. Mrs Jolly or Jude will see to that tomorrow. They want Guy to do a Lenten course for children at Polgrean.'

As there was no change of tone whatever on this obvious *non sequitur*, Laura attentively awaited its solution.

'You see,' the Vicar went on. 'Guy's Sunday School has naturally excited the Duchy. The general run of clergy are quite incapable of interesting themselves in Sunday afternoon pranks of that sort. They leave it to school teachers and the result is usually negative.'

'You mean there's not much chance of getting any proselytising done among the children.'

'No, the chapel is too powerful. They take strong measures

against that sort of truancy. Here it is different. Guy has an allure that no child can resist. A Lenten course at Polgrean would be packed. Midweekly, and he would be back here to keep the Sunday School alive.'

'I see.' There was a faint stir in her mind. She had watched the effect of Guy on the village children, and wondered at the magic spell he seemed to cast upon them. And when he inaugurated the Sunday School, it was done with concentrated zeal; it was a great project, yet as entertaining to himself and everyone concerned as the production of a new play might have been. It was amusing to introduce counters for behaviour and give each child a money-box to put them in, and not to know what virtue or sin they rewarded, until the monthly 'Day of Judgment'.

A great project, but a game for everybody, even for the mothers of delinquent children who stole away from Chapel Sunday School and risked a good hiding. The mothers were most of them under the spell. The Vicar watched Guy's progress with the children with a deep-seated satisfaction, weighted down, however, with an anxiety that irked him and set him wondering about himself. (He was always doing that. He often wished that he understood more of himself.) Apart from those Sunday gatherings, he was enchanted to see, and even sometimes to join in, the late afternoon walks when school was finished with and work over, and Guy with a child hanging or clinging to each hand and a troop of others following with ecstatic cries to the cliffs, led the search for wild flowers that was usually the avowed object of these peregrinations. Certainly, Laura would muse as she watched them going (she seldom went with them), this was not propaganda, but obviously a delight in children that he was at last able to indulge. He will love youth to the end of his days and he will want a big family. This was a stunning thought. It's not what I want. Memories of impoverished rectors and vicars with immense unwieldy families, bright boys and girls worthy of first-class education struggling for scholarships or exhibitions, clouded for a moment the prospect of family life with Guy, which she had so far hardly contemplated. She decided not to contemplate it at all for the present. Life at this vicarage was strange and amusing enough to stifle apprehensions.

Guy came into the study with a sheaf of letters. He was radiant.

'This is pretty good. I hope you think so, Father?'

'Of course. At the same time you might amuse yourself by spiking up some of the old codgers in the district who badly need it.'

'Oh, Laurie, two letters for you,' Guy diverged for a moment and threw the letters on her lap.

Laurie? That was a genial novelty. She liked it and glanced at the letters. 'Mother's' bold impulsive calligraphy, and a trail of pale sepia ink from Ariadne. Mrs Mallory was chiefly concerned for Guy's health since he had had another tiresome pain in his leg. 'A pity I mentioned it.' Laura regretted the exaggerated sense of duty which extracted careful weekly logs from her lazy pen.

Ariadne's concern was wholly her own health, the misery of wintering in her cold Chelsea room, the neglect of Clare Dobson, too busy at home with the sailor man on what seemed an endless leave. That was the worst of the mercantile marine. No sort of discipline or security. Poor Ariadne! Always at the back of one's mind, but what hope of being any use to her at this distance. What to do but send her a pot of Cornish cream every now and then or boxes of eggs, and a little commiseration which perhaps she might enjoy. Perhaps not. Her pride was so intense, perhaps unreasonable. She would scorn a cheque or the slightest hint of charity. That had been clearly evidenced in the Terence letter. She had not changed much since her youth in Dublin. Ah, well, no use to bother Guy about it, especially now with the prospect of Lenten discourses to enthrall his imagination.

Miss Want appeared a few days after the news, bringing the *batterie de cuisine* for sweet-making.

The Vicar was standing on the front doorstep when she arrived. 'What are all these depressing objects, Miss Want?'

'These,' said Miss Want with a faintly mocking glance, 'are Mrs Mallory's *batterie de cuisine*, as I believe you call it, for sweet-making. I suppose you knew that she was going to do it with me?'

'I suggested it,' he said with a far-away look. 'I think the first night she was here I asked her if she would be interested.'

'And she was,' smiled Miss Want in triumph.

'Oh, very well, very well — why not? And here is Jude to carry them in for you.'

'I can manage, thank you.'

'Oh no, you can't. I'd rather you didn't.'

Jude disappeared.

'Wretched boy. Where has he gone?'

'Beyond recall,' said Miss Want with a grin. 'Perhaps you would hold the pony while I carry these things in?'

'Not necessary. I know this pony. He never moves except under heavy pressure. Give me the enamel basin. I insist upon carrying that. The Mallorys are out, by the way.'

'Oh, and by the way, what do I hear about Mallory and children's Lenten talks?'

'I don't know. You always hear such queer things. No truth in it, whatever you have heard.'

Maddening creature! It was all over the village, and naturally she wanted to be up-to-date and hold her own with the gossips. That was the last thing he wanted, and she knew it.

'Why must you always tease me?' she dared.

'Tease you? My dear Miss Want, how can you suspect such a thing? What object —?'

'I've often wondered. You are a difficult person,' she plunged.

'I should hope so. Now put some of those strange rubber squares into the basin and I will carry them in to the house.'

'Those rubber squares as you call them are forms for fondants, new ones I bought for Mrs Mallory. My own are nearly worn out.'

'That all sounds very much to the point. And where will the art be practised?'

'Mrs Mallory thought the housemaid's cupboard, with plenty of running water, and room for my Primus on the ironing table.'

'Yes, yes, no doubt a good idea of Mrs Mallory's.'

'My Primus' woke an uneasy fear in the Father's breast. Did this portend an occupation? A moving in? He had seen the Primus crouching on the jingle floor; the significance of it had not struck him at the moment. But now — Mrs Mallory must have her own Primus as soon as possible. He regretted, in this newly-born mood, that he had ever mentioned the question of sweets. He was being hospitable on that first night, charmed by Laura, and anxious to suggest amusements that might appeal to an intelligent young woman who should be carefully discouraged from flinging herself into parish enthusiasms for lack of social excitements. This was soon proved unnecessary, long before dinner was over. There had really been no need to mention sweets. Of course the emergence of Miss Want into the conversation, because of the Looe Pool apparition, was really responsible for it.

Rather reckless, perhaps, on thinking it over, but one never thought anything over in time. While all this was trailing through his mind, Miss Want was briskly occupied in the housemaids' room.

'This is *capital*!' she was heard murmuring to herself. With a gasp at the sound he fled swiftly downstairs and quietly closed the study door, himself behind it.

Yes, certainly the Mallorys' sojourn at the vicarage had opened a wide vista for Miss Want, she declared to herself. She could stay the night now, after late sweet-making or an evening Benediction or Vespers, or even Compline, without compromising the Father. Wide vistas —but it was not long before disadvantages which would have daunted a less determined character than Josephine Want arose. *Whatever* happened she had decided, was, worth it.

She knew that she would be the centre of attention as soon as she entered the vicarage, and that, whatever it might mean, was in its way, flattering. She knew that Guy Mallory was organising practical jokes, carried out with enthusiasm by the household, especially on Saturdays when it was augmented by a gay youth from a neighbouring town, who came over to play the organ. He wore his hair in a fair wavy bang. While Miss Want was fussily playing two-handed bridge with the Vicar in his study after dinner, she knew there was tip-toed activity upstairs. Her bedroom was being prepared.

She knew also that when she went to bed, as soon as she shut her door, a silent group gathered outside it.

'I shall not make a sound, whatever happens.'

The carpet rolled itself up, pulled by strings under the door. 'Childish.'

From the water jug she poured a helter-skelter of newts and little frogs.

'All right, I shan't wash.' Defiantly.

Then the bed crashed when she got into it. A stifled giggle outside.

'Hang it all! Well, I shall sleep on it as it is. It's still flat. Apple pie, of course. That's soon remedied. Pepper on the pillow! I will *not* sneeze.'

She had settled down, if it could be called that, before

she discovered the last outrage, almost buried her face in it. But, damn it all, if she sat up all night holding her nose, she wouldn't give them that satisfaction.

Let them wait outside, the longer the better. Father St John would, of course, have gone to bed. He wouldn't approve of such pranks ... Or would he? No, no, no, of course not. He would never allow such liberties taken in his house.

No, no, of course not. Mallory was at the bottom of it all. She couldn't really like him. No, she couldn't. She admitted his fascination, even when he teased her, which he had begun to do almost at once. Why? He must like her or he wouldn't be bothered. It was quite good-natured most of the time; after all, she had brothers and knew what teasing was. She used to enjoy it, got a thrill out of it, and even now — it was better than being ignored. Not that there was any reason for that. No one had ever ignored her if she could help it.

What about Laura Mallory? She was a bit of a puzzle. Agreeable and pretty — no, not pretty — that was the wrong word, perhaps picturesque. Quite unsuitable for the vicarage and utterly incapable of running a house. Not that this house could be run by anybody — except perhaps herself ...

Bother! The bed had collapsed again. She was now lying at an angle of about forty-five degrees from the floor. She moved the mattress and bed-clothes on to the carpet. All but the pillow, of course, which she flung to a far corner in a cloud of pepper. She was a good campaigner. By Jove, she was!

Laura Mallory ... Yes, she was a puzzle. But safe. Too fond of Guy to be a danger to ... (Yes, that was the name she never did more than breathe to herself, this time with a roguish smirk at the glass.) Mrs ... No, no, no. After all, she believed in celibacy for the priesthood and blushed at the thought.

A knock at the window. Jude, of course, with a stick from below. No, *on* the window-sill — climbed up — a ladder probably. Let him stay there. Tiresome boy. He would not dare to do more than knock. The window was wide open at the top. She was a fresh-air fiend. Always had been since a girl. Out in all weathers. Her hair full of brine in sea mists. Her mac making puddles in the hall after one of her jolly rides around Helzephron with Rex in a full gale. Sailing along on its wings, or better still, fighting it tooth and nail on a bleak headland, sometimes actually being *blown backwards*, and once, indeed, nearly over the cliff in her madder moments. She knew the cliff road wasn't safe in a gale, but there! What was life without a spice of adventure, and unless one made it oneself, one mightn't have any. Those haunted, streaming nights on the lonely roads! Black as a pig, the night, sometimes, and her acetylene lamp always going wrong. And to think that she needn't be out at all only added to the fun.

'Very foolish, Miss Want,' was all the response she got from the Vicar after a vivid description of one of her perilous rides. 'Quite stupid, you know. One of these nights you may be murdered. There are a lot of queer people about. Yes, yes, queer people about. You can't trust these natives. Not at all. Don't blame me if you are murdered going back from the vicarage one night.'

Chapter Five

Guy happened to be present when this absurd suggestion was made about Miss Want's nocturnal risks. By chance she caught a devilish glint in his eye, so that when, a few nights later, she was just getting up speed outside the vicarage gate after a longish supper, she hardly jumped when a gun was fired close to her ear, from the hedge, in fact.

'Don't be silly, Jude,' she called out, only the faintest tremble in her voice. 'I know it's you. You ought to be ashamed of yourself.'

There was naturally no sound, and she turned back to the vicarage determined this time to let Mallory have a piece of her mind.

'Look here, it's not playing the game. I'm damned if it is,' she shouted in the hall.

'What is it, what is it, Miss Want? What game? Why have you come back?' Father St John came testily out of the study. 'I cannot have these disturbances at this time of night.'

'Where is Mallory? Where is Jude?'

Guy appeared at once in the study door.

'Back so soon?'

'Jude! Where is Jude?'

'Here be I, Miss Want.' Jude came out of the kitchen in his shirt sleeves, wiping a dish, his face alight with the innocence of a child. Altogether too innocent.

'Don't pretend. I know you fired a gun in the air as I went by just now. Deny it if you can.' She foamed at him.

'Now, now, Miss Want,' said the Vicar. 'We can't have these wild accusations at this time of night. You see, Jude is washing up in the kitchen. You must really go home quietly. If you like, Jude will escort you part of the way ...'

Jude indeed!

'Why Jude? You know he fired a gun just now,' she repeated, her voice shrill and uncertain with anger and a dreadful suspicion. Could the Father be in this dastardly plot?

'A gun? That's ridiculous. If there was a gun, it only bears out what I said the other day. You should really not be out alone at night. They stop at nothing in the dark. I was stoned once myself, if you remember, but only after dark.'

Quite true. Quite true. She remembered it well. How indignant she had been that those cowardly villagers had attacked the Father, and actually hit him, only the stones got lost in the folds of his cassock. The very thought of this outrage made her sick when she remembered it — yes, for weeks after it had: happened she suffered — yes, suffered as though the blow had been struck on her own body, even though it had missed his.

Why was she such a fool? The man was a fraud. Why couldn't he be honest and go over to Rome, where he should be? He simply enjoyed disobedience, mocking the Church with illegal practices, laughing in the face of his superiors. There was no excuse for him. But — her mind racing round like a Catherine wheel — whose was the outrage? Those chapel people, of course. Beastly hypocrites. Immoral fiends, hiding their wickedness behind bedroom doors and preaching purity twice of a Sunday. This thought always sent the blood rushing to her head and tonight it was already there, driven by anger with Mallory, and hideous doubts as to the Father's complicity. And then there was the possibility of the assailant's *not* being Jude after all. But yes, yes, they were all acting. Where was Laura? She stayed out of it, sniggering on the landing upstairs, no doubt. Oh, now they were driving her mad, all of them.

'This'll pull you together.'

'No, no, you know I never drink anything and I don't need pulling together,' as Guy, smiling benevolently, held out a glass of altar wine. 'No, not even a cup of tea, thank you. No, I can manage quite well alone, thank you. I am used to it, thank you.'

There was bitterness in her tone and in her exit. The Vicar walked up to the gate with her, his conscience not quite at ease. That was all very well, she thought, but it didn't cut any ice. They were all in disgrace. The whole vicarage was in disgrace. But did they realise it? They were so damned unperturbed. Their behaviour simply wasn't Christian, that was it. Not Christian. She plunged into the Cimmerian darkness and her lamp went out. There was not even Rex for company. He was whining for her at home. Courage, brave heart! 'Go it, Jo,' as her brothers used to shout at her when they played mixed hockey and she was an intrepid forward, bashing the ball and everything else in sight. *Go it, Jo!*

The pig-like blackness of the night seemed impenetrable, but gradually the hedges took on a blotted shape against the low-clouded sky: wind-shorn trees, her landmarks, revealed themselves grim figures in the gloom. Here was the twisted one warning her that she had reached the gate of the golf-links. This was the worst part of the journey, at any time, but without a light and with the bike to push, it was a bit of a problem. Well, she wasn't nervous, thank God, though at the bottom of the links was the beach over which she must pass to reach the road to her cottage. A little hamlet it was, just a few thatched houses.

Sometimes the tide was in and she had to keep well up on the dry shore among the prickly sea holly. Once when she thought the tide was low the sea had come softly foaming over her feet in the dark without the slightest warning. That did give her a turn, she had to admit. It wasn't like the sea, but something creepy-crawly, like milk boiling over, so soft in a great white spread, and silent, for there were no waves that night.

'Rather like one of Mallory's tricks,' she had laughed to herself.

This night — the gun night — she found the golf-links gate, and after a good deal of fiddling got herself and her bicycle through it. Stumbling along the cart tracks over the links, she saw a light ahead. Someone walking with a lantern. A faint shiver down her spine. Who would be out as late as this? Perhaps it had *not* been Jude with a gun after all? But no, that was absurd. She would be glad of a light.

'I shall take the bull by the horns,' one of her favourite clichés, she decided, 'and shout.'

For once there was no wind and her voice rang out over the darkness. The lantern stopped, hesitated, and went on. She shouted again. Drat the man; he was afraid of her. That gave her courage.

Now he was waiting.

'Miss Want! I recognised your voice the second time. Let me take your bicycle, if you will carry the lantern.'

'Good gracious!' she peered short-sightedly into the face illuminated by what seemed to her now a flood of brilliant light.

'It's you, Mr Potter! What on earth are you doing out at this time of night?'

'I might return the compliment, Miss Want,' he replied with rather heavy joviality. 'This is my time for a constitutional, you know.'

'I didn't know. Well, as we take the same road, perhaps it's fortunate we met. You see my light has failed again.'

'You must really let me have a look at it tomorrow. I'm quite good at these things.'

'Thank you. That is very kind.' She suddenly became *Grande Dame*, as far as was possible on such a pitch-dark night, blundering along beside a young man whose outlines were dim. He was rather common, and being a near neighbour, staying in one of those thatched cottages, must be kept in his place. She knew *nothing* about him except that he was some kind of an artist and was *decidedly* common. He had a wife — at least a woman living with him, and a child who made rather too much noise in their scrap of a garden, which they were trying to cultivate in a feeble ignorant way. She had looked in on them one morning — not called, exactly — just looked in, really to see what they were like. They were grateful for a few lettuce seeds and some highly coloured sweets from Mrs Bonython's shop for the child. Poor souls, they didn't look well nor particularly happy. Mr Potter's face seemed to be dragged down against his will. His smile was bitter and his eyes without hope.

Yet his manner was cheerful and friendly. An odd mixture. The little woman was anxious, pleasant and flabby. It was not quite clear whether an addition to the family was on the way or not. She had that kind of a figure.

How and why had they come to live here? Mr Potter was said to be writing a book. He spent some of his leisure doing pretty little sketches of the countryside and sea-shore. Miss Want could *not* discover what their means of existence was. As they had no woman from the hamlet or anywhere else to help in the house, it was difficult to get any information about it.

She actually bought one of his sketches to see what he charged. It was a guinea. A great deal more than she had bargained for. She had figured no more than five shillings. It was a silly waste of money in any case, because how could she know that he wasn't putting it on for her, or even letting her have it cheap? It was not a bad little thing to stick up on the wall. She had to have it framed because it was so expensive to begin with, and to tell the truth she had chosen the picture because, on that particular bit of road, under rather a nice tree, she had had one of her long altercations with Father

St John, in which she had had the last word. At least … he had stopped arguing.

Tonight, Mr Potter saw her to her door, declining the offer of a cup of tea. Rex's shrill bark of greeting could not be shouted against nor silenced. Having swept his mistress into the house and seen that the front and sitting-room doors were shut on the threatening intruder, he gave her that eager look and special swing of tail that she knew so well —

'I've been shut up here for four hours at least. If you don't …'

She jumped up from the chair into which she had sunk exhausted.

'Little walkie porky for poor little Rexie boy? Tummy on, old Tiddles.'

She picked up his lead, a mere formality, but also a sign, and fought her way through his frenzy to the front door, and he rushed screaming into the night.

'That bloody dog,' said Mr Potter locking his front door.

'Those poor things,' said Miss Want to herself. 'I must really do something to help them, if I can only think what.'

Mr Potter had been quite chatty and her curiosity on several points had been satisfied.

'Come along Rex. To heel, old man, *to heel, to heel*!' Rex, who regarded this as just silly talk, leapt onward through the darkness and spent the night out.

Chapter Six

The question of Ariadne lay heavily on several consciences. She was fading away in Chelsea, so proud and poor, her purse still yawning exhausted on the chimney-piece with the dead rose for company, her rent in arrears, and only one poem accepted by a literary weekly in six months. In justice to the enlightened weekly, it must be conceded that it was the only poem she had sent in. Inspiration was drying up. She lay on her camp-bed without even her pencil poised, gazing at her precious Beardsley, solitary on the whitewashed wall of her room. Aubrey himself had given it to her and it had never been published. A delicious riot of fauns and satyrs. What drawing! What a mind!

But oh! she had said that long ago. Now it didn't inspire. Aubrey was dead. Life was surely over. She was tired, she wished someone would do something for her. Off-scourings from the dregs of her Paris life were to be found in England. She had seen some of them. They were all poets or artists of some sort, wrapped up in themselves, more than ever wrapped up in themselves now that they realised there wasn't much left for them in the way of fame or fortune. She felt that they were saying to each other that they must do something for poor Ariadne, but they never did. No, what they said was that something *must be done* for poor Ariadne, which amounted to a complete evasion of responsibility.

She had relied so much on Clare Dobson. She, after all, was not an artist in any sense, except that she knew how to live fastidiously, had good taste in decoration and people. But now there was this baby, a ridiculous intrusion which had disappointed everyone but Clare and her infatuated husband, by being born healthy and screaming like any middle-class child. It was almost indecent, thought Ariadne. One day she had gazed at the King of Rome cradle, in which the month-old child lay asleep; she was artistically impressed by the spectacle. But she had later observed a row of nappies hanging on a line in the bathroom when she went to powder her nose.

This had so sickened her that she had forgotten to ask whether it was a girl or boy. She had not been to the Regent's Canal since. She had not been *asked*.

Clare's painfully normal husband had been on leave for what seemed like months, and Clare was never herself when he was about. Her intellect seemed to fly out of the window. There was no *conversation*. If it were possible that anyone so crudely service as the sailor man could rather subtly mock, that was certainly the impression he managed to convey in his encounters with Ariadne. So naturally she ignored him so far as one politely could. And now she wasn't even *asked*. Another illusion blasted. She had had such faith in Clare. True, Clare wrote occasionally and once visited her, but seemed depressed and had no ideas that were of any use.

And what about those Mallorys? Always in Cornwall, utterly indifferent to anyone else's fate. Wrapped up in themselves like all the rest. Ariadne could fade right away for all they cared. Poor Ariadne, consumptive, starving, and still bursting with genius. But too — too tired. She would lie here until somebody came to rescue her.

So she lay, inconsolable; unconscious of the fact that Regent's Canal and Cornwall were all the time engaged in earnest correspondence. All through Lent, all through the excitements of Guy's Lenten Course, Laura and Clare were in close communion, almost secret, for Guy must not be disturbed in his work which he was taking so seriously, and which was proving such a startling success. Finally, at Easter, when comparative peace reigned at the vicarage, came Clare's most despairing letter:

What *can* we do for Ariadne? I have just been to see her again. The case is getting serious. She is in a terrible state and thinks she is neglected by everyone, which I suppose is true. You see, I have the sailor man at home and this baby who takes so much more time than I expected. Ariadne does not like a domestic atmosphere so I don't ask her here. And in any case she is practically bed-ridden. What shall we do?

Guy, relaxed at last, was allowed to see this letter.

'Of course,' he said without a pause. 'Ariadne must come here as a paying guest.'

'Who will pay?' asked Laura who had vaguely hoped some such solution might present itself.

'I will, of course. Put her in the little spare room and Miss Want can use the maid's room when she comes.'

'What about the Father? Mustn't he be asked first?'

'If you like. But I think he would be glad to meet her. She's just his type, and they will understand each other.'

'Well, if you think so.' Laura was not very pleased with this simplification of the problem.

'I'm quite sure of it,' settled the question.

There were now no servants in the house beyond Jude. Mrs Jolly had made an hysterical exit in Holy Week. The Vicar hastily advertised again for a couple of deaf and dumb servants. Meanwhile a simple half-daily woman came in from the village to help. She was of low mentality and did not know one thing from another, but she could scrub floors and gave no trouble. Father St John took temporary charge of the kitchen. His was a delicate art. Laura got a smattering of the *haute école* before she knew anything about first principles, so that she progressed without roots, and her dishes were more flights of fancy than the real thing. Yet edible, and now her French dressing was approved.

This was the state of the household when Ariadne arrived on a spring day. The problem of paying her fare had swelled the correspondence between Regent's Canal and Cornwall. How persuade the proud creature to accept it? A solution was found. What about her doing drawings of the Mallorys and perhaps of Father St John (if she felt like it)? This commission, which was suggested to Ariadne as though the generosity were all on her side, Mrs Dobson had been glad to report, had been at last accepted. The Mallorys would pay.

Every necessity for the undertaking had been ordered from Messrs Winsor and Newton, and entered to Mrs Dobson's account. It seemed that Ariadne had but the one pencil and that an HB, no paper or drawing-boards and no india-rubber. Charcoal and crayons were added to the list in case she should care to use them.

Chapter Seven

It was a spring day, but it was cold and wet. Ariadne stood on the platform of the little station, her famous black cape clutched about her, the saffron scarf she had tied round her head now sagging at the back of her neck, her faded auburn hair blowing across her face. There was a wild distinction about her as she stood lonely and peevish in the rain, surrounded by the paraphernalia of a country station, crates of indignant poultry and sporting dogs on chains.

Laura was a little bit late. A fly had had to be ordered because of the rain. The new jingle and pony Guy had lately bought in the market, all had agreed would not be hospitable on such a day. The fly, manure scented, had been late picking up Laura at the vicarage. The horse, with broken knees and a spavined hock, could not be hurried on any account, not even Ariadne's.

An old porter, as soon as he saw Laura, came forward and took Ariadne's shapeless holdall. There had been something too strange about that apparition for a superstitious Cornishman to approach it without support. Ariadne had stood remote and uninviting until Laura appeared. Uninviting and peevish.

In fact, if Laura had been in a less enthusiastic and hospitable mood she might have compared the expression on Ariadne's peaky face to that of one of those indignant hens. But Laura was bursting with loving-kindness. Nothing was good enough for Ariadne: it was disgraceful of the weather to behave as it did, and as for that old fly and its smells — it was a hideous insult to genius.

She had dreamed of driving Ariadne through the sweet lanes, with Edward the pony groomed and shining, transfigured by a wise diet of unaccustomed corn, spanking along, while she flourished but never used the whip, the sky a rich Cornish blue and the hedges pink with dog-roses.

Ariadne sank back into the dusty shadow of the fly. She was really very tired and this didn't seem a propitious beginning to the new enterprise. She would go straight to bed as soon as she reached the vicarage, she decided. That would save the bother of sitting up and talking and being introduced to the Vicar. Not that she found the prospect of meeting him at all alarming. No solemnity in the encounter; on the contrary she was well prepared to meet a kindred spirit; she knew he had edited an æsthetic magazine when he was at Oxford in the 'nineties. She knew about his nonsense verses and how as a freshman he had accepted an invitation to breakfast with a prominent undergraduate, in coal, for lack of a pencil at the moment, on a sheet of Bromo.

All the more reason for being at one's best for the introduction, which she decided should take place the following day. Tomorrow she would get up leisurely, at about three-thirty, yes, *about* three-thirty, and make her first appearance at tea. This she was revolving in her mind while Laura was nervously regretting the weather, fly, smells and her own lateness at the station. She was obviously desperately anxious about Ariadne's comfort, and that was all to the good.

'I think you should go straight to bed when we get in. You must be awfully tired.'

Almost thought-reading, smiled Ariadne to herself.

'Oh, no,' she protested, turning her smile to wanness. 'I shall be all right.'

She knew that was quite safe. Still protesting, she was urged up to her bedroom by Laura, Guy following, actually carrying her luggage, the holdall and a large tapestry bag,

The Vicar was out, nervously postponing the encounter with Ariadne. Not that he was afraid either, for he had heard enough about her to know that here was no menace of the dreaded church fowl. His acquaintance with Laura had been allowed to ripen into friendship immediately, with an assurance that she would not ever take an undue interest in parish matters. He was frightened, even shocked, by religious women. Let them be nuns, by all means. There was nothing more delightful in theory than a good nun. Let them remain enclosed if possible until death. But the church fowls, pecking about the altar steps with farmyard familiarity. No! He would like to have it trespass. He had even considered the possibility of erecting a board to that effect, for the discouragement of Miss Want, who seemed to think the church was at all hours her pleasaunce.

He was fond of the company of women out of church, so long as they were intelligent, presentable, and, for choice, happily married. Artists, too, were preferred.

He had prepared a special little dinner for Ariadne to eat in bed, because he knew that Laura was going to insist upon her retiring there at once. It was a tentative message, a taste of his quality, he hoped. Laura carried it up to her. Sole garnished with hard-boiled eggs stuffed with caviare and a dish of his own bottled cherries, which he and Laura had watched turning over slowly like ducks in their syrup, bumping gently into each other without disturbing their shapes. A dash of liqueur, and beside them a little bowl of Cornish cream, which the Vicar hoped Ariadne would not allow to blur the clean perfection of his cherries. But she did.

A simple little vicarage meal, a glass or two of Chablis to wash it down. There was, after all, something besides altar wine in the cellar.

✖

It was no one's fault that Miss Want had not been warned of Ariadne's presence at the vicarage, or perhaps it was that no one considered himself responsible. Her existence had for the moment been blotted out in the excitement of Ariadne's installation, for that was almost what it amounted to. It so happened that on the very day of the arrival, Miss Want had been struggling against wind and rain over Goonhilly Downs, determined to hear Mass properly celebrated at a reasonable pace, somewhere in the Lizard district which was notable in those days as an Anglo-Catholic stronghold. She was away ten days, longer than she had meant, then stayed at home tidying her cottage for another three days — just to tease Father St John and keep the vicarage guessing.

I shan't even tell them where I've been! I shan't! So there. Let them wonder. Let them be surprised when they hear! Very good for them.

But they didn't wonder; her absence was simply a blank. And when she appeared at the vicarage gate, more than a week after Ariadne's arrival, Laura, looking out of their bedroom window, said:

'Hullo! There's Miss Want ... I'd forgotten all about her.'

'Good Lord!' said Guy. 'So had I.'

It happened also that as Miss Want propped her bicycle up against the clematis by the front door (a deplorable habit of hers), the shrill voice of Ariadne struck like the ping of an arrow on her ear. A moment later the Vicar emerged from the porch, smiling his charming smile, at what Miss Want was perhaps justified in describing (on first glance) as a weird looking female wrapped up in veils.

Father St John must have forgotten, too, for his smile faded swiftly into the startled-deer look that Miss Want knew so well. Good heavens! she had never been told.

'Ah! Here you are, Miss Want! Quite a stranger. You haven't met Miss Berden, have you?'

'No, I haven't.' Miss Want peered through the veils, then, fixing the Vicar with a severe glance —

'Father, I have a message for you from Father Marston and that is why I am here. May I see you alone for a moment?'

'So sorry, Miss Want, but I am just taking Miss Berden up to the church. She is going to paint a fresco for me and we are going to settle exactly where, and do measurements, probably,' he added inconsequently. 'We will be back for tea, I expect. Pray go in. You will find the Mallorys. Your dog, Miss Want. Please leave him outside. He smells.'

This maddening compound of courtesy and downright rudeness was only too familiar, and in the face of the extraordinary being who was gazing at her with lifted veil and glittering curiosity, it was intolerable, humiliating. Each lady was dumbfounded by the appearance of the other, for neither had been warned. Just vicarage carelessness.

Josephine Want could not make up her mind. Should she seize her bicycle and make a dignified retreat or accept the invitation to tea, whereby she could probe the mystery of this new arrival? The dignified retreat would deprive her, *possibly for days*, of any information beyond village gossip. This was, she declared to herself, her *natural* impulse. Yet, there was a stronger one, unacknowledged, a throbbing curiosity which won easily, and she walked in, mumbling:

'I may as well see Mrs Mallory for a minute about another sweet lesson, as I'm here.' She knew she would stay to tea.

Mrs Mallory! Why not Laura? Long ago she had wished that the Mallorys would call her Jo. She had even hinted at it. 'Everybody calls me Jo!' she had said brightly, striding beside Laura on a windy walk, but there was no response. They were familiar enough to play tricks on her. But she remained Miss Want. Ah! Perhaps it was simply respect? But no, those silly tricks which she always took in such good part? Not much respect there, but mostly playful. Except, of course, for the shooting incident of the gun which she could *not* forgive. It was not a question of the social side of things. Heavens, no.

She was an officer's daughter, born and bred in the army.

After all, who *were* the Mallorys? That flamboyant creature had a queer background, artists and actors and such like — fairly well-known ones, it must be admitted.

As for Laura, she was a clergyman's daughter, but was that a criterion? Street women had up for soliciting constantly described themselves as daughters of clergymen or actresses. There wasn't much in it really.

She found Laura in the kitchen, looking less like a street-walker than usual, dressed in a pretty red blouse and a grey tweed skirt, getting the tea-things ready. She greeted the visitor with one of her most engaging smiles, because it had really been too bad of them to forget poor Miss Want, and then the shock of Ariadne in the front door without any warning must have been shattering. She must be nice to Miss Want and arrange another sweet lesson, and Guy must not tease her. He, too, knew that, and came out of the study to greet her. They put her in the only armchair unoccupied by books and papers. Ariadne would expect to sit on it when she came in from her walk with the Vicar. Miss Want took out her tatting (for that was what it was) as she did when she first called on the Mallorys to find out why they were there. Laura who had never seen tatting before, had thought it was nervous excitement, but the Vicar had explained later when asked:

'Tatting, lady, tatting — just tatting.'

In moments of agitation it was a great help to Miss Want. She could fidget as much as she liked and produce some very pretty work at the same time.

Conversation was restrained. Friendly questions about her absence were met with vague generalities such as the state of the roads and trippers on the Lizard beaches.

Tatting increased in violence.

Then it came out.

'Who is the lady I met in the porch?'

'That is our friend, Ariadne Berden.'

'Your friend? Oh, your friend …' Her wild eyes roved from one to the other. Were they teasing her?

'We asked her down here to do our portraits. She is a good artist.'

Now she was lost again in a maze of suppositions.

'Oh, your friend,' she repeated, swaying to her tatting.

'She's been ill and needs a change of air.'

'She certainly looks quite washed out. Has she begun your portraits?'

'Not yet. She's not up to it yet.'

'I see,' slowly. 'Father St John said something about a fresco in the church. She is able—?'

The tatting fell to the floor and was swiftly recovered with a weatherbeaten hand.

So she knew about that already. Oh, naughty Father, thought Laura. What a rogue.

'Oh, that's not got very far yet.' She realised that she said this as though she were soothing a feverish patient.

'She was a friend of Oscar Wilde's,' Guy said to ginger up the conversation.

'Goodness! Had he any women friends?' This she considered a rather smart remark. It showed that she knew what it was all about, though she was fundamentally a bit hazy.

Well, really, to meet a friend of Oscar Wilde's … that would be something to talk about and think about. So when the high-pitched voice of Ariadne was heard in the hall, Miss Want quivered with a new sensation, and watched the door.

Ariadne, unswathing her scarves and veil, entered with a frail smile. A chair had been hastily cleared for her so that Miss Want need not be disturbed in mind or body. Ariadne sank into it with only a glance at the usurped seat — a glance which turned into a stare at its occupant. She also had never seen tatting before. Nor had she ever remembered to have been in a room with anyone at all like Miss Want. Interest was kindling on both sides. Something new! Ariadne the artist was always in search of it and Josephine needed it desperately.

The afternoon mellowed surprisingly: the invitation to tea launched by Miss Want as she rose to go was accepted by Ariadne almost eagerly.

The Mallorys were, of course, included.

'And you will come, Father?' She twitched at him as she went out.

'Perhaps. Perhaps. Thank you. Don't expect me.'

'All right. Just as you please,' she retorted, proudly grasping the handle-bar of her bicycle. They all stood and watched her push it up the circular drive.

'Incredible,' murmured Ariadne, appraising the lines of that determined back. The Vicar, nervously relieved at the success of this encounter, retired to the kitchen, resolving to cook a calf's head for dinner. It had been waiting for him all day in the larder, its glazed eyes shaded by long thick lashes.

'Most unusual.' He had stared at it fascinated. 'Poor little dear.' Now it was prepared for him, but there was much to do, and Laura was called upon to make a vinaigrette sauce for the brains.

'Quite easy. I've hard-boiled the eggs for you. You've only to make an ordinary dressing, cut up a few gherkins and shallots, throw in the brains and give it a good beating at the end.'

'It sounds very simple.'

'So it is. You can't go wrong unless you use malt vinegar.'

'You know there isn't any in the house.'

Dinner was begun at ten-thirty.

After dinner Ariadne amused herself and everyone else with lightning sketches of Miss Want in various attitudes, tatting, walking up the drive and leaping on to her machine.

The small cloud that had gathered almost imperceptibly over Ariadne's relations with the Mallorys had been turning into a cumulus, but it melted under the charm of her cleverness, the spell of wit that flashed at her pencil point.

Guy said, 'You should do us all.'

She put her pencil away. 'Another time.' She blushed faintly.

The small cloud had gathered while Ariadne argued with Guy about art, especially at meals, her voice shrilling into a scream of dissent. It had darkened when Ariadne came wandering in from solitary country walks, laden with wispy and ragged wild flowers for which she demanded jars and jars of water, spilt in transit to window-seats soon littered with floral debris and earwigs.

Then the Vicar got tired of preparing Ariadne's breakfast and Laura's eager servitude slackened in a heat wave. It was now June. Herring roes on toast, streaky bacon grilled dry and crisp, the only way Ariadne could eat it, every possible egg device — all this was very well in the first flush of pity and admiration.

Ariadne always lay abed until she smelt lunch. Then she would trail down, smiling wanly, just in time to have the first helping of whatever was on the menu. Her appetite was good, though she ate daintily. Laura was glad of all this, though she was apt to remind herself of the proud genius starving in a Chelsea garret. It was surely doing Ariadne good to be down at the vicarage, whatever happened.

If only Ariadne had alluded, however vaguely, to those portraits. If only she could have shown the slightest intention of doing them, how the Mallorys would have forbidden her to do such a thing. They had never really wanted her to do the work. It was simply a way of getting her out of London and into some comfort. Laura was well aware that Guy had been sceptical, that it was to please her that he had suggested the plan. Doing a kind thing, sitting back and watching and suddenly getting tired of it.

Then Laura would get nervous and susceptible, and now here were more clouds gathering in this queer ecclesiastical outpost. Guy was already in demand as a preacher. He had plenty to say and knew how to say it. The rule that Lay-readers should not preach from the pulpit was naturally ignored. He took the pulpit as he would take the stage. His Sunday School had the village children more and more enthralled. In fact there was no doubt that Mallory was making a stir in the High Anglican community.

Chapter Eight

Father St John, despite his vague aloofness, was but human. A premature distribution of Popish medals had closed his own Sunday School with a sharply directed bang from headquarters three years ago. Guy's idea of opening a Sunday School had salved the Vicar's conscience. It would please the parents who liked to have Sunday afternoon to themselves. Conscience being damped down, jealousy quite unexpectedly flared up. This was so strange an emotion to the Vicar that he hardly recognised it and thought that he merely disapproved of secular devices to attract children — such as counters and money boxes.

Then those walks on the cliffs, with Guy like the Pied Piper leading them along with tales of fairyland and flowers and birds. All this had nothing to do with religious teaching, declared the Vicar, who was afraid of children when he was not bored with them. Child-like himself he could not understand them.

Devoted though he was to Guy he began to think that perhaps he was too big for a quiet country parish. Even Jude did not resist the fascination. In fact, Jude was at Guy's beck and call.

'Where are you off to, Jude?'

'I belong going to village for Mr Mallory's post.'

'What about the garden? Have you finished the job I gave you?'

'Ah, garden can wait. Mr Mallory's in some frizz about a letter as didn't come.'

Colour rushed to the Vicar's pale face. He seized Jude's wrist violently. 'You are *not* — you are *not*. You are to work for *me* — for *me*, do you understand?'

'Oh, yes, right enough.'

Jude wrenched his wrist away, his dark hair fell over his eyes. Father St John, breathless, stared into his face. What did it mean? 'You are *not*,' he repeated. 'You are *not*.'

Jude gave him a saucy look and leapt on to his bicycle. He was going to the village.

Humiliation! How dared Jude defy him?

Oh, yes, he had done it before, been cheeky often — a growing cheekiness. The Vicar found himself in a whirl of warring emotions.

'My head is going round. Perhaps I am going mad. What is the matter with me? God help me.'

It seemed fortunate that at this moment Ariadne appeared. She had been painting in the church. One look at the Vicar and she knew something was wrong. And she knew what it was. Jude had flashed past her on his bicycle, with a naughty glint in his eye.

'You spoil Jude,' she said in a teasing voice.

'Nonsense, nonsense. Don't say such things. I shall give him notice tonight. His behaviour is quite abominable. Quite atrocious, dear lady.'

But he was already soothed by her presence.

'Let us go and see your work,' he said.

They strolled up to the church and sat in the Lady Chapel on one of the few pitch pine seats that he hadn't thrown into the sea when he first became incumbent. Simply because authority fussed about the whole idea and there were threats which were serious enough to be respected, so he had desisted. That there was a Beardsley nuance in the pose of the crowned Virgin did not displease him. It was not going to be banal at any rate. They sat there some time.

'Still a lot to do?' he quizzed charmingly.

'A lot. But I can't get on till they send me everything I need from London. I've never done a fresco before, you know. It seems to me rather a mess so far.'

'Oh, no, no, no. At any rate there is plenty of time.'

'I'm so glad to hear you say so. I had begun to think Guy and Laura were getting a little tired of me.'

'Ridiculous,' said the Vicar.

A benign calm had stolen over his troubled spirit. Really Ariadne was just what he sometimes needed.

Her last remark, however, had roused a rustle in the displeasure which had been tormenting him and which she had so gently annealed as they sat on the pitch pine bench.

The church door had been open all the time and they had not heard Miss Want enter for a little quiet meditation. She had been teaching some of the village children a few German words, just for fun, and they had accompanied her ever so gaily almost to the church, shouting 'my fahter! my fahter!' in a glad chorus. She wondered why this simple word for father amused them so much. She was glad to have given them pleasure.

She had knelt down and made the Sign of the Cross and was gazing wildly at the altar, whose flowers wanted at least weeding out, when Ariadne and the Vicar emerged from the Lady Chapel. She buried her head in her hands as they passed close to her.

'What on earth was Miss Want doing there?' said the Vicar with disgust when they were outside.

'Saying her prayers, I suppose.'

'But why? She has no business to be fussing in and out of the church at all hours. It will have to be locked.'

'Come, come, Father, cheer up! Here is Jude, back from the village,' she added, to change the subject, which bored her.

The Vicar's head began to go round again. He rushed home and left Ariadne smiling to herself, but not wanly.

He heard the Mallorys talking in the study. He could not face them. Jude was in the kitchen. He could not face him. To his little bedroom he went, flung himself down by the bed and prayed for light. That this was denied him was no surprise. He was not worthy. He was in a state of sin and deserved to be rejected. That was always so, was it not? God's face turned away for sorrow, one hoped not in anger.

He rose, and lit a cigarette. He ventured into the kitchen, empty of Jude who had stoked up for the evening cooking. It was his night off. A small leg of mutton awaited the Vicar and he stuffed more garlic than usual under the bone.

Cooking was more beneficial than prayer. That was, of course, because it was more absorbing. Alas, for vagrant thoughts that beat like moths against a window pane! He made a complicated savoury while the joint was in the oven, and by nine o'clock all seemed serene: Laura's presence helping in the kitchen had not distracted him. Nerves no longer jangled — Ariadne did not argue, Guy was in high spirits and the joint was done to a turn.

All seemed set fair when they went to bed that night. Set fair it remained for a halcyon fortnight in early June. Visits were exchanged in perfect weather, sweets were made in the housemaid's cupboard. On a fine day even the Father deigned to dip fillings into the warm chocolate, later to appear as a peppermint cream in an elegant plateful of dainties, gaily coloured fondants some shaped in a Homeric bearded form, the latest novelty from London, to be toyed with on the lawn after tea,

It was the Father's duty to fetch Ariadne from her fresco work in the church, to carry her impedimenta (for fear perhaps of marauding enemies) and settle her in a garden chair to rest after her labours. The garden was so peaceful in the evening light, and sometimes Josephine Want would be able to stay the night, and sleep in the empty maid's room, the smaller spare room being sacred, of course, to Ariadne. The Trinities being in full blast, there was not much activity in the church. The Corpus Christi procession had given much pleasure to the villagers. The Sunday School girls had worn Mary-blue ribbons with their white frocks and one little boy led the procession as John the Baptist clad in a little muslin garment which had caused a sensation in the village and for him a dangerous cold. For the rest — an agreeable monotony spread beneficently. Freedom to think and act as you pleased seemed to be the order of the day. Miss Want, if she did not stay for the night, never failed to watch for the advent of the Vicar and Ariadne at early dusk, bidding a bright good-bye to all when she mounted her bike.

Guy, free now from ecclesiastic duties beyond the Sunday School and Golf Visitors' Mass, would vanish into the dining-room some afternoons for an hour or two — writing, it appeared. Letters, Miss Want presumed. She was the only person who showed any curiosity about this occupation that kept him in on beautiful days.

On one of these days, Josephine Want suggested, not exactly shyly, but with some diffidence, that she and Ariadne should take a walk along the cliffs for a little change. Ariadne rose to it.

'Perhaps the Father would come too?' Josephine queried with one of her side glances that never caught his eye.

'Not today. I am superintending Jude's work in the garden.' This was said without assurance but with firm intention and opening the dining-room door, as though to escape.

Laura was playing the piano while Guy wrote. The Vicar put his head in.

'That is very nice, lady. What is it?'

'A Schubert Waltz.'

'Delicious. Like grapes. Sweet, rich and juicy.'

He was completely unmusical, could not intone a note in church, and had never tried to whistle a tune. He enjoyed, however, playing two-handed bridge to Laura's piano and when there was rare chamber music to be heard in Oxford days he would listen with pleasure, especially when a clarinet interposed as in the Mozart Quintet in A, with virile energy. He rather wished he could learn the clarinet, but his friends had discouraged him from such foolishness.

'But surely, alone in the vicarage, I could make as much noise as I liked? I can imagine being very happy with it. I can see I should have to be quite alone, for I should love to blow very hard. I should find it a great relief and being quite unmusical, I should not mind what happened. Oh, yes, I feel it would be a mellow spiritual adventure.'

This was long ago. The ambition had faded.

Ariadne, with a heavy old tropical sunshade inherited by the Vicar from his grandfather and a brand new sketchbook, set out for the famous cliff walk with Miss Want, who at first carried nothing but a stick and a real Panama hat of her brother's. 'He wore it out East,' was her nonchalant reproof when teased by Guy on its first appearance at the vicarage.

It was not long before she had exchanged her stick for Ariadne's parasol.

'I think I shall faint unless I sit down now and open it.'

'A great mistake bringing it. I advised the Vicar not to burden you with it and hoped you would refuse. It would have spoilt the walk. And here we are only half a mile from the vicarage and you are tired already. I can manage it quite well. I can put your sketchbook in my string bag and then you will be quite free. I always think it's a mistake to carry a lot of paraphernalia on a walk … And after all I think I shall risk dumping the parasol in the hedge. No one will notice it and if they do they won't want it.'

Ariadne, having flattered the Father by accepting his impossible parasol for the walk, was now delighted to sit watching the efforts of Miss Want to conceal it in a dry ditch.

'Well done,' she said when Miss Want, red-faced but relieved, relinquished her stick to her. 'Now I feel ready for anything.' Ariadne flourished the stick with youthful energy.

'I'm glad of that. Now we can make straight for the best point which is really most exciting on a rough day, but as today is calm we shall see it in a mild pretty mood. The sea pinks and campions are always a sight this time of year ...'

'Ah, you love flowers?' Ariadne probed with a twinkle in her eye.

'Of course, of course. Didn't you know? One can't very well live in this part of the world without loving them. Besides, I was once a great gardener. I grew dahlias and supplied my family with vegetables.'

'How generous when you were wrapped up in dahlias.'

'Not all the year round,' Miss Want corrected with severity. 'There's lifting and replanting of course, but plenty of time to spare for peas and cabbages till the dahlias bloom.'

'A full life, anyway.' Ariadne firmly decided to put an end to what was threatening to become a life history. She was not interested in Miss Want's past; her queerness had been a shock and a delight and that was enough. Except, perhaps — how she had come to be bedevilled by the Vicar — how, when and where? But no — too much bother; she was not really comic. Simply boring. Her background? A peppery colonel with ever-rising blood pressure, the mother, a poor soul labouring patiently under the disadvantage of an utterly unmarriageable daughter.

No, it was not worth diving into.

'Well — shall we move on?' Miss Want picked up her string bag, which now contained Ariadne's sketchbook and the tatting apparatus that she always carried with her. And off they went.

Whatever Ariadne had decided to avoid in the matter of family history Miss Want was inquisitive about Miss Berden's past. In this eager quest she had not been encouraged by anyone, least of all Miss Berden. She had lost hope on this point, but her interest in Miss Berden's present was acute.

'And the fresco?' she questioned brightly as they stumbled together over the tussocks. 'Does it progress satisfactorily?'

'Slowly,' said Ariadne. 'There were such delays from London. Now that I have got all that is necessary I can get on with it. In a month or so it should be finished if there are no interruptions.'

'Interruptions? I shouldn't think there would be many here which you could not avoid.'

'Oh, one never knows. One never knows,' sighed Ariadne, her voice suddenly drooping.

'Ah, how true. One never knows,' agreed Miss Want heartily. 'You might be called to London and that would be sad for the fresco.'

'That is most unlikely. The most unlikely thing that could happen.'

'Really? And why is that? There must be plenty of friends waiting for you in London,'

Ariadne sensed the eager nose of Miss Want's curiosity again at work.

'Oh, no, there's no one I need bother about in London. Or anywhere else for that matter.'

'Anywhere else? Surely here? The Mallorys? Father St John? They seem to be very devoted to you.'

'You think so? The Mallorys are nice and kind. They want me to do their portraits but I've put it off. I haven't known them long enough and haven't quite got into the mood. There's plenty of time.'

'Oh! Are they likely to become permanent?'

'Till he finds something bigger. I'm sure he won't be a clergyman, or priest, as they like to call them here.'

'Good gracious, why not?'

'Several reasons. First, because his wife would hate it.'

'Would he mind that?'

'Of course he would. He is quite a sensitive creature really, easily discouraged, and would hate to drag her into anything she didn't like.'

'You do surprise me. He seems to me a mass of conceit, overbearing, and very often obnoxious — extremely so.'

'That's true,' said Ariadne nodding her head.

'But, of course, one can't deny his charm. They both have that,' said Miss Want.

'Laura, too?' (Miss Want winced at the familiarity.) Ariadne was hardly conscious that Christian names were denied to Miss Want, who seized the occasion.

'Yes, Laura too, *I* think, don't you?'

Ariadne hesitated.

'She has a kind heart, at least.'

'Is that all?'

'Not quite, perhaps.'

'She has taken on a big problem in her marriage if you are right about her objection to the Church for him. He is bound to be a great figure. He might rock the Church of England to its foundations and then where would she be?'

'Who can guess. This is silly woman's talk. Let us get on with the walk,' said Ariadne.

They had sat leaning against a green hump with their destination, the Point, in view half a mile or so away. The sun had disappeared behind a cumulus that seemed to have risen mirage-like out of the sea.

'That is worth coming out to look at,' Ariadne murmured.

'Quite ominous,' laughed Miss Want, and swung her string bag as she forged ahead. 'The sunset ought to be interesting.'

Ariadne dawdled a moment to store in her memory the enchantment of the scene, the great cloud that seemed to have sprung like a mushroom from the horizon, building itself up in slow cauliflower shapes of shining alabaster.

'Come along,' cried Miss Want. 'Do you want your sketchbook?'

'Not at all. I couldn't draw it.' She did not add, 'I shall never forget it.'

At last they came to the Point, skirting along a low wall boundary, and uphill all the way till they were standing at the apex of a triangle, and looked from what Ariadne called a dizzy height at a frightening sea-stack surrounded by rocks like crouching rhinos.

'This is a place for wrecks,' pronounced Miss Want. 'The Cornishman's joy, with his donkey light.'

'Oh, dear,' said Ariadne. 'Were they so bad as that?'

'Of course they were. It's in the blood. Always on the look out.'

'You take a very poor view of these fascinating people.'

'I can't help it. I know too much. But do forget about the rocks and wrecks and look at the sea pinks. They are growing in great clumps all the way down the cliff. Do look.'

Ariadne turned to do so, but after a glance behind her whispered, 'There's a man looking over that wall.'

Miss Want looked round.

'There's no one there.'

'Yes there is. Let's go and see.'

They went to the wall and looked over.

'No one there. You imagined it.'

'No I didn't. Unless it was a ghost. He can't have escaped in this open country.'

'Where is he then?'

'Let's look again.' She climbed over the wall which was bordered on the other side by a ditch. Miss Want, unbelieving, hesitated.

'Hullo,' Ariadne called from beyond the wall. 'Here's a dead man.'

And there he was, in the ditch, on his face.

The obvious thing was to keep him there. So they sat on the wall, not too near him, and kept up a long extremely dull conversation, their eyes daring him to move. They sat on until the sun began to set in splendour so that there was no reason to hurry, and now the conversation was dilatory — just enough to keep him static. Then Ariadne indicated that she had had enough and that it was time to go. But first she would have a last look at the prone and enormous figure.

'Now I suppose,' she said, 'we ought to go and inform the police about this poor fellow. I wonder how long he's been here. How huge he is. You may know him. Better not to turn him over. We can't guess how long he may have been here.'

With such pleasantries Ariadne teased the imprisoned giant, while Miss Want, unusually pale, looked on with growing agitation and no chance of getting at the tatting which she always sought for relief. For she was now in a quandary.

'Come along,' she whispered. 'Let us get back. I am chilly. I don't feel well.'

'Really?' Ariadne had little sympathy for such sudden frailty in others.

As soon as they were over the wall and away, Miss Want gasped:

'I had no idea — and then when I joined you and looked down upon him I realised that he must be the farmer who owns all that land. I don't know him well. I always understood he was a decent sort of man. To think of him spying! It's appalling. You see you never can trust them.'

'After all, if he is the man you think, he was on his own property, and why shouldn't he have a look at whoever was passing by?'

'And why should he hide in his own ditch!' countered Miss Want briskly. Having recovered from the initial shock her indignation was paramount.

'There is that, to be sure. Not quite usual. He was quick

getting settled in the ditch before we got over the wall, wasn't he!' laughed Ariadne.

'So like them! So like them! Hypocritical, double-faced spies, cowards, pirates, wreckers!'

Ariadne was amused, and played up.

'Why should he want to spy on us? Did he want to listen? If that was all why did he have to hide? Why not stand where he was and pass the time of day with the usual Cornish good manners, especially as he probably knew you.'

'Very strange, very strange. I agree. But there's no understanding of their motives. With all their charm they can't be trusted. In fact I know only one person in the village one can rely upon and that is Mrs Bonython of the shop. I don't know if you have seen her?'

'I have been to her shop occasionally and she has always been friendly. She has beautiful manners and a lovely face.'

'Lovely face? I hadn't noticed that.'

'Look again,' said Ariadne. 'Great character. A Dürer. Passionate, I should say … in her beliefs I mean,' she hastened to add when a peculiar look swept across Miss Want's features. 'Brave, and knowing her own mind.'

'More than her husband does. A nice fellow but not up to her standard of intelligence. She's above her station altogether,' Miss Want concluded, dismissing the Bonythons.

'I'll come in for a minute,' as they reached the vicarage gate. 'I must go back to my poor Rex, all alone in the cottage.'

'He would have enjoyed the walk. You should have thought of bringing him. Poor old dog.'

'A little discipline is good for him.' Miss Want turned away and peered into the dusk which had begun to gather. 'I shouldn't be surprised if he has found his way here after all.'

But no, there was no Rex at the vicarage. Miss Want delivered up the tropical parasol, and the spy story was a lively diversion for the study.

'A queer habit. John Williams, if he was your man, I believe is a good farmer, but a better preacher. They tell me he can keep it up for an hour at a time and no one in the chapel dozes. I should like to be able to do that. More than ten minutes in the pulpit and I and the congregation would be sound asleep.'

'Thank heaven for that,' said Guy.

'I've known you stretch it out to twenty yourself,' retorted the Vicar. 'And in my pulpit too.'

This was not the moment to mention the unfortunate occasion when a golf lady visitor in a smart hat fluttered the leaves of her prayer-book so ostentatiously, while the Vicar preached, that he descended from the pulpit, picked up a reed-bottomed chair, with difficulty and a good deal of noise dragged it up the steps and half sat on it, watching her until she desisted and shut her eyes instead,

This was not one of the Father's masterpieces. The problem of rising from the chair with dignity and continuing the address in the overcrowded little pulpit had not been faced. The gesture was conceived in rage and not worked out to an elegant finish. An error of judgment. A triumph for the Philistines ... there was sniggering ... mockery. It was unbearable for priest and faithful people. It was best forgotten.

✕

Miss Want had by this time lit her lamp and set off on the journey home. Her mind, now that solitude enwrapped her, dwelt uncomfortably on that motionless figure stretched on his face along his own ditch. It was so very odd to see such a sight, she pondered, so very odd. And so uncanny. It gave one the shivers. That he had been peering over his low wall one moment and was hiding the next flat on his face in his own ditch. Why, as Ariadne had said, why not have the gumption to pass the time of day over his wall and leave it at that? No reason why he shouldn't be looking over his wall on a fine evening. Nothing to be ashamed of. Well, she decided, there was no accounting for people's behaviour, especially in this queer haunted part of the world. As she was pushing her bike up the slope to her cottage, the despairing bark of Rex from his prison rent the air. At the same time the wife (or woman?) of Mr Potter could be seen carrying a lantern in such a way that the outline of her shape cleared up any doubts about her condition. They exchanged a good night greeting.

'Just as I thought, t-t-t. How improvident these people are. Come, Rexie boy, a little toddle!' and, as usual on these occasions, Rex was gone in a flash.

Chapter Nine

A few days after the cliff walk Miss Want encountered Mr Williams of the ditch by chance in the village street. She need not have bothered whether boldly to bid him good morning or rush into the nearest doorway. Mr Williams, striding towards her, gave a genial greeting, passing the time of day in a normal manner — which was all she ever received from him — and marched on about his business without a flicker.

There was no mistaking him all the same, thought Miss Want. No man was so tall in the neighbourhood. She had almost forgotten that he was one of the farmers who had knocked her up on a dark night with the silly threat to shoot Rex for sheep maiming. And this morning he had not even glanced at Rex sloping along beside her.

Well, well, there was no knowing what these people would be up to. She would like the episode to be kept dark if possible and decided to go up to the vicarage, to beg for silence on the subject. It might start all sorts of gossip and make things uncomfortable for herself. It was probably too late. She should have done it before. Botheration! Mallory at any rate would have delighted to jollify about it in the village. 'Yes, I think I've probably left it too long,' she muttered, 'but anyway I'm due to pay another visit to the vicarage.'

After tea on the next day she set off with Rex. Weather was fine and warm so she made straight for the garden where she expected to find some sign of life. Silence greeted her.

'No one here?'

The chairs were spread about as usual, reminders of tea lingered. Guy had left his pipe lying about beside a book, which she recognised as a copy of *Emma*. She had always wondered why they were so fond of Jane Austen — such a waste of time. 'We don't see eye to eye in our literary tastes,' she mused deeply, after rummaging in her spacious store of clichés. As she looked round at this conclusion, she saw Rex sniffing round an object which she had not noticed. After all, there was someone there. A little woman asleep in one of the most luxurious chairs.

It was too late to call Rex off before he had licked the little woman's hand and woken her with a start.

'Good gracious, what is this? Go away, you dreadful dog. Where is everybody?'

For the second time in twenty-four hours Miss Want had to make a quick decision. To run away, hoping Rex would follow without being whistled, or to face this alarming little person boldly. She chose the latter.

The little woman confronted by Miss Want did not actually repeat *What is this?* but her large blue eyes were expressive enough to suggest fastidious dismay as though perhaps this were a waking dream. For Mrs Mallory, Senior, was very tired indeed. She had decided suddenly that she must see Helzephron and her son. She had sent a long expensive telegram announcing that she would be staying for a few days at a hotel in a neighbouring town, and would come over to Helzephron for tea probably in a hired car. They were not to worry about her. She was taking a short holiday alone, and was again at Helzephron for tea on the day Miss Want found her.

Rex, overawed, was soon lying down at his mistress's command and Miss Want, who was never self-conscious, seated herself with clumsy ease in the next chair to Mrs Mallory.

'I am here to see my son,' announced Mrs Mallory with firm emphasis. 'We had a tiring drive and after tea they must have left me sleeping. I dropped off, it seems. There was some talk of a walk, and I was not inclined to see anything more today. We have enjoyed driving about in the motor-car I have hired from my hotel. I suppose you are a friend of Father St John's.'

That was a good opening for Josephine who, undaunted by the cold gleam of those watchful eyes, launched out on a long story of her acquaintance with the Father.

'So you took up your residence in these parts soon after Father St John was appointed here? No doubt you are wise to choose Cornwall for your home. I cannot imagine anything more suitable. And as a high Anglican myself I can thoroughly sympathise with your choice of Helzephron as the ideal retreat for meditation and prayer. Peace of mind, you will agree, is one of the first conditions of the religious life. I am convinced that you have it here.'

Miss Want was taken aback by Mrs Mallory's pronouncement, spoken solemnly, yet with a scarcely veiled mockery in her plangent voice. Why should she be 'convinced' indeed? What did she know about life in Helzephron! Life in Helzephron was constant turmoil and, Josephine flattered herself, all the better for that. Even the vicarage 'teasing' was stimulating with all the uncertainties as to the Father's complicity to liven it up.

She had half a mind to give a lighthearted description of Guy Mallory's pranks, which might give his mother a little discomfort, and shed a new light on her son's character. This would check the high-minded conversation that Mrs Mallory had evidently decided to inflict upon Josephine without the slightest warning and with such a winning smile. Josephine was at a loss. She would have liked to get up and run away with Rex bounding beside her to give her confidence. But that could not be. It would be too obvious. She would *not* discuss meditation and prayer with a perfect stranger. That should have been plain to anyone, surely. It was most irregular, she comforted herself when a doubt assailed her as to her capacity for discussing such an intimate theme at all.

No need to worry … the Mallorys appeared, back from their walk.

'Oh, here is your son at last with his wife.' Miss Want struggled to rise from her low chair.

'Ah, do not go yet, Miss — er — Miss — forgive me, I did not catch your name!'

'Miss Want, Mother.' Guy helped Miss Want to her feet with a gallant gesture. She was weakened, she felt, by the sudden outbreak of religious fervour from his extraordinary mother, and the ghastly threat of a heart-to-heart talk on church matters, when all she wanted to do was to warn the vicarage about Farmer Williams of the ditch, then to go straight back to Chollow, and avoid seeing the Father and Ariadne returning from the church, where they surely were, closeted in the Lady Chapel admiring the fresco.

Miss Want, having excused herself with a promise to have another talk in the near future with Mrs Mallory, drew Guy across the lawn to the drive, and there opened to him the subject of Farmer Williams.

She was relieved to know that the Mallorys had been motoring about the country with his mother for the last few days, devoting themselves entirely to her, for she was tired out with the journey, but was anxious to see some of Cornwall in comfort before she returned to London. Miss Want gathered that Ariadne had not accompanied them on any expedition, the Vicar once to Fowey, where he had ecclesiastical interests of a pleasing nature long deferred for lack of transport. The rare chance of a motor-car was worth seizing. So the cliff walk had been forgotten in the thrill of Mrs Mallory's elaborately planned visit.

Miss Want detailed to Guy her encounter with Williams in the village street as they walked up the drive.

'Oh, don't worry, Miss Want. It's nothing unusual, I should imagine. To hide in one's own ditch is probably quite an amusing local habit. Just for fun, you know, like hide and seek or I spy. Did you ever play I spy?'

'Never, as far as I remember.'

'It's more exciting than hide and seek. The hider catches the hunters, vice versa. We'll try it one day.'

'You're joking!' she laughed. 'I'm too old for that sort of thing now, I'm afraid.'

'Oh, we'll get the Sunday School to come and play. Then you won't feel too old.'

Miss Want could sense that Guy was attracted by this idea, and feared some mischief was behind it.

'Then the Williams business shall be forgotten?' she changed the subject swiftly.

'Oh, we won't talk about it, if that is what you want. That doesn't mean that it won't get about somehow. You know what it's like in this village.'

Miss Want nodded wisely, mounted her bike and Guy returned to his mother.

'What a strange woman! She seems to be obsessed by Father St John. Is that usual?'

'Who told you this?'

'She did, not in so many words but it was easy to penetrate the obscurity of her copious logorrhea. I was not prepared for such revelations and was much struck by them. The contortions of her face as she spoke convinced me that she is an unhappy rather tortured person. Do you agree about that?'

'Perhaps.' Guy showed no embarrassment at this. 'She's rather a nuisance, but on the whole not a bad soul. A fervent Anglo-Catholic.'

'So I gathered. But when I tried to probe her sincerity, she seemed to hold back — and then you interrupted and she got away. I quite realise that she is a lady by birth. That was obvious in spite of her peculiar clothes and wild appearance.'

She paused for a few moments and Guy sat down beside her.

'Now your other friend, so very queer, and also quite certainly of good family. I understand from Laura that you picked her up in London.'

'Not exactly picked her up but met her by chance in a private house. Laura was rather moved by her charm and poverty, and we got her to come down here for her health.'

'So Laura told me … She seems a little bit preoccupied about the plan, but was reticent enough over it to keep me in complete ignorance of what it is all about. All I can see is that Miss Er — is engaged on a fresco for the Lady Chapel, and that Father St John spends a good deal of time discussing it with her. That is only natural, and I am hoping to be allowed to see the work before I return to London.'

'Of course you must. The fact is that Laura has been a little put out about an arrangement we had made with her to do drawings of us, but we are neither of us really keen on it, only it was held out as a pretext for her coming to stay here.'

'From which I gather that you offered to pay her fare and keep her here and she, being poor, would have been too proud to accept without that pretext. No doubt Laura has suffered a disillusion.'

'All that is quite true,' agreed Guy, beginning to think this was enough about Ariadne: but he added, 'I was responsible for the suggestion, not Laura.'

'I have no doubt about that. It was generous of both of you — of you especially — taking the financial responsibility without being particularly interested in the lady. Laura, of course, appreciates that, I am sure. She has a great admiration for Miss Berden's personality and talent. That I gathered from her.'

'Now, Mother,' was Guy's inward reaction. 'That's enough. Not even a hint, please, of criticism, none of your insinuations *against my beloved Laura. You're a very naughty old woman sometimes.'* Aloud he said simply: 'She's quite right. There's a great deal of talent there.'

'To be sure. One can see that. There must be talent.' Mrs Mallory was decisive and Guy knew what she meant.

'She is very poor and has a few precious clothes, like the black cloak she wears, and the saffron silk scarf. They have become so much part of her that one can hardly imagine them on anyone else.'

'I *quite* agree,' was all Mrs Mallory said at that, with a smile.

This was her last day but one in Cornwall. She wished that she had seen Miss Want again, not because she liked her, but she would have enjoyed further diagnosis. She would go and look at Miss Berden's fresco tomorrow in a good light. She was anxious to get the hang of the Helzephron situation, which was not altogether to her liking. Miss Want was possibly harmless, though her obsession with the Vicar was a little unpleasant. Nothing in it, of course. Father St John was far above anything of the sort. The other woman had led an eccentric and possibly immoral life in Paris. A friend of that dreadful Aubrey Beardsley, not to mention Oscar Wilde, must be suspect. These were apparently the only women that Laura was seeing, to judge by their social environment. This plan for Guy was not encouraging, though they both seemed happy enough in their marriage, and no doubt that was all that mattered to them. It was unlikely, however, that Guy would be contented for long in such a narrow environment, nor indeed would Laura, so perhaps it would be wiser to say nothing before leaving tomorrow. So Mrs Mallory's mind ran on secretly. She said nothing to Guy or Laura, and when taken to see the fresco in the Lady Chapel on the morning of her departure, she merely said:

'This is not a very good light. I feel sure you are taking pains,' graciously to Ariadne who had stood aside to let her examine the work.

Nothing could be worse than this, and she knew it. Ariadne did not do more than show her wan smile. She did not mind at all what old Mrs Mallory thought about anything. Only the Father's interest in the fresco and herself saved her from despair. The Mallorys were tired of her. Even Laura seemed preoccupied. What by? How could she guess? Something she herself had done or said, surely Laura playing while Guy wrote was alienating them from her! They were self-sufficient, had passed into a new phase. That was it! Perhaps a baby, or some nonsense of that sort? Anyway, the atmosphere was changed in a subtle way and she was very unhappy.

But after Mrs Mallory's departure there was a change. A week, ten days went by without any discomfort to anyone. No one quite knew why. Could Guy's mother have left an influence behind her, a good one to salve infectious irritations? Then one morning Laura carried Ariadne's breakfast up to her bedside, looking happier than usual.

'A heavenly day! We must have a picnic for a change.'

'Without Miss Want? Do let us. Oo!' she gazed at the tray. 'Hot scones, and strawberries and cream! That's heaven! Any post yet?'

'It's late.'

'I was hoping to hear more from Clare about her going to France. I can't think how she can give up the Regent Canal house. And now she's going abroad I suppose she's completely lost to me.'

'Oh, don't say that. You will stay with her in France, surely?'

'Not with that dreadful sailor man about. I expect she's going there to escape from me.'

'Good heavens, what egotism,' thought Laura, and went to

answer the postman's ring. There was nothing for Ariadne, a budget for Guy and one letter addressed to Laura.

She laughed when she opened it.

'Look at this. It's a joke of Ariadne's, I suppose.'

Guy looked. A hideous caricature of Ariadne, sitting back in an easy-chair, her feet firmly planted on the roof of the vicarage, her footstool.

'Here I am and here I mean to stay,' was its message. The drawing was not bad, reminding them of Ariadne's quick characteristic sketches.

'Rather a macabre joke, considering the state of things here. Can it be a prelude to her going?'

'But she's been so cheerful lately.'

'That may be part of the joke. Posted in London, SW. Why did she bother?'

There couldn't be any mystery about who sent it and yet how queer that she had. It was, when they considered it, acutely embarrassing. Perhaps it was *meant* to be? 'If so, better not to allude to it, and tear it up or burn it,' said Laura.

'Nonsense,' said Guy. 'Take it in to her at once and see what she says.' Laura did so.

Ariadne stared at the drawing and her pale cheeks flushed.

'I shall leave at once. You might have found a kinder way of getting rid of me. And how dared you accuse me of drawing anything so feeble!'

Large tears followed each other slowly down her face and dripped on to her nightgown.

Laura was appalled by such an unexpected reaction. She flung herself down by the bed, protesting:

'You mustn't say that. You mustn't think it. How can you? We thought it was a joke. You did send it, didn't you? Oh, tell me that you did.'

'Of course I didn't. Why should I? It wouldn't be a joke. I've been so unhappy, knowing that you both hated me.' ('Oh!'

moaned Laura.) 'Only Father wanted me to do that fresco and I stayed because of that. And then things got better. And now — this! I know who sent it. There's only one person, and God knows who he got to do it and post it. It was Guy, of course. Guy! Guy!' she cried loudly.

Tears were now pouring in torrents and there was no handkerchief to mop them up.

The only answer to this was to fetch Guy, who was already on his way, urged by the shrieking of his own name, and the certainty that a scene was in progress. The end of it found the Mallorys kneeling on each side of Ariadne, wiping her eyes and nose with Guy's clean handkerchief, and imploring her to stay as long as she liked, declaring that, of course, they loved her, and she mustn't think such dreadful things.

How endless and exhausting that scene to all concerned! Ariadne would have lunch in bed; the Mallorys would discuss the affair from all angles with the Vicar, who took a light view of it.

'Anonymous? Why not? I've had scores of them. I keep them all in a special drawer. I suppose it wasn't you, Guy?'

'Nor you, neither?' was Guy's reply.

Chapter Ten

When two more arrived next morning for the Father and Ariadne, this time faintly pornographic, the atmosphere became unpleasantly obscure. Suspicion lurked in every corner. Even Jude was questioned. The village was aroused. Everyone had a theory. What about the dwarfish brother of Farmer Williams who liked to peer into other people's windows on dark evenings and spread evil reports? Mrs Bonython of the shop would not discuss it, but her dark eyes held unutterable secrets. Miss Want was sure that it was an enemy of Ariadne's in London until she had one herself. She broke the news at the vicarage two days later.

'What was it like?' asked Laura.

'I've got it here.' She fumbled in her bag. A rosary fell out in a tangle of household keys … But there was no need to caricature Josephine Want. She was floating in a flood of her own tears holding a large handkerchief. 'Poor old Joe!' A faint outline of the Vicar and Ariadne at the altar adorned the background, It was cleverly done. Had Miss Want any theories? N-no. She couldn't understand what it was all about. From the look in her eye when Guy came into the room, it was made obvious that she suspected him. Well, that was not surprising under the circumstances. Laura was uneasy again, for Ariadne's first cry of 'Guy!' was very hot in her memory. His delight in practical jokes made him suspect even in Laura's eyes, though this was not a joke at all. It was silly, but it was horrible. No one was at ease though each pretended to be.

At the end of ten days Ariadne heard from Clare Dobson, who wrote urgently that she must come at once to London, as there was news from Ireland that would surprise and she hoped please her. Her Aunt Grizelda, the only survivor of her family, having sold the big house, was now settling into a little home in the neighbourhood which she would like to share with Ariadne. She had had to wait a long time before she could get in touch …

'Poor Aunt Grizelda, she was the best of them all, in fact the only one with a trace of humanity in her, the only one who ever wrote a friendly letter to me and that was only once soon after I left home. Of course, I never answered it.'

'Never answered it?' marvelled Laura.

'Never. Why should I? I wanted to die for my art. Now that I'm not dead I'm alive enough to look forward to a peaceful life with the old dear in a comfortable little home. What could be better? — or more surprising?'

'What indeed!' Guy echoed with one of his crooked smiles. 'And the fresco?'

'No good. Left as it is, the Father can do what he likes with it, unless I sponge it out tomorrow. It was fun doing it for him, though. I shall do wild Irish abstractions and have a show in Dublin. No one will remember who I was, or understand what I mean. And I shall be rather vague about it too. It will be like a rebirth. Aunt Grizelda will leave the cottage to me and life will begin all over again. Who'd have thought it! I shall stay with Clare for a week and not mind a bit whether the sailorman is there or not. And you will all come and stay with me in Ireland. Clare will bring her baby, Laura shall have a piano and play waltzes and Guy will write a great book. What a dream!'

Ariadne was dreadfully excited. Eyes glowed, a bright spot of hectic colour gathered on each hollow cheek. The Mallorys gazed at her and each other in amazement. She was transformed. Here was an end of self-pity, it should be hoped, so long as Aunt Grizelda behaved herself, would not expect Ariadne to conform to old-fashioned ideas like breakfast at eight downstairs. Ariadne would live exactly as she liked.

Aunt Grizelda would soon be under the spell. Ariadne would see to that and keep her under it until she died. This was superb.

'I must leave you all at once. There's no time to waste. A week in London will be too long to bear, but there will be a lot of things to attend to. I might leave tomorrow. Send a telegram today. Perhaps Guy will see to that while Laura and I are packing.'

At this moment Father St John passed the study window, his puzzled baby expression predominant. Soon he was in the room.

'What's this, what's this. Are you leaving us so soon?'

'Tomorrow. If you can get me to the station in time. I trust you all to help me. It will be a good riddance for everybody.' She smiled gaily to make it a joke.

'Not for me. What about my fresco?' The Father put it that way.

'Fresco will fade away. It will look better so. Perhaps I'll blot it out tonight in the gloaming. Shall we have a gloaming party?'

'Certainly,' said Guy, and 'Certainly *not*,' ruled the Vicar, his face a study in exasperation. Then from another angle he attacked: 'And you care to leave us before the caricature mystery has been solved?'

'Why not? I have my guesses, and it will give us a reason to exchange at least one letter, when you do know the truth. I *don't* really care. I am beginning a new life, Father, as I was telling Laura and Guy — it's a rebirth, so that I shall be able to demolish the past. Not that I shall want to forget any of you as you don't belong to my past but are stepping-stones into this new one. You will all visit me in Ireland,' she concluded as she went to the door with a sweeping gesture and shut it behind her.

'Decidedly rebirth,' remarked the Vicar and said no more.

He went out and was not seen until Ariadne had left next day. No bustle and fuss for him. No good-byes. The fresco was dead. It had been dead from the start, he assured himself. Against his early convictions, enchantment had faded, the saffron scarf which he found lying on the lawn, and asked Laura to forward, was grubby and dull. Laura had taken it from him with delightful insouciance.

'That must go at once. She'll be lost without it, poor girl.'

'Lost — poor girl,' he echoed with a derisive laugh, turning away as he said it after glancing for a moment at her face.

The vicarage was obviously not quite itself now that Ariadne had gone. The sense of loss was soon ousted for the Mallorys at least by a spiritual release from what had become a useless gesture of compassion and in Laura's case certainly of affection and admiration.

The Father was sad, disillusioned, particularly because the fresco had been abandoned so light-heartedly for the prospect of a comfortable life elsewhere. In a moment everything was changed for Ariadne. And why should she not be glad after the hopeless humiliations of the last few years, Guy and Laura insisted when they all talked it over after the saffron scarf had been posted by Jude.

'Quite right,' agreed the Father. 'Quite right, my dears, of course we must look at it that way. Confound her,' he added, and then, 'I wish we knew who sent those caricatures,' with the usual smirk at Guy, which had begun to bore Guy and worry Laura. 'Perhaps it was herself after all. Perhaps she already knew what was coming to her and thought this would really be a good joke on us.'

'I'm quite sure not. That's a nonsensical idea. She's much too lazy to bother about anything so complicated as having the things sent from London. Local posting might not deter her, but I deny that she has the energy for anything more complicated. She would fade away in the middle of it.'

'Perhaps we shall never know. At any rate, I beg you to let me have yours, Laura, and perhaps Miss Want will let me add hers to my collection in the special drawer. Then I should have the whole series.'

'You can certainly have mine,' said Laura. 'Here it is in my pocket. No. 1 of the series. I don't know why it came to me. It should have gone to Ariadne. I ought to have torn it up and saved an exhausting scene.'

'And the pornography wouldn't have mattered so much, yours and hers. Just a comment on an imagined situation and rather amusing. Ariadne wouldn't have minded that.'

'Yes, it was really a pity that the first caused such a to-do.'

'Well, it's all finished now. Ariadne is happy and we are at peace.'

'Ah, yes, Guy,' said the Vicar. 'How right. How right.'

Guy rose and looked out of the window.

'Raining. But I must go to the shop for my tobacco. Mrs Bonython promised it. Want a walk, Laurie?'

Laurie again! So rare. 'Of course.'

It had been a squally day when Ariadne had left, and again not fit weather for the jingle and luggage.

So the old cab had called to take her to the station with Laura, but there was no lassitude or wanness, no apologetic feelings about the drive and relief on both sides when she had waved from the train, wearing an old cap of Laura's which she had taken to.

Again a squall when the Mallorys opened the door of Mrs Bonython's shop at dusk.

'Ah, here you are, sir. Here's your tobacco, just arrived.'

'Just in time. My pouch is empty.'

'Let me fill it.' This was Mrs Bonython's privilege which she took with a warm blush.

The pouch was filled, when the shop bell tinkled and a wild figure entered, followed by a dripping dog.

It was Miss Want, in search of biscuits and envelopes.

'Ah, here we all are again,' she said heartily. Rex shook himself over everybody. 'Lie down, Rexie boy.'

'Yes, here we all are, except Ariadne,' said Guy, surprisingly.

'Ah, well, she wouldn't be out on a night like this.'

'You haven't heard, Miss Want. She left for London yesterday.'

'Good gracious! How sudden. Not bad news, I hope?'

'On the contrary, good news.'

'Had she finished the fresco?'

'No, she hadn't.'

Suddenly Guy picked up the one candlestick and held it in Miss Want's face.

'You sent those pictures. Don't try to deny it. I know. The truth, now, the truth.'

Miss Want's distorted face was cruelly illumined by that single candle. For a moment she drew back; the candle was jerked nearer. 'The truth now, the truth!'

'All right. You've won. I did. I hated you all and I didn't care. I wanted to get that woman away, and now she's gone.'

'Her going had nothing to do with you. Don't imagine it.'

Mrs Bonython now retired quietly from the scene. Laura in a maze of astonishment at Guy's attack on Miss Want was moved by the agonised face of the poor woman. 'This is awful, awful.' She wanted to follow Mrs Bonython but Josephine Want suddenly recovered her balance.

Anyway, she declared, she had had her fun. It was just a little joke in which poor Mr Potter was glad to join. He was very hard up, his wife was having another baby and she had paid him handsomely for his sketches. 'Ten shillings apiece to be exact. Potter resented the existence of such people as the Mallorys and Ariadne and was glad to have a go at them. She herself disliked Ariadne Berden so much that she had thought of pushing her over a cliff when they were having a friendly walk and an opportunity occurred. Only just in time she had looked round and seen one of the farmers spying on them over a wall. They had gone at once to see who he was but he had disappeared. Ariadne looked over and saw him lying flat on his face in a ditch and laughing called out:

'Hullo, here's a dead man.'

It was rather quaint to think how nearly someone might have called out, 'Here's a dead woman!' instead, and have been right.

Well, now the squall was over. She would sally forth. 'Come, Rex, old man.' She was really glad it was out. When all was said and done, it was only a little joke … 'These are my biscuits, I think. Say good night to Mrs Bonython for me.'

'Your envelopes, Miss Want.' Guy handed them to her.

The shop bell tinkled again and she was gone.

'How did you know?'

'I didn't. It was just an idea.'

Mrs Bonython came back,

'I was as sure it were Miss Want as I stand here. So I says to John, and he shut me up. A sad business. An ill-wisht person, ill-wisht, poor lady.'

The Vicar received the news with equanimity.

'Good for you, Guy. Looking back at it, we ought all to have known that she must be at the bottom of it. But who did the drawings?'

'Potter, of course.'

'Who is Potter?'

'One of your parishioners who never goes to church. But would like to know you, I expect.'

'I must call on him. What does he do and why is he here?'

'He wants to be a writer but makes a few shillings with watercolours which he sells occasionally to local people. A wife and one child and another on the way. It would probably embarrass him if you called after all this. He is a neighbour of Miss Want's.'

'That doesn't matter at all. You noticed, I expect, that I shut myself up a good deal while the posting was going on. Embarrassing. A new angle, you understand. So I shut myself up and did some not bad nonsense rhymes. Miss Want has cleared the air. I'm feeling better and healthier all round. What about a glass of altar wine to celebrate. Let's drink her health, now that she need never come to the vicarage again ... Or will she?'

Jude brought in the wine with a pleasing smile. There were four glasses on the tray. The Vicar poured, and after handing the fourth glass to Jude, half turning away as he always did under the stress of emotion:

'Here's to our better behaviour.'

The front door bell clanged.

'And if I am not mistaken, here is Miss Want. Jude, another glass.'

Mandolinata

Fourteen Stories

The original publishers of the 1931 edition, Cope and Fenwick, made grateful acknowledgment to the editors of *The American Bookman*, *Eve*, *The New Coterie*, and the *New Statesman* for permission to reprint five of these stories.

To M C M

1 The Angle of Error

Half past five. Spiaggia was waking up. All through the glowing August afternoon, silence had brooded over this little city of tired bathers. Only the olive trees were alive with the regular scream of the cicale — the dry heart beat of a summer day. Sometimes a dog had got up, barked, and lain down again, exhausted, no other dog even bothering to reply. The sacred siesta had not been desecrated, even by the English visitors with their barbarous habit of noisy walks in the full sun. The heat had triumphed, and everyone had retired behind jalousies to sleep through the burning hours.

Damiano Chilosà, being a Neapolitan and very tired, had gone frankly to bed, which he considered the coolest and most restful place. He was very tired because, besides trying to teach the Duchesse de Sans Souci to swim, he had cooked a wonderful picnic lunch for ten people. He knew that if he did not cook an occasional lunch or dinner he would not be teaching duchesses to swim. That was life: he accepted it. It was all very well to be a successful singer, and to have the entrée into the houses of the Great on that account, but it was not enough for Damiano. He knew pretty well what the Great really thought about the poor devil of a singer, and Damiano did not regard himself as a poor devil of a singer. It was only by the merest chance that he was a singer at all. Just lack of means and a natural gift for singing had led him into what was the easiest profession going. He regarded himself, and wished to be regarded, as the Barone Chilosà, scion of one of the most ancient families in Italy.

The noble family of Chilosà had long been drained to its dregs, and Damiano found himself among the dregs. But family pride dies hard. The Palazzo Chilosà, only one of the many strongholds of this once eminent race, had gone through centuries of changing fortune, till now, as the Hotel Paradiso, it sheltered a large party of London's lightweight set and a featherweight Parisian or two, who, by force of what they considered character, managed to keep the hotel to themselves.

It was in this society that Damiano wished to shine, and it was his fine culinary gift as well as his delightful voice that had captured the heart of the Elect. He imagined that the 'Barone' helped, but really it had no effect at all. They didn't care a bit what his family was, or whether he had any right to the title (which he hadn't), as long as he sang and cooked so divinely. They might have got tired of him if he had only been able to sing. There were few things they could concentrate on for more than ten minutes, but one of them was food, and that was where he came in. They demanded his presence at all their al fresco parties. His ravioli at midnight! His spaghetti at dawn! It was food for the gods.

And he was such a dear, so obliging — always there when he was wanted to interpret and advise on boat-hiring, wine, barbers, villas, and where the best exchange could be had. They were always sending for him, and he always went — but with dignity, as though he had just dropped in as one of themselves, not with any subserviency. *Per Dio*, no!

Damiano dressed leisurely, and, opening his bedroom window, stepped out on to his little white terrace. It was cool there now; the sun had left its roof of dried broom. He sat down and looked out over the vineyard and olive orchard that he wished were his — over the orchard to the great mountain which wore the bloom of a purple plum against the dense blue sky.

'*Un bel di!*' he murmured. Never could a singer make, or at any rate keep, enough money to buy that orchard and possess that view. But — one fine day! He had hopes of Zio Alfredo, a bachelor uncle who was making a fortune in South America, and had been impressed by his nephew and his performance in *Traviata* at Buenos Aires. As to saving anything himself — it all went jingling through his fingers before ever he got home to Spiaggia. He could not even afford to marry the poor Carolina, who had been waiting for him nearly fourteen years, her youth and looks ebbing away. No one understood why he persevered with this childhood's engagement to the simple peasant girl, and no one, except Carolina herself, believed that he would ever marry her. Still, he never failed to visit her each day, whatever his social engagements, and his letters and presents came pouring in regularly when he was singing abroad.

'The *giovannott'* of yesterday has arrived.'

A small boy like a bright brown bird made this announcement; Giannino, Damiano's only servant, and his assistant at all the cooking parties; swift and agile bearer of pots and pans, and fanner of obstinate carbone fires.

'He may enter.'

The young man of yesterday came by appointment. He had been sent by a friend of Damiano's who had heard him, somewhere near Naples, amusing a few friends with his guitar. The result of yesterday's interview was satisfactory, and here he was for his first lesson.

He entered. He was about nineteen, and of a god-like beauty: of the best period, fifth century, BC.

He wore, in spite of the heat, a closely-fitting jacket of enormous check, much cut in at the waist after the fashion of the less informed Neapolitan tailors, white trousers, a red tie spotted white with a large horseshoe in the middle of it, a striped waistcoat, and three diamond rings. His feet were shod in boots apparently made of bright yellow paper, with shiny black pointed toes and welts. He wore no hat, and his mass of sable hair had been carefully trained to rise vertically a good half foot from his sloping brow. His appearance, in short, was the beau ideal of the Neapolitan *vuappo*.

Yesterday this had saddened Damiano, who hoped that he would be less gorgeous today; instead he wore yet another diamond ring. Damiano understood that it was in his honour that all these hot clothes were worn, and the extra ring signified grateful appreciation. 'Some day perhaps I shall tell him. He has much to learn.'

The lesson began. The voice of Marco Tale rushed into his throat because he was nervous. He sang flat, and grew very hot, and nearly burst into tears. Yesterday he had brought his guitar, and sung with perfect musicality and a thrilling voice the Neapolitan songs he had known from his childhood. This was quite different. He had never sung a scale in his life. Discipline was unknown either to his voice or to himself. It was a painful hour, and after such a fiasco he would not be surprised to be told by the Barone that he need not come again.

This did not happen, however. He was merely advised to arrange with the Spiaggia organist for lessons in the theory of music and to come at the same time tomorrow for another lesson.

'That is, if you are *appassionato*; if you wish to be a singer, I will give you a lesson every day for a month, and start you. But if not —' he shrugged his shoulders.

'If you have faith in my voice, Signor Barone, I will work day and night. Today I sang like a dog, and feared you would *buttarmi via*.'

'Yes; you did sing like a dog, and I am glad to know that you are aware of it. But I shall not "throw you out". I understand enough, *figlio mio*, to know that never again will you sing so like a dog. You have the voice and temperament of a great artist, but you have much — very much' — with a glance he could not control at the coiffure and the rings — 'to learn.'

It was soon manifest that Marco, who came from a very poor home, had spent his all on the new clothes, which had been bought expressly for that important interview with Damiano. For lodging and food there remained nothing to speak of. As soon as Damiano discovered this, he cleared out a small cupboard, where Marco established himself with his belongings; these consisted of a few rags of peasant clothes, a metal comb, a bottle of pungent hair pomade, and his guitar.

There was no happy mean between the peasant clothes and the garments which gave Damiano such pain. So one of his own discarded flannel suits, a white shirt with turn-down collar, and a pair of rope-soled shoes such as everyone wore in the summer transformed Marco from superficial vulgarity to distinction. Only on occasions he still wore his diamond rings.

'Why, my friend, do you wear those false diamond rings?'

'Because I cannot afford real ones,' Marco replied simply.

Damiano held out his plump hand.

'This is the only ring for a man. You will find no Englishman of any breeding wears anything else.'

A heavy signet ring was the only decoration. It bore the Chilosà crest, with the simple but pregnant motto 'Per Bene'.

'Of course, you are not of noble family, and have no coat of arms.' Marco sadly assented. 'Still, it is possible even for a commoner to wear a signet ring.'

The diamond rings disappeared. They were given to Giannino; Giannino gave two of them to his girl, aged ten, who appreciated them very much; he kept one for himself for *festas*. They served, in fact, to heal the wounds of jealousy caused in Giannino's breast by the unknown *giovannott*'s occupation of that cupboard; so they were not bought in vain.

Marco's slim, brown hands went unadorned.

His education progressed. Not only was he advancing in the elements of musical theory and voice production with astonishing swiftness, but he was apprehending the finer shades of behaviour, with the example of Damiano, that stickler for the correct thing, ever before him. He had, of course, good manners and address, as all Italians have, but he had to unlearn a number of customs to which he had been bred from infancy, such as spitting on the floor and eating *maccheroni*, however skilfully, with his fingers. Damiano had stirred his social ambition. He saw him go out, perfectly dressed in clothes of English cut (they were made by Poole) to parties given by those *inglese pazzi*, who, for all their mad behaviour, were said to be the cream of English society. He longed to join them, to have a little 'flirt' with one of those pretty blonde women who were so strangely thin, like matches. He strongly suspected that it was not only in their thinness that they resembled matches. Damiano forbade his meeting anyone for the present.

'I shall know when you are ready to meet them. Till then you must not be seen by them. Mr Adolphus Nerely is giving a select party in his garden when the moon is full. For that I hope you will be ready to appear, singing Neapolitan songs with your guitar. I shall cook the supper. I shall not sing. I have already told Mr Nerely that I have made a discovery, and he is anxious that you should appear at this party.'

He did not tell Marco all that he had told Mr Nerely, for fear he should become conceited. He was at present singularly free from this failing.

'Your hair you must really control better. I have already told you that it must be flat — flat. Such coiffures as yours are not seen in the houses of English gentlemen.'

'My hair is a desperation' (he called it *dishperazione*). 'I cannot keep it down.'

'Pomade and more pomade, and a handkerchief tied round while dressing. Enrico the barber shall attend to you before the party.'

Stile inglese was preached at Marco from morning to night.
'The English are the only people who can dress. Next come
the good Italians, but only because they have the intelligence
to copy the English. In dress and bearing follow the English,
but in little else. They have no manners because they have
no imagination and are without altruism. But the finest
gentleman in the world, perhaps, is the Englishman who
has made Italy his home. Mr Adolphus Nerely is an example.
True, he must have been born with unusual sensibility. A
hater of sport — a lover of art. He began to build the Villa
Glaucus when he was twenty-four. He is now fifty, and lor
years that house on the edge of the sea has been a temple of
the arts. A man of wealth, he has never had to work, and his
life has been spent in the collection of beautiful things and
the friendship of artists. Observe him well.'

Damiano was on his favourite subject. He puffed at the
Havana cigar he had chosen at the tobacconist's with the
fastidiousness of a connoisseur.

'None of your stinking Napolitani for me,' he had said, 'and
a Toscano is little better. For me always a Havana *del primo
ordine*, which you do not find here. This miserable cabbage is
the best in the shop.'

The tobacconist, an old friend accustomed to Dumiano's
ways, had only laughed with good-humour.

'The best we can do here, Maestro,' giving him a light.
The 'Maestro' implied more respect than 'Barone', a title not
insisted upon by Damiano among his intimate friends, for
many reasons. Marco's Macedonia cigarette was lighted with
the same match, while he vowed to himself that never would
he yield to the lure of the common Neapolitan cigar.

So Marco learned. As the moon waxed his store of worldly
wisdom grew, and, by the time it was full and the night of Mr
Nerely's party had arrived, Damiano felt no misgivings about
introducing his protégé to the distinguished company.

Marco wore a white silk shirt open at the throat, and, to enhance his picturesque beauty, Damiano lent him a black Spanish cape, which he immediately put on as though he had worn Spanish capes all his life. Together they walked down through shining olive groves, with Giannino behind carrying the guitar and a bundle of freshly-gathered herbs for Damiano's cooking. Marco was pale and thoughtful, while Damiano nervously plied him with last injunctions as to behaviour.

'Above all, be cool. Show no fear.'

'I must admit that my heart is going tup, tup' (*tup, tup fa 'o core*).

'That is only right. So it is with all true artists. Courage! You will make a furore tonight.'

Their arrival at the Villa Glaucus was the first sensation.

The villa was high and solitary above the sea, but Mr Nerely and his guests were gathered on the spacious terrace of the *foresteria*, or guest-house, where Damiano was to cook the supper. The *foresteria* was right down on the sea, which lapped the walls of the terrace in fine weather, and in a storm broke right over it. This terrace was approached by a long and dignified series of steps, and it was as he walked down these that Marco was first observed by Mr Nerely and his guests, who had just finished dancing to the delicious music made by three barbers and three tailors, expert performers upon the mandoline and guitar.

Damiano, who led the way, they could recognise, but the strange figure in the cape, moving with slow, young dignity, intrigued them.

'Signor Tale!'

Who was Signor Tale? Mr Nerely, all in white, with snowy hair, drooping moustache, and hawklike aristocratic countenance, began immediately to present him.

Damiano noticed with pride how gracefully his pupil

kissed the hand of the Duchesse de Sans Souci — just the flutter of the lips, and perhaps the faint pressure of the hand which might or might not have been intentional.

The Duchesse de Sans Souci had the largest eyes in Europe and the smallest feet. She wore a Chinese coat and chiffon trousers gathered in at the ankles with gold bells which tinkled when she moved. Marco had never seen anything like her before, but he kept his head. He kissed all the ladies' hands, and warmed to his work. It was not necessary to speak much, as the English ladies, naturally, did not understand Italian; he had only to look serious and interesting. His hair was smooth as a raven's wing, and his classic features were like carved ivory in the moonlight.

'My dear! I've never seen anything like it!' — 'Look at the profile!' — 'The slant of the eyes.' — 'I'm all unhinged!' — 'Too marvellous!'

'Is it right? Is it kind?' murmured someone from the shadows.

When the excitement of Marco's arrival had subsided, and the barbers and tailors had struck up again, Mr Nerely took Damiano and his pupil into the *foresteria* and gave them some champagne. Marco was only allowed half a glass. 'Till he has sung. After that —?'

The host produced a large box of cigars.

'Ah, look, Marco! These are the cigars of cigars!' Damiano took one and fondled it between finger and thumb. 'This is the kind you must smoke when you are a great singer. They are the best in the world.'

Marco looked at the box.

'Corona Corona,' he read. 'What a beautiful name! That I shall never forget.'

The few drops of unaccustomed champagne gave Marco the courage he needed. On the terrace he took his guitar and, leaning against a pillar, began to sing without a trace of nervousness. He opened with the hackneyed 'O Sole Mio' and went on through 'O Surdato 'nnamurato' to 'Tu Sola!' which he sang with tragic intensity. Everyone was enchanted, except one man, a husband, who had been brought out by some stupid piece of carelessness and was always threatening to leave, but, unfortunately, never did. He was heard to mutter:

'By Jove, you know, I think these foreign chaps rather overdo it, what?'

He was the strong, military type of Englishman to whom Italy and its inhabitants make no appeal. When everyone gathered round Marco after 'Tu Sola!' he was muttering:

'Dam dagoes, you know. All right to engage 'em to sing if you like that sort of thing, but — make pets of 'em — no. It doesn't do, my dear fellow. Believe me, I know. It doesn't do.'

No one took the slightest notice of him.

> Vicin' 'o mare
> facimme l'ammore
> a core a core
> pe ce spassa!

sang Marco, and the barbers and tailors were so carried away that they all sang it with him. The rosemary-scented air rang with rich Italian voices and the rhythmic twang of mandolines and guitars.

Damiano tore himself away from the scene of triumph to the *foresteria*, where his dishes awaited him under the watchful eyes of Giannino. It was even better than he had hoped. Marco's success was his own, and his good-natured face was radiant as he lifted the lid of the *pollo cacciatore* which was simmering over a gentle fire.

The husband disapproved of this supper mania. Cooking, he felt, should be done by servants, and certainly not by greasy singers. The whole atmosphere of the party was deplorable, and he was really getting fed up with Italy and its exaggerated moonlight and silly stage effects. Thank God, the moors were not far off!

The supper roused as many superlatives as Marco's singing. The *maccheroni* were cooked five minutes beyond Damiano's regulation, in deference to British taste, which he understood accepted macaroni pudding done to a pulp (and sweetened, too, if such a thing were to be believed). This concession was painful to the artist, but he had once heard an English guest whisper, 'Not quite cooked, is it?' That was enough for him.

The *pollo cacciatore* was followed by exquisite *crêpes Suzette*, which Damiano flapped about in champagne on a chafing-dish and tossed on to plates greedily extended. He could have gone on flapping them till dawn — no one had ever had enough.

Marco sang again after supper with more feeling and less voice, and Damiano was persuaded to give Tosti's 'Luna d' Estate' and 'Pecché?' which he sang as well as they could be sung, in spite of the excellent supper he had eaten. He was no exception to the rule that all really inspired cooks are greedy.

It was not till the east was rosy that Damiano and his pupil, both flushed with triumph, left the Villa Glaucus. Together they watched the sun's path of gold across the star-sapphire sea.

'A symbol!' cried Damiano. 'Yours will be a golden path. The gods have given you many gifts.'

'The best is your goodness to me, *caro* Maestro,' said Marco humbly. 'How can I ever repay you for what you have done for me?'

Damiano waved this away.

'I should not have helped you if I had not known it was worthwhile.'

Marco hesitated a moment, evidently wanting to say something.

'Well, what is it?'

'Maestro, I have longed to show in some way my appreciation of your goodness to me, and I have always been wondering how I can do it. I have no money. I cannot buy the wonderful present I should like to give you. But these I have for you.'

From under his cape he produced a large handful of cigars. They were Corona Coronas.

'How — how did you get those?' Damiano felt a creeping of the scalp as though his hair were beginning to stand on end.

'Oh, it was quite easy. When I went to fetch your watch from the kitchen. It was the work of a moment. No one saw me.'

Damiano at first could only stand helpless with his teeth chattering and his underlip quivering.

'You are not pleased, Maestro? You do not like them?'

'Pleased —!'

Then he found his tongue. There are no English equivalents for the phrases that poured from it. Enough that Marco shuddered and paled beneath them. When the first flood was exhausted —

'Ruin! Ruin! You have ruined me! I, Damiano, of the noble family of Chilosà, to be suspected of such a petty crime! Never, never can I show my face among *gente per bene*. What will they say? He will miss the cigars — I had shown I liked them — what can he think but that? — Ah! and that *antipatico* Englishman who was there. "Dagoes", I heard him say. Dagoes! and now this! I am shamed before the world.'

Marco was appalled by the effect on his noble friend of what he considered a simple little act of friendship.

'I will take them back now,' he said eagerly. 'I will say I took them by mistake. Or I might even put them back without anyone knowing. I could creep down on to the terrace — they will be all in bed —'

Damiano seized him.

'Do not ever go near the place again. If they saw you they would think I had sent you for something else. *Dio mio, Dio mio!* Even if they do not suspect me, they will think it is either you or the little Giannino stealing for me. Leave me! Go, go, and never let me see your face again!'

Marco fled, sobbing, and was lost among the olives.

✕

Damiano Chilosà's social ambitions died that morning. This dreadful incident cut them off sharp, as the stem of a flower is cut and wounded by a steel knife. Marco was one of the blooms that fell.

A strange series of coincidences combined to change completely the pattern of Damiano's life. First, the *inglesi pazzi* disappeared like gipsies in a night, leaving nothing behind but a few discarded bathing caps, and one of the Sans Souci's famous beach shoes, which were garnished with red and green silk seaweed to go with her bathing wrap of wide amber ciré ribbon. This shoe was presented to Damiano with a wink by the owner of the bathing establishment. He was not displeased by the implication of the wink, but put the shoe away in a drawer and tried to forget all about it.

The English party left without a word for Damiano, nor did he, in fact, ever hear from any of them again. This had a sinister significance for him, though it really meant nothing at all except that they had found someone else to do odd jobs for them. The soldier escaped to the moors without a backward glance, and the rest changed partners and moved to the Lido, whose star was just beginning to rise (or set, if you please).

Then Zio Alfredo died most unexpectedly, leaving Damiano quite a decent little fortune. He broke his singing contracts, bought the vineyard and olive orchard of his heart, married Carolina, and settled down to a peaceful domestic life, all in the space of three months. No one, not even Carolina, knew the true history of Marco's disappearance. The general opinion was that he had been captured by the *inglesi pazzi*, and indeed there were persistent rumours that he had been seen bathing at the Lido. Whatever happened, Damiano has never seen him again, but he follows his career very closely.

Nothing but the loss of his voice or an accident to his face could prevent the success of Marco Tale. As neither of these things has happened, he is now the idol of the two Americas.

✻

Last Christmas Damiano Chilosà sat on his terrace gazing out at his orchard and his vineyard, and away to the mountain that was like a damson against the blue winter sky. It was a mild and lovely Christmas day. Little Damiano, aged three, was blowing his new trumpet, his great brown eyes rolling with delight. Carolina was in the kitchen, where all good wives should be, preparing delicious food for Damiano's Christmas dinner. She has not wasted her fourteen years of waiting. She never errs as to a leaf, a pinch or a minute, and now Damiano doesn't so much as put his head inside the kitchen door, unless, of course, a delay occurs.

Giannino is doing his military service, which bores him extremely, and his place in the Chilosà household is only being filled by a stop-gap.

The flesh is creeping over Damiano's bones like an oncoming tide. He heeds it not. Of what use is a figure to the owner of a vineyard and an olive orchard? The garments of Poole have long passed on to the backs of slimmer friends. One has been dissected by Ferruccio the tailor, to his own profit and the benefit of his clients.

Ferruccio the tailor and Enrico the barber were coming to share the Chilosà Christmas dinner — friends of Damiano's boyhood. He sat there waiting for them, puffing at his cigar.

It was a Corona Corona.

He had taken it from an enormous box which had arrived that morning, free of duty, from America. A photograph had also arrived. It was inscribed:

To my beloved Maestro, with the gratitude and eternal affection of Marco Tale.

There were the gay eyes, the sweet, serious mouth, the classic lines, the hair like a raven's wing — unchanged. But there were also perfectly cut clothes, discreet collar and tie, and, on the still slim hand that rested on the beautifully creased knee, one handsome signet ring.

'*Ebbene*,' Damiano smiled serenely. 'We have both learned something. No harm done.'

Little Damiano, having just discovered that the harder you blew the more noise you made, gave a piercing blast.

A delicious aroma was wafted up from the kitchen.

2 Mandolinata

The Miramare Hotel sleeps, or at any rate pretends to. Two hours ago the band shut up and went to bed; the dancers have wandered home along moonlit alleys or upstairs to the Miramare bedrooms. The barman downstairs has been allowed to go to bed. Even the night porter sleeps.

A ferocious bang on the locked front door rouses him. Behold outside the *maresciallo* and two *carabinieri*! At half-past two in the morning! *Mamma mia*! Giuseppe trembles, though for the moment his conscience is clear. Still, one never knows …

'A Signor X. Is he staying here?'

Giuseppe gasps with relief.

'Yes, Signor X has been here a month. He occupies Number 426.'

'Take us up to his room immediately.'

Giuseppe cannot but hesitate an instant. Disturb a guest at this hour! Whatever his offence, it seems hardly decent.

'*At once.* Every moment is of value. It is a matter of life and death.'

To this there is no reply but to throw open the doors of the lift and usher in the three representatives of the law. Excitement communicates itself to Giuseppe as the lift rushes up to the fourth floor. Even the *maresciallo* seems to bristle with anticipation. He glances at his watch.

'It is already the half-hour,' he mutters.

At the end of the corridor is Number 426. The *maresciallo* hastens towards it and bangs on the door. No answer.

'Too late!'

He bangs again.

After several violent bangs they hear sounds within; the thud of a heavy body getting out of bed followed by footsteps approaching the door. The *maresciallo* stands expectant, his eyes fixed on the spot where the face of the inmate of the room will probably appear. The door is opened cautiously, but the *maresciallo's* eyes are fixed upon a large expanse of purple silk pyjama. The face is at least a foot above. The *maresciallo's* gaze travels up and discovers an enormous visage with gargantuan nose looking down upon him, crimson with annoyance.

'What do you want?'

The door remains half open.

'Are you Signor X?'

'Of course I am. What is this joke of yours?'

'It is not a joke, *signore*. Kindly let me into your room. By now, if this message is correct, you should have committed suicide. But I find you in bed.'

He hands the message to the purple-clad gentleman. It is from the wireless station:

Message from Budapest. Prevent Kolya X staying at Miramare Hotel from threatened suicide at two-thirty am on June 14 urgent.

'This message was brought down to me from the Marconi station only fifteen minutes ago. I collect my *carabinieri* and by a miracle of haste we arrive at two-thirty, only to find you in bed. Please have the goodness to explain, *signore*.'

'This is from my father. It is true that in a letter I told him I should commit suicide this morning at two-thirty. But as you see, I have not done so. I have changed my mind.'

'Ha ha! That is very good indeed. That we should be called from our beds to save a suicide who has changed his mind. Pray understand, *signore*, that you will hear more of this!'

'I am very sorry that I have not been able to oblige you, but you understand that I am quite ready to do anything you may suggest, within reason, to compensate you for your disappointment.'

The *maresciallo* smiled graciously as though to say, 'Ah, now you're talking!'

'As for disappointment, that is not quite the word. We are delighted to see the *signore* standing before us in florid health. Delighted indeed! Our haste was to prevent so sad a calamity as the death of so brave a *signore*. Fortunately this was not necessary.'

'How will it do if we meet and talk this over later on?' asks the purple gentleman, who is beginning to yawn. 'I have only been in bed an hour and am confoundedly sleepy. I apologise for my father's impetuosity, and wish you all a very good-night.'

He holds the door open in so compelling a fashion that the three men, with the hovering Giuseppe, retire with an obsequious 'Good-night'. The purple gentleman locks his door and gets back into bed. He sleeps till mid-day.

※

The news of this nocturnal adventure thrilled Spiaggia. The tall, lonely young man who for a month had sat silent in a corner of the ballroom after dinner, watching with melancholy preoccupation the antics of his fellow-guests, became a public figure. A large number of unusual people dined at the Miramare to look at the hero of the day. They could have seen him more cheaply if they had gone to the café after dinner; for it was there he was to be seen, not in his accustomed place at the hotel. Eager inquirers at the Miramare were informed that he had interviewed the *maresciallo* in the afternoon, and that the *maresciallo* was completely satisfied with his explanation. He had behaved in a manner *molto signorile*.

Kolya X was laboriously writing a letter to his father. The café ink and the café pen, combined with the café paper, made this task even more distasteful than usual. His huge well-clad form sprawled over the narrow table. An enormous crossed leg protruded on the side opposite him. Every now and then he would lift his eyes in gloomy meditation, and invariably met the lively gaze of some interested observer. He seemed unconscious of the attention he was attracting:

Dear Father,

I had to tip the police heavily on account of your wireless message. The consequence is that I am harder up than ever. If you would telegraph me some money it would serve a better purpose than rousing everybody in Spiaggia at two-thirty in the morning. Excuse me! I know you meant well. I am in a desperate state, and unless you send me something I shall kill myself, but I shall not tell you when, next time. You cannot prevent me.

Your unhappy son, Kolya.

Kolya was the son of a rich Jewish merchant. He had early shown a disinclination for work of any kind, a disinclination that had been indulged and even encouraged by his doting parents, who, after giving him an expensive education, had supplied funds for luxurious vagrancy. He had wandered round the world seeking happiness, he said, but could not find it. His lather suggested that he might be happier if he had some occupation, something that would anchor him somewhere.

'Very well,' said Kolya. 'Find me something to do, but not in Budapest.'

He was sent to England with introductions to one of the leading Jewish merchants in that country. He was at once engaged as a clerk, as a first step to learning the business. He turned up on the first day of his employment and sat, at a table much too small for him, through a long morning of extreme boredom. The afternoon was worse, and went on until six o'clock. At the end of the day he visited the head of his department and asked how much salary he was going to get.

'Three pounds a week.'

'Three pounds a week to sit at that small table and be bored to tears? No thank you, it is not interesting enough! That is the end of my engagement. Good afternoon.'

His father was so indignant at what he considered his bad manners that he cut down by half the liberal allowance he was still making him. Kolya continued his travels in search of Nirvana, but with straitened means it was even more difficult to find. By the time he drifted to Spiaggia he had sunk into a state of melancholy which he wore, however, with such a comic spirit that no one believed in it.

For he made a good many friends after the episode of the wireless message, and was known by the natives as *Il Signorin' Suicidio*, or simply as *Lungo-lungo*. He used to go picnicking up on the mountain, and would amuse the company by his ridiculous talk about suicide and his threats to throw himself there and then from a rocky peak. One day after lunch he stretched his whole huge length on a rosemary-scented cliff-side and cried:

'Why can I find nothing worth while? My life is a wilderness; I wander and wander about in it and arrive nowhere. Should I have stayed in that office? Should I have been happier because I was working? No, NO, dear madame, I should have died of ugliness. I, the most hideous person you have ever seen, adore beauty, and the sight of those clerks sitting round me, doing ugly work they must hate, would have killed me. Not that way would I wish to die. I would like to die of beauty — smothered, intoxicated, asphyxiated by it. I would like to die loving some glorious woman or enchanting boy. This can never happen, because glorious women and enchanting boys will not allow me to love them. I am too ugly and I am no longer rich enough.

NOW IS THE TIME!' he shouted, suddenly leaping to his feet, waving his great arms and rushing to the edge of the precipice.

Everyone ran laughing to pull him back.

'You can't commit suicide till you've digested your lunch,' said someone, pushing him back on the grass.

'That's true. Such a good lunch too! Besides, it would be rude to end such a charming picnic thus. I must postpone my happiness!' He lit a cigarette.

Little Anyuta threw herself upon him and began stroking his face.

'Ugly man! Great big ugly man!'

'There, you see! Even Anyuta at seven years old finds me hideous. Oh, Anyuta, have pity on me! Will you marry me, please, and save me from suicide?'

'Yes, yes. I love you, great ugly Lungo-lungo. You are so — queer. May I marry him, mama?'

The pretty Russian woman laughed. Kolya looked at her reproachfully.

'She laughs! The idea is too ridiculous. Three times in this week have I asked your mother to marry me, Anyuta, and now when you say "yes" — she laughs. She has laughed three times before this.'

Since Anyuta had met Kolya she had delighted to climb about him as though he were some exciting rock. She flung her arms about him now.

'*I* am not laughing.'

He held her tiny head in his great hands.

'Someone who does not laugh!' he said, and, because she kissed him spontaneously, he blushed.

The Russian widow was regarding him darkly.

'You know, it is all bosh about wanting to marry. You do not want to marry me — or anyone else.'

He sat up.

'How brutally you understand, you dark woman with witch's eyes! I do not want to marry, it is perfectly true. But I passionately want to *want* to marry. I have a deep longing to love a woman like yourself and to have a family, and to live for ever in a house with my family and enjoy it. After all, I am a Jew, and sometimes I feel I should make a great patriarch — but the rest of the time I know I should not. I know too well that, if you of your graciousness were to accept my proposal of marriage, I should be frightened and run away. But I know that you will go on refusing me because, first, I am a Jew, and you are pure Slav and hate Jews, and second, because I am ugly and foolish and because God, besides making me ugly and foolish, has pleased to make me tall like a tower so that all men should see this great hideous Kolya. Nowhere can I hide my stupid, unnecessary body. How could a woman like you look at me, even if I were rich, as I am no longer? So I go on safely asking you to marry me, because it gives me a wonderful feeling of normality to pretend that I want you in that way. I do not. I adore you, and I should like to spend my whole life with you.'

The Russian woman, who had wisdom as well as beauty, was not offended.

'Alas, Kolya, that will not be possible,' she said with a smile. 'After next week we shall not meet again — at least for a very long time. I am going back to Russia.'

Something in her tone told him that she was going to meet some man — perhaps going to be married.

'To Russia! You leave me?' He leapt up again.

'You will come too, *Lungo-lungo!*' cried Anyuta, clinging to him.

'No, no. She does not want me. I can see it! It is just my luck. Let us go down the mountain quickly and have large drinks at the café.'

For the rest of that week Kolya devoted himself entirely to

his Russian friends. He disappeared the day before they were to leave.

'Ask me no questions,' he said. 'But you will not see me. Perhaps I am going to throw myself over the cliff. Perhaps not.'

'He talks of nothing but suicide,' said someone. 'That kind never does it.'

Kolya could have been found on the Marina, where he spent the whole day decorating a large boat with flowers. When he had finished, the boat was like a flower itself. He had cleared the two horticulturists' shops, and had made garlands of myrtle and orange, Florentine fashion, to hang from stern to mast and from mast to prow.

'*Carin' assai! Com' ha fatto bene il Signorin' Suicidio!*' An admiring crowd had been watching him all day.

The same crowd, augmented, was also there the next day when the Naples steamer hooted its warning. It saw *Il Signorin' Suicidio* leading the Russian widow and her child down the quay to the flower boat; it heard the cry of wonder from Anyuta as she jumped into it and seized the huge doll that looked out from the roses in the prow like a figure-head. It heard the *mandolinata* of the three barbers sitting in the stern, and it gave a slightly derisive cheer as the boat swung away from the quay towards the steamer.

'Kolya, you are mad!' exclaimed the widow, laughing a little self-consciously. 'How could you do such a thing!'

'You do not like it? It was to honour you. Another failure!'

'It is delicious. I love it, of course. But so much time you must have spent on it!'

'What is time?' said Kolya.

She felt that it was not the moment to begin an argument on this subject, so she cried:

'Anyuta will never forget this adventure, will you, Anyuta?'

Anyuta, laughing, clasped her doll.

In five minutes they were on the steamer, and hung over the side listening to the *mandolinata* of the smiling barbers in the boat below. Another curious crowd gathered round and listened. When the time came to go, everyone watched Kolya climb into the flower boat and wave a large yellow silk handkerchief.

How bleak it was, going back in that gay boat, alone with the mandolines which had become barbers again and looked at him with kindly amusement. He felt a little foolish as he came ashore into the large crowd that stared at him.

'Perhaps I have made a fool of myself again,' he thought. 'But at any rate it pleased Anyuta."

He left the quay hurriedly, feeling very lonely. The decorated boat was soon full of screaming children tearing the flowers and oranges from it.

He spent the next three days lying in the sun on the beach. Then he wrote to his Russian friend:

Darling, daring Friend!

No news for you, because nothing happens since you left. It's just my luck. So shortly after meeting you I am left broken-hearted. How I wish to be near you. Don't laugh, please! But suicide is near. I have been burnt from the sun. Such terrible pains! My nerves are in a fearful state. I must find courage to make an end, because so the life is rotten. How I envy you to travel! How long I had such a life. But now I must stay here and wait for my father to send money to pay my bills. Fortunately Spiaggia is a wonderful place full of thoughts of you, so I do not suffer so much as I would. A kiss to my dear, dear Anyuta and much love to your beautiful self.

Your faithful friend, Kolya.

I think this is the last letter you will get from me.

He never saw the answer to that letter, telling him not to talk such nonsense about suicide, because in a week he was dead.

Peasants going to work on a crystal August morning found him lying outside the cemetery, shot through the heart. He had sat in the café talking to acquaintances all the evening before, had drunk four double whiskies, and for a change had not talked of suicide. He left when the café closed to go for a walk in the moonlight. Two people met him on his way down to the cemetery, and he said 'Good-night' cheerfully. No one heard the shots.

He had prepared everything carefully. Evidently funds had come from his father, for his table was neatly arranged with envelopes containing money for the tradesmen. A letter to the manager of the hotel contained this:

> I hope I shall not inconvenience you very much. I am going down to the cemetery to shoot myself, at the gate, so that my body will not have to be carried far, and you will not have the displeasure of receiving it. Please let my father know at the enclosed address. I ask, please, that when I am buried a mandolinata shall be played at my grave. Thank you for your kindness to me.

In spite of the heat, everyone went to *Lungo-lungo*'s funeral in the Protestant cemetery, some from curiosity, but many because the strange creature, with all his oddness and the *modo signorile* in which he had finally carried out his threat, had pleasantly impressed the inhabitants of Spiaggia. They did not laugh when the three barbers came forward, and standing over the open grave played *Se chiagnere me siente* and *Torna a Surriento*.

The thin notes of the mandolines tinkled through the radiant air. The solemn resting-place of willing exiles seemed to stir as the unwonted sound floated among the cypress-trees — a futile, pathetic tinkle.

3 La Bonne Mine

Gluck! Dear winsome Gluck! For once that rather tiresome adjective is the only one to use. Winsome! Look at his photograph at four years old. '*Oui, c'est moi. On dit que j'étais beau a cet age. Voila ma soeur — nous étions l'un tel comme l'autre.*' Fair curls, round innocent baby faces, delicate hands — they smiled, those gentle creatures, from the formal little chairs provided by the German photographer.

And look at him now. Fair curls, round innocent baby face, and the slender white hand holding his cigarette. Though in expression a baby face, in form it was of the age of Praxiteles. It was not his fault that he was the Hermes come to life. He could not help knowing it — too many people had told him so. His soft blue eyes fluttered apologetically under the stare of admiration to which he was so used. 'I know what you're going to say,' they seemed to plead. 'But it's not my fault. I really don't care about it. I'm not at all conceited. Please like me!'

And who could help it?

He appeared from nowhere, like most people at Spiaggia. There he was one day, walking up and down the Piazza, alone, with his overcoat slung Neapolitan-wise over his broad shoulders, his head bare, his cigarette between his girlish lips, and his air of dignity and diffidence mingled. He knew, of course, that he was attracting attention, as he must wherever he went.

Grazia and Mafalda had managed to get out this evening only half an hour late for our appointment. Somehow they had unearthed a hat each from their untidy sparrow's nest, shoes hastily whitened for their slim feet, powder and lipstick for their pretty faces; the frock of Grazia on Mafalda, and the frock of Mafalda on Grazia, just to make a change.

And here they were, fresh and lovely, walking the Piazza, and there was Gluck, passing and re-passing.

We three went arm-in-arm. I loved the pull of their slender wrists as they leaned over, chattering both together so that our conversation was a delicious confusion. They both exclaimed as Gluck went striding by, his shining head held high and a faint self-conscious flush on his finely-moulded cheeks. Next time we met him face to face, and he was enveloped in a triple gaze which he could hardly ignore. The blush burned deeper, and he looked carefully away.

'*Un amore!*' Grazia exclaimed under her breath. '*Ma proprio un amore!* And how modest! Not a glance in our direction.'

'*Un ragazzo per bene,*' said Mafalda with conviction. 'One sees at once that there is nothing common about him. Let us sit down.' Mafalda was sometimes quite practical, and it was obvious that sitting down we should have a better opportunity of studying the new arrival with modesty.

We speculated upon him. Grazia thought he must be Swedish because he reminded her of a Swede who had courted her *accanitamente* till he suddenly disappeared with a Russian woman, the mother of a large family, and none of them was ever heard of again. '*Ma, pero, fui contenta, perché ha comminciato di annoiarmi, assai, assai. Un seccante del primo ordine.*' Mafalda curled her lip at this, saw no resemblance to the Swede, and, moreover, protested that Grazia had been *mortificata assai assai* when her *corteggiante* had run away with that black Russian woman, without even letting her know that he could not keep his bathing appointment with her as usual. A *brutta figura* he had made of poor Grazia on the beach that morning last year. Grazia's eyes flashed, but she disdained an argument which might leave her the loser. She found at any rate that the young stranger was a *simpaticone*, and she was sure that he was the sort of person one ought to know.

'But one never can say. Tomorrow he may be gone.'

That's how it was in Spiaggia. Something flashed and was gone. Hardly a memory — so uncertain and eventful was life in that little city of pleasure. They went, and forgot, and you stayed — and forgot, because something else always happened so quickly.

But Gluck was not gone on the morrow. Nor a week later when Grazia and Mafalda came down to dance at the villa was he gone. They came twittering into the studio with bright, excited eyes. Gluck was to follow later with Basilio, with whom he had wisely made friends at the café. Basilio was slim like a paper-knife, his narrow face had an immense nose and a gay mouth that smiled from ear to ear, glittering teeth and brilliant, intelligent eyes. He danced like an Argentino, and few women could resist him if he really put his mind to it. He never missed a dance by moonlight at the villa. We were the best of friends, and could have danced together to the moon.

Every week we used to meet in the studio — sometimes not more than six of us, but always Grazia and Mafalda — in the studio and on that roof outside, which was also terrace — tranced under the moon or stars, with the sea below and tall limestone cliffs cleaving the indigo sky above us. Remote from the world in that villa standing high and lonely, it seemed as though we were indeed dancing on the moon, and the figures of Grazia and Mafalda in their white frocks were like summer moths flitting to and fro, intangible. Sometimes one wanted to stretch out an arm and hold them — to be sure they were not wraiths of fancy — these delicate, elusive ghosts waving beneath the moon.

Basilio was to bring Gluck tonight. This afternoon two cards had lain in the hall, Basilio's and Gluck's.

'*E molto scrupuloso,*' Grazia said as she changed her rope shoes for a silver pair. 'He refused to come tonight unless he first paid a call upon you, even after your invitation.'

'*Un ragazzo molto fino,*' chimed in Mafalda, arranging her hair with a fierce frown at herself in the mirror. '*Ci piace assai.* You will like him too. He is your type and worthy of the villa; or we would not have suggested bringing him.'

That was how it began.

'I am a Prussian,' he told me in pretty French, sitting on the parapet of the terrace and gazing at the moon's path across the sea. 'Yes, a true Prussian on my father's and my mother's side. But one should not talk about oneself here on this terrace. One certainly seems hardly worth discussing in the face of all this beauty. Yet if I do not assert that I am a Prussian, I am likely to forget that I really exist on such a night as this. I feel somehow that I have wandered into another world. How beautiful are the two *signorine!*' he broke off suddenly.

My heart warmed, for I agreed with him.

'You will love one of them.'

'I fear I already love them both.' He did not smile as he said it.

I understood that too.

I told him about Prince Marini and his choice of the artist's life, of his romantic marriage, and the enormous family that resulted — of the estates in Calabria, that had now dwindled to nothing; how poverty stalked the crumbling Marini home, and pride walked with it. Grazia and Mafalda, the youngest, had not shared the advantages of their elder sisters. By the time they arrived there were no English and French governesses. A year or two at a convent school provided all the bringing up they had had, but, though they never read a book, they had in their sixteen and seventeen years captured somehow the secret of life and a shrewd understanding of people.

'Ah, yes. That is true. They are wise — strangely wise, I find, for such young people. And such charming irresponsibility, with, underneath that sadness — I cannot define it.'

Gluck did not know Magna Graecia well enough to see beneath its radiant smile, to hear the minor moods of its favourite music, to sense the tragic despair at the heart of a civilization too old to be deluded.

His own good manners sprang from something more than breeding and education.

'*Il faut avoir toujours la bonne mine,*' he would say. 'It is useless to hurt people's feelings, and, if one's own are hurt, what is the use of showing it!'

It was certainly difficult to imagine a situation in which Gluck's *bonne mine* would fail him.

Someone had paid for a visit to Italy — a mysterious friend of the family — to study pictures and architecture.

'I am an architect. This is a wonderful opportunity, as we are poor, and travel would have been impossible for me if this good friend had not come forward. I have seen Florence, Siena, Perugia, and Rome, and on my way home shall go to Venice.'

The spring of 1914 blazed along, blue and silver, into summer, gold as a Sorrento orange. Spiaggia was full of lovers making bright pages of history for themselves. Gluck did not go to Venice, but lingered on, always protesting that he must leave next week, but only weaving himself more firmly each day into the pattern of that memorable season. Admirers flocked for Grazia and Mafalda — lithe Neapolitans with mahogany bodies swam with them in the blue grotto where they all turned into silver fish, or sailed them dexterously in lovely yachts, themselves clad in astonishing blazers and trousers even more immaculate than the sails of their craft.

Gluck found that there were too many Neapolitans.

'As time goes on they increase,' he said with a frown. 'Each day a new one, and one does not know which —'

'None,' he was assured. 'They mean nothing to Grazia and Mafalda. They have known each other all their lives. What the girls like best is the villa, and our evenings together. Now do you know which one you love?'

The blue eyes flickered. 'Please do not ask me. Let us be happy together, and not ask ourselves or each other questions that are unanswerable.'

Once when we sat drinking our cocktails in the dusk, while the young moon and Venus hung in the paling sunset, he leaned forward and looked at us all three intently.

'But now,' he said, 'in this light, there is no difference. You are all the same. First when I saw you on the Piazza together I thought you were mother and daughters. Ah, madame, do not laugh! It was only for a moment. Then I thought you were sisters. The likeness is extraordinary. I cannot believe that there is no relationship.'

White figures in the dusk; our cigarettes like fireflies; we sat silent for a moment while somewhere near Destiny stirred.

'We are sisters,' Grazia declared, and came over and kissed me suddenly. Mafalda sitting near me took my hand. 'Sisters,' she echoed. We laughed, and the spell was broken. Maria announced that dinner was ready.

Gluck was in a serious mood that night. His shapely brow was clouded as he talked platitudes about war, and the girls' attention began to wander. War was a dull subject for a summer night in Spiaggia.

'There is no doubt, alas, that my country has for long been determined to fight someone.' His eyes rested for more than a moment with anxious gaze upon me. 'Though I am a Prussian I am profoundly anti-war. But do not imagine,' he added hurriedly, 'that I should not go willingly to fight for my country when the call came.'

La bonne mine! 'Bravo, Gluck!' The girls raised their glasses.

Next day Maria brought me a bouquet of drooping pink roses, tired June flowers.

'The Signorin' Biondo has left these. He would not come in, though I was just making tea. *Com' é simpatico, quell' signorin'!*'

Maria's motto might also have been '*Toujours la bonne mine.*'

'The English flower for the English lady,' said the card. '*Pardon pour hier soir!*'

What was it, last night, that needed an apology? Mother and daughters — no, not that. Ah, yes, talk of war, and that long look at me, the Englishwoman. Poor Gluck had spent a sleepless night.

※

Half-way through July Gluck wrenched himself away from Spiaggia. A farewell dinner at the villa and departure by the early boat meant that we sat up all night and saw the dawn spread over an opal sea. We watched a school of dolphins playing round the great rock below, plashing silkily. Then came the sun, almost breaking the unearthly silence with his triumphant emergence from the sea.

'*Dio!* One must powder one's nose.'

Grazia and Mafalda had chattered through the night, but an hour or two before dawn flung themselves on a divan in the studio and slept like kittens. And the sun took them unawares when they crept out sleepily at a call to watch the dawn.

Then coffee and rolls and some tears.

'Good-bye, Grazia! Good-bye, Mafalda! Madame, good-bye! Grazia —! Mafalda ——!'

He was gone. We watched him along the narrow path and as he turned the corner he waved and made as though to come back. The boat sent out its long, dreary hoot of warning. Whither, Gluck?

※

Postcards for Grazia, postcards for Mafalda, postcards for madame, all the way along to Germany. No time to stop in Venice. Then a letter to madame:

> … I am in despair because I feel I have not behaved as I should. I could not declare myself to either, because even now I do not know which I love. And if I did, would she have me? No, it is that one cannot separate them, and therefore one cannot have either. One can only look back at those hours on that terrace as enchanted hours outside life. Here in Germany we …

Then came the war. A letter to Grazia:

> … I dare not even send a message to that lady, our friend. Who knows what she may be thinking? War plays such havoc among friends. Enemies now! That I cannot believe. With tact, dear Grazia, find out what she feels, and then if possible tell her how unhappy — how unhappy is poor Gluck. Thank God at least we are not enemies, dear Grazia and Mafalda — as yet.

One more letter on the eve of joining his regiment — and then nothing more from Gluck.

※

I see him bravely marching among his fellows, shorn hair under the hideous cap, his girlish mouth set, his blue eyes troubled and perplexed. Out and away from dreams, trudging endlessly till the release comes. *Toujours la bonne mine!*

'*Povero* Gluck! It is so long since he wrote. Perhaps he —?'

But, as nothing was ever heard, there was no moment to shed a tear for Gluck.

4.1 Variations on a Theme: Miss Mabel Ebony

Bron Edge in her white cape climbed the rocky grey mountain. Her path was decorated with anemones, cyclamen, and orchids like small minarets. Sometimes a solitary olive tree gave her a moment's delicate shade. Rosemary and lentisk filled the air with a bitter-sweetness; the shadows in the rocks were blue as the few trails of lithospermum that still lingered. She pressed forward eagerly, as though a lover were awaiting her up there in the azure. She was filled with the glamour of the Italian day. In Spiaggia one's senses play a quintet in a thousand movements; there is no hour that is not filled with some sensuous delight. The delight of today was to be the mountain garden. In this sweet enclosure the tulips would be in full bloom, the irises, and the last of the daffodils.

The garden was not quite at the top. There was an untidy little shrine strewn with dead and dying wild flowers; then the path branched to the right for the topmost height where one could get gloriously drunk on half a glass of wine if the peasant who sold it happened to be there. But Bron's path was straight on towards the hermit's chapel. Half-way along this flat path a valley appeared to the left, and down in the valley was the garden, which was flung over the spare peasant cultivations like a gay rug. Bron always stood on the path above and contemplated the strangely fascinating landscape before she descended to the garden. On each side of the valley the mountain grimly pierced the blazing sky, and between these austere battlements there was a vista of sea in the distance, softly and meltingly blue, and Vesuvius wearing its white plume, always with an air, and always at a different angle.

Here in the mountain valley was complete solitude and a silence that held the heavens in its lap. Not a bird sang — the cicale were silent as yet. It was for this ecstatic moment of the first vision of her valley that Bron always hurried up the mountain path. Today she stood and breathed the exquisite beauty, letting her eyes wander from sky and sea to rocky peaks, and last, always last, to the valley and the gardens. Then she stared. Someone was there. Someone like a large fungus sitting among her tulips. Her mood changed, and she hurried down to the gate of the garden, which was locked. The creature must have climbed the wall. It was a woman, who rose in embarrassment when she saw Bron.

'Do you know you are trespassing?" asked Bron with some indignation.

'Yes, I'm afraid I do,' said the other disarmingly. 'But it didn't seem possible that anyone could be within miles of me, and I couldn't resist climbing over. I am so sorry. I will go at once. Please forgive me. May I say that I have never seen anything so beautiful as your garden?'

Bron melted at once.

'If you really think that, please stay a little longer. I will get some cushions from the *casetta* and we will sit on the wall.'

She was eyeing with some curiosity this young woman in the hideous mud-coloured clothes. How dared she wear such things in Spiaggia? She was between twenty-five and thirty, a tall, drooping creature with large, hysterical blue eyes, a sallow face, and an abundance of colourless hair arranged untidily about her ears. She was a perfect example of the un-loved spinster. She had come to Spiaggia, she said, because she had seen a picture of it in a paper four years ago. She had made up her mind to visit it if she ever went anywhere. Her small income was not enough to live on, but by working she had saved enough, and had taken a month's holiday.

'What from?'

'I work for the Charity Society and since my mother died I live at a residential club for professional girls.'

'You mean, it's a holiday from both?'

She smiled. Certainly life wasn't very exciting, but she was less lonely living in the club. No, she was not at all disappointed in Spiaggia. She had never imagined anything so lovely.

'It makes you feel quite a different being,' she said.

'It does indeed. Are you alone?'

'Quite.'

'No friends here?'

'I talk to some old ladies and a clergyman who are staying at my little hotel on the Marina. That's all.'

Her thin, claw-like hands were playing with the tulips Bron had given her; her narrow shoulders were hunched.

'No men to speak of?'

'No, I never meet any men — to speak of.'

Bron thought of a letter she had had this morning from a woman friend:

> As for the Mediterranean — did it get me? My dear Bron, it got me to such an extent that I cannot live in Italy alone — it's not possible. No, one needs a man in Italy. Climatically, it is impossible for spinsters. Like the rose, the Mediterranean has very sharp thorns. *Basta*!

Here was a type, interesting not in itself, but in its reaction to the lure of Spiaggia. Would this spinster too be driven forth by mutinous repressions?

Meanwhile, it was time for her to go. The tulips must be enjoyed alone.

'Come to tea at my villa tomorrow,' suggested Bron. She explained where it was.

'*That* villa. Why, then, you must be — are you Mrs Edge?'

'Does it frighten you?'

'No, *no*. Only, it interests me tremendously.'

'Will you come?'

'Of *course*. Do you really mean it?'

Bron laughed and nodded. The drab figure sheered off, but came back again.

'I forgot to tell you my name. It is Mabel Ebony.'

'How nice,' said Bron.

※

Next day Bron was on her terrace at tea-time, and saw Miss Mabel Ebony plunging along the narrow path which led to the villa, nearly as lonely as the mountain garden, but not so remote. She seemed to be in a hurry. When she was announced by Maria (who glanced at her as much to say, 'Well, whatever the *signora* does is right, but this is not *my* style') it was evident that she was agitated.

'Please forgive me if I seem bothered. I ought not to have come, but I want your advice — at least, I should say, I want to see you before I leave. I am going tomorrow.'

'What! going tomorrow? You said you were here for three weeks.'

'Yes, yes, I was. But I must go. I have had an experience. Dreadful. I don't know what to do. Oh, yes. I must go tomorrow. There's no doubt about it.'

'Can you tell me what has happened to make you change your mind?' Bron was burning with curiosity.

The globe-like eyes were feverishly bright.

'Well, when I left you yesterday I didn't go home, but wandered about the mountain till dusk, and then went down to the town and bought a few things before I started to walk down to the Marina. By that time it was quite dark.' She gulped. 'I hadn't been walking long down the steps when I realised that I was being followed. He was just about three yards behind me all the way down the first stretch —'

'How do you know he was following you? If he happened to be walking behind you —'

'He was talking to me. I don't know what it was, most of it, though he said a few words in English, but it was all *whispered* — and terrifying.' The colour rushed up and down her neck. 'Of course, I took no notice of him but hurried on. Then when I got to where the steps cross the road and the road makes a curve and joins the steps again, I thought I'd got rid of him, for he didn't follow me. But when I got to the road again, there he was waiting for me, facing the steps! He must have run round quickly to get in front of me.'

'Then what happened?' asked Bron as the narrator seemed to collapse.

'Then he offered to carry my string bag —'

'String bag!' thought Bron. 'How like you.'

'And walked beside me all the way to the hotel.'

'And you let him carry your string bag?'

'What could I do? I was much too frightened to refuse. But wasn't it awful! Have you ever had such an experience?'

'Hum, well, not exactly the same perhaps. But it's not uncommon, especially here. There are lots of queer people about who don't mind being followed as much as you do.'

'I could never stay here alone after that, could I?'

'Of course not, if you feel like that about it.'

'You do advise me to leave, don't you?'

'Certainly. Is that all you have to tell me?'

'Nearly. It was queer, though, when he was eating his *maccheroni* —'

'*What?*'

'Oh, didn't I tell you? He said he was hungry, and when he asked me to give him some food I didn't dare refuse. So I took him into the hotel and gave him something to eat. I didn't eat with him, of course. But as I was saying, it was queer, because the landlady of the hotel knows him quite well. She told me he was a boatman — rather a bad lot, I think.'

'What's he like? Perhaps I know him.'

'I hardly looked at him. But he's young, and I suppose, good-looking in a dark Italian sort of way — big brown eyes and very white teeth. But he didn't make much impression, except that in the dark he was a frightening, menacing figure. There was no one about. How was I to know he wasn't going to murder me?'

'Or worse,' suggested Bron, simply to see the sallow face crimson.

'Oh, Mrs Edge!' she quivered. 'Wasn't it terrifying, though! I shall never forget it. The darkness and not knowing what he was saying, and the feeling that at any moment he might — touch me. He did bump into me once when he was carrying my bag and I wasn't sure whether he did it on purpose. Then as he gave me my bag at the hotel he touched my hand, but that might have been an accident too. What do you think?'

'I should say that if he bumped into you *and* touched your hand it was not an accident.'

'I'm dreadfully afraid it wasn't. What *could* he have meant by such behaviour? I'm sure no Englishman would do such a thing.'

'No, I'm quite sure he wouldn't,' agreed Bron, faintly smiling.

Two spots of crimson had settled permanently in Miss Ebony's cheeks.

'I know you must think it exaggerated to take it so seriously —' There was too much accent on the 'you'.

'Why should I?'

'Oh, because you have — you must —' she faltered.

'I've had so much experience, you mean? Probably, however, I haven't had quite as much as you've been led to believe.'

'Oh, forgive me! How tactless I am. But what I meant was — you must have — I mean — Oh, please believe I don't believe everything I hear.'

Bron would have loved to know what she had heard.

Spiaggia gossip! It was stupendous — on the grand scale. A Tower of Babel, Gothic in tendency, but richly decorated with rococo improvisations of Latin origin.

'So you're going tomorrow.'

'Yes, by the early boat. He has threatened to come to the hotel tonight with some corals, but I certainly shan't see him.'

'No, I certainly shouldn't. Now come and see my cliff garden, which is nearly as good as the mountain one.'

Miss Ebony was able to give a fluttering attention to the wild beauty of the garden in a cleft of the sheer cliff and the huge limestone column that dominated it, shedding a long shadow over the house. When she said goodbye there were tears in her eyes.

'It has all been so wonderful,' she said fervently. 'I do hate going.'

'Safer to go,' smiled Bron.

'Oh, yes, there's no doubt about that.'

Bron sniffed a bit of rosemary when she had seen Miss Ebony through the gate. 'Poor outraged virgin,' she sighed. A pity she was leaving. But she was probably too deeply rooted in respectability to yield even to the siren call of Spiaggia. On behalf of all starved females Bron invoked the god whose symbol towered with such majesty above the garden, and then she forgot Miss Mabel Ebony.

Three weeks later Bron went down to the Marina. It was a grey and primrose morning. The sea, as if to show it need not always be blue to be attractive, had become quicksilver and still as a lake. The air was just touched with sirocco — enough to make one pleasantly languid. Wistaria hung from old gates and terraces, filling the air with sudden perfume, as though a goddess had brushed by on her way to some celestial tryst.

A line of girls passed, moving like young leopards, barefooted, each one as she swung by under her load saluting with a smile from bright, wanton eyes.

'Everything that happens here, everything one sees, is an event. There is nothing without significance. That little cab trailing up the hill, with its driver half asleep inside it, has intense individuality. Every day is a different flower. Yesterday was a peony; today is a columbine. How wonderful it all is. One never gets used to it, thank God. If one did one wouldn't deserve to live here.'

The delicious languor of the day demanded a vermouth, and from a terrace over the Marina Bron sat watching the movements of the little port. Sea and sky met in a lavender stillness, and orange boats were floating like gold-fish in a bowl. Maria had said, as she bade Bron *'buona passeggiata'*, that the sun was sick. *'Il sole à ammalato.'* She considered it was sick if it was not blazing from a cloudless sky.

From one of the houses on the Marina a bright figure emerged — a girl with two fat pigtails, bareheaded, barelegged, brown-necked. She wore a home-made but expressive little frock of gay cretonne. Probably one of the Swedish party that was so much talked about, fair young men and women who, when they were not swimming or doing incredible gymnastics on the beach, were rooted like brilliant anemones to the rocks, sun-bathing.

'Ecco la signorina inglese,' remarked the waiter, pouring out another glass of vermouth. 'She occupies the *casetta* of our *padrone*. They say she has taken it for a year.'

'English?' Bron said, and looked again at the girl who was approaching up the road.

'Yes, English. Very rich, they say, and chooses to be at Spiaggia for the rest of her life. She bathes — not on the Marina. She prefers to go to distant beaches. My cousin Luigino is her *marinaio*. She has engaged him for the season.

A *simpatica signorina*, he says, but a little mad, like all the English, if you will excuse me.'

It was Mabel Ebony, transformed, transmuted, blooming like a rose. She would wear pigtails and dress strangely for the rest of her life and be perfectly happy. And all because an impudent fisherman followed her home one night.

'*Ecco Luigino*! He is preparing the boat.'

Untidy black curls, flashing eyes, mahogany skin, and a rich tenor voice. Blithely he sang as he threw the cushions and bathing things into the boat.

> Vieni sul mar!
> Vieni a vogar
> Sentirai l'ebbrezza
> del tuo marinar!

to the tune of Two Lovely Black Eyes.

'At any rate I am not responsible for this,' thought Bron, 'I did advise her to go home.'

She forgot the invocation to that god whose symbol towered with such majesty above her garden.

4.2 Variations on a Theme: Lillie in Rome

'The pink one for me,' said Sister Lucy Ann, holding up the silk nightgown. 'Look at the butterflies on the shoulders! Yes, I'll have this one, please, Mrs Edge.'

'I like lace,' said Sister Dora, who could not have been more than twenty-two. 'And lots of ribbon. This blue one's my favourite. I think it's lovely. Tassels and all at the end of the ribbons. So carefully thought out.'

'I don't agree with any of you,' said Mother Kate, who had called them in to see the box of things on approval unpacked on Mrs Edge's bed. Her kindly face with its severe lines and innocent blue eyes beamed at Bron Edge as she held up a snow-white crêpe de chine garment over her grey habit. 'This is my choice, please, I shall wear it when Dr Lari comes tomorrow for the big operation!'

All the nuns laughed like children. They were full of jokes, and none was too foolish to provoke laughter. Last night Sister Lucy Ann had been sent in to take a new patient's temperature — a serious case, she was told — and she had gone in with her best professional manner, only to find that a bolster and a woollen shawl occupied the bed. This was one of Sister Dora's successes. She had come from Australia six weeks ago.

'Well, I find Rome very different from Sydney,' was all she said when they asked her how she liked Rome.

The nightgowns were being packed away, when a pink face under a bright blue hat appeared round the doorway.

It was Lillie, who came nearly every afternoon. She was the daughter of one of Bron's worldly acquaintances, staying for singing and Italian lessons with a noble Roman family who fed and chaperoned the daughters of the English aristocracy in order to keep a roof over their own poverty-stricken heads.

Lillie's round, copper-coloured head was set on a white neck like a flower stalk. There were freckles on her small nose, and her slenderly full figure was carried in a slight exaggeration of the fashionable gait. Lillie pursued fashion with comic eagerness. Her shoulder-knots were always absolutely placed, and she knew to the hundredth part of an inch where the latest thing in buttonholes should be pinned. She was not pretty, but almost excessively elegant, and had no knowledge of the world at all.

She stood at the window of Bron's little room when the nuns had gone out.

'I like this view,' she said.

In the drive of the convent a yellow cart with a blue hood was discharging its load of fresh vegetables; two cream oxen lay between the shafts, contentedly chewing the cud till it was time to go home. The ancient rotundity of St Stefano was close at hand; beyond were the baths of Caracalla, and over across the Appian Way stretched the limitless Campagna.

'It's not a bad view,' Bron agreed.

'I love Rome!' cried Lillie.

'Original child.'

'Oh, but I didn't at first. I was bored stiff. Only lately —'

'On Thursday we will lunch together in Rome, and you shall tell me why. I drove along the Appian Way this morning, and tomorrow I am allowed out for three hours. Don't you think it's rather lovely that one's first drive after an illness should be with Golden Cynthia down the Appian Way?'

'Oh, yes, how absolutely topping! But do let me lunch with you on Thursday. Will you call for me at the flat? What time? Goodness, I must go now —' looking at a ridiculous watch.

'But you've only just come! Your visits are getting shorter

and shorter — oftener but less. What does it mean?'

'It's these beastly singing lessons. I have to rush off. As I'm only allowed to drive in an old cab, it takes such a time. I can't see why a car should be improper for me. Anyone could jump on to one of these silly old cabs and steal me if he wanted to. Anyone could. I think they're much more dangerous than cars — much more dangerous. That's why I'm always in such a hellish rush,' she finished lamely, but firmly leaning over and kissing Bron good-bye.

'Something up,' thought Bron, leaning back and watching the silver spring light turn to gold over the Campagna.

The fair Russian girl who was a secular probationer came in as usual for pulse and temperature. Neither was ever very exciting, and they talked of other things. Calm, contained and beautiful, this girl with her dark eyes and sunny hair would never be a nun, though she might possibly be a saint. She it was who had accompanied Bron on her first drive — along the Appian Way.

Then dinner — always good food. Then the Neapolitan bride's nine o'clock hysterics when her husband left her to the company of her mother and sister, who were accommodated on camp-beds in the sick-room. Most Italian women take part of their families with them to hospital because they simply cannot be alone.

Then night closed down upon the convent. A guarded peace. A soft step outside sometimes, a sense of protection from evil bodily and spiritual, and outside far, far away in the Campagna, a thousand ghostly dogs barked like echoes of themselves; a muted symphony of dogs on the shores of Lethe.

'But I'm glad I don't live in the Campagna,' thought Bron as she turned over to ponder the question of Lillie and sink to sleep on it.

The flat which sheltered Lillie was off the Via Boncompagni

and approached by the usual dingy stone stairs. As Bron reached the third floor on the Thursday of their lunch appointment, the door of Number Six opened swiftly and a young man came out. He wore a well-cut blue suit that would have looked shabby on anyone less distinguished. He should have been clothed in a slender doublet and hose of costly silks, with jewelled belt and sword clanking delicately, a black velvet cape swung from his left shoulder.

A clarissimo!

As Bron advanced he saluted her with a grave smile. He was evidently just going out, but turned and opened the door for her with a latch-key.

'*Favorisca, signora!*'

With a gesture he ushered her in. It should have been a Palazzo by Valvasori, instead of this particularly wretched flat. The hall was dark and smelt of garlic and umbrellas, and the *salotta* into which he guided her was gloomy and furnished in waiting-room taste. He flashed an adorable glance at her as he bowed himself out.

'Well!'

Then Lillie entered in her blue hat.

'Who on earth was the boy that let me in?' demanded Bron without preliminaries.

'Oh, that,' carelessly. 'That must have been Mario, the son, you know.'

'But I *don't* know. And does your mother know about Mario, the son, you know?'

'I don't know. Why should she?'

'We'll talk about that at lunch. Let's get out of this. It's depressing me.'

'This flat? I think it's a lovely flat.'

'Oh, you do, do you? Then it's just as I thought. We'll lunch out of doors in the Borghese. The food's bad, but the sun is all right.'

At lunch Lillie was driven to confess that she was madly in love with Mario.

'Your first love affair, I suppose?'

'Well, of course, I've thought I was in love with boys at home, you know, but they're rather dull to look back upon.'

Bron was puzzling in her head whether it wasn't a good thing to get one's Latin experiences over at seventeen, or would it make those nice boys at home seem rather tame when the time came to choose one of them for a lover? She was looking hard at Lillie, but she was seeing Mario's slanting eyes, his deep-cornered mouth, and remembering those supple, unfaltering hands.

'Why didn't you tell me about him before?'

'I was afraid you'd tell mummy and I might get teased.'

Lillie was always teased.

'Promise me you won't tell anybody!'

'Oh, I promise. But you must be a good girl.'

'I am, I am!' cried Lillie fervently. 'But I did hate deceiving you. You will probably be surprised to know it wasn't singing lessons —'

'Not very much surprised.'

'You see, you are the only person they would allow me to visit alone. So —'

'So you met somewhere?'

'Yes, On the Palatine. So close to you. And then tea sometimes. All quite harmless, you see.'

'I see.'

'The trouble was, we didn't dare to speak hardly at the flat. Donna Laura is fearfully strict. So he suggested meeting outside.'

'And the Palatine? What did you do there?'

'Oh, mooch around. You know — and sit about. It's all ruins. I expect you know it. Mario explains everything to me.'

'That must be delightful.'

'Yes, he is brilliantly clever, you know. He's an engineer and is going to build marvellous bridges. It's in the family apparently. An ancestor of his built a marvellous bridge hundreds of years ago across the Tiber, called the Felice or something, somewhere outside Rome — at least, some emperor built it first and he rebuilt it later on. I can't remember any names.'

'I think you've got it marvellously clearly.'

'Ah, now you're laughing at me.'

'How did Mario get an opportunity of — suggesting the Palatine, if Donna Laura is so strict?'

'Oh, that was funny and rather exciting. The first — no, the second time I was driving out to see you he suddenly jumped on to the cab! I was so thrilled. He said he had been waiting for me, and he drove all the way to the gates of the convent, and that was when we made friends. He said he couldn't help it —' Lillie bridled.

'I'm sure he couldn't. Now that I'm going to Spiaggia, how will you manage?'

'I can't imagine. It's all getting simply desperate.'

'You mustn't let it get too desperate.'

'I know, I know!'

'If it gets too desperate, if I were you I should tell your mother you're coming home.'

'Father's fetching me in a month. She won't let me travel alone.'

'Still —'. There was a dutiful note of warning in Bron's voice.

'Yes, oh, of course, you're quite right. If it's necessary. But I'm really much too happy to want to go away. I've never been so happy in my life.'

'I can well believe that,' said Bron with a sigh.

✕

There was no Lillie at the convent next day, and Bron spent the afternoon packing for her return home on the morrow, with the help of Golden Cynthia, whose afternoon off it was. When the chance of Lillie's visit had evaporated, they went for a drive along the Appian Way, and came back to the convent in a velvety dusk. All through the day Lillie was lurking at the back of Bron's mind — Lillie and her brilliant engineer who was going to build marvellous bridges, whose eyes slanted under wistful brows and whose hands were long and unfaltering.

Why had Lillie not come today?

Before Bron was up next morning Lillie appeared, pale and agitated.

'I say, I'm going to ask you something awful, but can you lend me five hundred liras? You see, I've decided to go back to England and I haven't got enough money, and I simply daren't ask Donna Laura. She would think it quite mad. I've wired to mummy to send me a wire telling me to come back at once, and I ought to get an answer tonight or tomorrow morning. I thought over what you said, and this morning at dawn I came to the conclusion that if I stay I shall go off my head or something. I didn't realise till last night how terribly in love Mario is. It's really ghastly. I think it will kill him if I go away, but we shall both die if I stay — and, anyway, I'm frightened. You know, it's like being all the time in a terrific thunderstorm. I think my nerves are being shattered. I haven't told him yet that I'm going. I hardly dare. I ought to get away the day after tomorrow, I should think, and I shan't *move* out of the flat till I do go, unless Donna Laura goes with me.'

'How wise. Here is the five hundred. Is it enough?'

'Oh, heaps. It's only in case of stopping over. I've got a return ticket — Cook's. So you're going today. I should miss you terribly if I weren't going too.'

'Why didn't you come yesterday?'

'I simply hadn't the nerve after what I'd told you. lt would have been so obvious if I had rushed off to the Palatine.'

'So you didn't go to the Palatine?'

'Oh, yes. I said I was coming to you as usual, but went straight there. All rather a muddle. And then we were frightfully late for dinner. We stayed in the Palatine till it was shut, and then had tea, and you know how late tea is in Rome. It hardly begins till six. And after that we went for a long drive …'

'And then?'

'And then it was half-past eight, and I rushed in alone and said I'd been helping you to pack.'

'I'm so glad I really seem to have been useful.'

'Oh, you've been a perfect angel! And now I must rush, because I honestly have got a singing lesson at eleven o'clock — my last, I hope. I can't see to sing, I'm so excited and queer, and I believe the silly old teacher thinks I'm in love with him!'

Sister Lucy Ann came in as Lillie made a breathless exit.

'I expect your little friend is sorry to lose you.'

'She's decided to go to England herself.'

'Ah, poor child! I expect she's homesick.'

It was sad to part from Sister Lucy Ann, from Mother Kate and even the foolish Sister Dora. Saddest of all to wave to Golden Cynthia, who, enchained by an operation patient, could only lean from a corridor window high up and send her deep, radiant smile floating down. Sad to leave the simple white room with its sublime view, and the dog symphony which would surely haunt her dreams; but wonderful to be landing in Spiaggia, to be walking home along the narrow path. The happiness of reunion with her beloved house was so intense that she walked in a dream through it, touching everything as she went by, forgetting Rome, forgetting

Lillie and her passionate lover, forgetting even Cynthia the Golden.

When, later on, her thoughts did turn to Lillie, she was glad to think that the love-sick child was on her way to England. Too much, oh, far too much to endure at seventeen. How wise Lillie had been — so unexpectedly strong-minded, or perhaps only terribly frightened?

Two days after her arrival home a registered letter came from Lillie. Five hundred-lira notes dropped out,

> ... I am sending back your notes with many thanks. I shan't want them after all. Mummy sent a wire saying 'absolutely forbid travelling alone wait for father to fetch you as arranged', so there's nothing to be done about it. Mario was dreadful when he thought I was going. It was frightful to see him.

> All love from Lillie.

Such a careful mother! So Lillie stayed in Rome after all.

5 The Suit

Boris Ivanovitch Petrov raised his eyebrows. One would not have thought this possible, so pointed a gable did each make over his deep-set, somnolent eyes. But up they went, wrinkling the good square forehead to his sleek blue-black hair.

They were not raised in surprise, because Boris lvanovitch had long passed the stage of being surprised at anything. They were raised in deep contemplation of a dark blue suit. It hung over a chair on the vine-covered terrace — a decent enough suit, made by the best tailor in Rome three years ago, when its wearer had a really good job for the first, and, as far as he could see, the last time in his life. He had worn the suit a great deal, but it was made of honest English serge and was not even shiny at the edges; the problem was whether, in the present state of his finances, his conscience would allow him to give it away.

He had been with the Ruggieri family for nearly a year, inhabiting a small whitewashed room under the roof of their old house, writing poetry on the little terrace in his exquisite hand, and waiting for a job which never came. Spiaggia was certainly the best place to be poor in, for one could almost live upon its beauty — the soul, at any rate, could thrive on its rapturous sunsets and opal dawns. Boris used to sit for hours in a yogi-like trance, contemplating the vivid sea and landscape that stretched before his terrace.

Angelo Ruggieri and Maria his wife had been brought up with this view, and scarcely gave it a glance; only sometimes Maria would exclaim sympathetically, 'Che bellezza! is not the sea blue this morning, Signorin'? Otherwise they were much too occupied to notice it, and a great part of their time, especially Maria's, was spent in taking care of the Signorin', whom they regarded as a helpless baby giant. They fed him with good *maccheroni* and, occasionally, special dishes cooked by Angelo, who had been a chef. Maria was a tiny wisp of a woman with a neat little figure, much corseted, a benevolent wrinkled face with bird's eyes, and a genius for cleanliness and order. This was just the lodger she loved — a real *Signore* — oh, yes, in spite of his poverty Maria was not deceived — and pleasant in his ways. Boris had never been more tranquil than he was now, though never, perhaps, had he been so disastrously poor. He found courage in their good hearts, and this was the nearest thing to home he had known since he was a youth at Moscow University — before he was sent away to Siberia and his strange, sad, homeless life began.

He had suffered intense horrors of loneliness during those years in Paris after his escape from Siberia. He was never meant for a bohemian life, for he was domesticated, and his longing for a home was beyond ordinary longings. Wherever he was he always built a nest for himself, and when he rented a new room, however unpromising an attic it might be, he was at once busy with tintacks, hanging bits of antique stuff on the dull walls, and neatly arranging his scant possessions. In the place of honour, among the score of books that he always carried about with him, was the photograph of his beloved friend — his Dorogaia — whom he would certainly love till death. It was just his luck that she was not, and probably never could be, his, but she was his soul mate. It gave a lustre to his life when she was far away from him. He had always been beset by women, and was continually getting into desperate complications, but when the situation got beyond his control he simply went into a kind of trance until they had evaporated — which was often a long process.

The relentless way in which he was pursued by ill-fortune made him almost a comic figure, much as Don Quixote was comic, and he was able to laugh at himself, with a bitter laugh, so ingeniously did Fate contrive to make him ridiculous. But poetry strode always beside him, heartening him through despairs, and nowadays his Dorogaia shone like a bright star, wherever she might be.

Now, here was the question of the suit. Easter was approaching, and some mark of appreciation was demanded by the feast for the great friendliness and devotion of Angelo and Maria. They had been generous in waiting for the rent and feeding him without question when he was in their debt: Maria had nursed him like a mother when he was ill for two months. A really solid proof of his gratitude was necessary. It was utterly impossible to give them a good tip, or any tip; as they knew. Maria herself was a problem he did not attempt to solve; he had nothing he could give her. But she would be more than satisfied, he knew, with a gift to her brilliant husband, the *bel uomo* against whose lowest rib she could just rest her proud head. Angelo's best black suit had been brushed nearly out of this world, and each time he put it on he wore it with less assurance. This suit of Boris's would fit him well enough; and it would surely bring gladness to the house of Ruggieri. It was the only thing at all adequate to the situation. Yet it was a sacrifice. There was such a lot of wear in it still, and, though he had newer suits, this one could still be very useful. Besides, the Dorogaia had helped him to choose it, and had come to the fitting and said the collar sat abominably. He would never have noticed how the collar sat, and had always blessed her for her care to get it right. All this only enhanced the beauty of the sacrifice, and — his big gentle hands fingered the pocket-flaps — it was assuredly the right thing to do.

Easter came, with its gift, and Angelo was produced by Maria as a large doll might be, turned round and patted, in his wonderful new suit. It hung rather loosely, but he grinned as Maria pulled and patted, her bright eyes flashing with pride.

'Look, *Signorin*'! It has been made for him. Never has he been so *chic*. *Che magnificenza! Evviva il nostro caro Signorin*'! This will only be for *la festa*. He can hold his own with the mayor now. There is nowhere he cannot go!'

Boris was consoled for the loss of his suit by the genuine delight of the couple. He even felt a dash of spiritual pride.

For two months Angelo paraded in his new suit on the piazza every Sunday and saint's day. It was talked about, and everybody agreed that it was a *bel gesto* on the part of the *signorin*'. There were even a few who wondered whether he had any more to give away, and Boris was not surprised when fruit and flowers began arriving from unaccustomed sources. He had no illusions whatever about fruit and flowers.

Suddenly some mysterious internal malady asserted itself and Angelo died within a week. Maria retired to mourn her dead, and Boris sat disconsolate on his terrace, eating his lunch and dinner at a little restaurant. On the evening of the day Angelo died, a niece was sent up to ask Boris to visit the death chamber. He entered the high white room downstairs. It was ablaze with candles, and Maria, looking tinier than ever, with her head enveloped in a black mantilla, came forward as a hostess receives her guests.

'*Buona sera, signorin*'. *Facciamo la festa del pov' Angelo*. Come in, come in, I beg of you.'

She had done her weeping for the present, and was now doing her best to enjoy the importance of owning a dead husband. She would weep again; but this was the social side of mourning: this was the widow's hour.

A dozen or so of relations and friends were arranged in silent black groups against the white wall.

Boris approached with reverence the body of Angelo. The sick man's beard had been trimmed to a fine point, and he looked like a diplomat lying in state. Candles at his head; candles at his feet; a rosary on his breast. His hands were folded. He was fully clothed for burial on the morrow.

Boris's eyebrows suddenly flew up like two butterflies.

Maria, ever alert, touched his arm.

'*Si, si*, you are right. Your suit, *signorin*'. It was his best. For the journey to Heaven nothing is too good. You have been honoured —'

'My suit! *Boje moy*, my suit!'

Maria wondered why the *signorin*' laughed as he went upstairs to his room under the roof.

6 The Wedding Present

James, Mrs Chalvey's butler, mounted the staircase which led to the studio with more than his usual air of importance. At the door he turned on the pair who were humbly and silently following him, and demanded their names, with a look which was intended not only to annihilate them but at the same time to deny their very existence. He conveyed both admirably.

'Mr Kosminski,' the young man stammered.

'And Miss Isaacovitch,' added the young woman with spirit.

'Yes, and Miss Isaacovitch,' the young man agreed hastily.

'*Good* Lord!' James conveyed, and opened the door with a slightly overdone flourish.

Mr Kosminski carried a violin and a case of music. He was small and rather shabby, but carefully brushed and heavily pomaded. James had rightly considered quite deplorable the hat he had handled in the hall with such exaggerated care.

Nina Isaacovitch was tall and sallow. Her black hair trailed down her long neck on to her shoulders, thick and straight. Yet she was picturesque with her discoloured blue velvet frock and the flowing cape which, though poor as to material, was cut by a master hand. A velvet cap was pulled down over a pair of gleaming eyes.

It was evident that the visit to Mrs Chalvey was regarded by these two people as of immense importance. There was a tenseness about them, a summoning of all their forces, physical and moral, as they were delivered from the unfriendly hands of James, and launched upon the shining floor of Mrs Chalvey's famous studio. Mrs Chalvey herself, in a stiff grey gown enriched by ropes of pearls, came graciously forward to meet them, just in time to save Mr Kosminski from slipping on the endless parquet. She was an Edwardian survival, but still had the ear of the big impresarios, and her influence could help or hinder a career.

'Now let me see,' she said with the kind, vague air that can be so chilling. 'It was Mr Duren who wrote to me about you, wasn't it? Yes, of course. He heard you in Paris. You are a violinist and your wife the pianist? Is that right?'

'My fiancée, not my wife; and she is the violinist.'

'Ah, yes, to be sure. Now perhaps you will play at once?' She smiled bleakly at Nina, who wondered why she was reminded of an iced cake with silver decorations that could be seen in shop windows but had nothing inside.

It was a little bit depressing to realise that to Mrs Chalvey this visit was of so little importance that she was scarcely aware of their identity, but they cheered up when they reached the sanctuary of the piano and Nina took out her violin. As she stood tuning it she glanced round the room and observed that there was an audience of about ten people and notably a lady of Mrs Chalvey's age and type, who sat beside her hostess with an air of importance.

Nina had developed plenty of bad habits in the Montmartre cabaret where Duren had heard her play. He was an amateur musician always in search of original talent, and he was impressed by the rather diabolical personality of the girl. There was something of Paganini in her. He recognised a true gift under the slap-dash interpretation of cheap music, and concluded that necessity had driven a good artist to such work. Sitting at his table sipping champagne she had told him a lurid life history of which he believed much less than half. He was familiar enough with the exuberant temperaments which have to romanticise everything, most of all themselves, and his inductions from her spirited narrative of spies and revolutionaries were that she was Polish Jew by birth, had, judging by her English accent, grown up in Whitechapel or thereabouts, and had learnt her art from a well-known violinist who was interested enough to teach her for nothing, but who had unfortunately died.

'That is my fiancé, Mr Kosminski,' she had said as the little man sat down at the piano and played some brilliant syncopation. 'It's not his job either. Joe is a fine pianist and studied at the London College — got all his diplomas too. We're only just filling in here a six weeks' engagement. Then we go to London for some serious concerts. No, we aren't engaged for any yet, but we got letters from Joe's teacher to some agents. So we ought to be all right.'

It was then that Duren thought of Mrs Chalvey, who was always so delighted to discover unusual artists. He was a little dubious, however, for in spite of the girl's striking appearance they were hardly presentable. The little man, having finished his turn, had come and sat at the table. There was an eager, anxious look at the back of his full brown eyes, and his gratitude at the suggestion of an introduction to Mrs Chalvey was embarrassingly fervid. Duren always acted on impulse, especially in Montmartre, and the musicians had gone to their lodgings that night with a letter to Mrs Chalvey in Nina's handbag.

And now here they were in her studio, playing the first movement of the Spring Sonata to an audience which, until the first repeat, had been attentive enough, but showed signs of boredom that were not lost on Nina, as soon as the novelty of their appearance had worn off. It was a mistake to play Beethoven; neither artist had recovered from the cabaret, and their own consciousness of this subdued their playing, so that their interpretation of the sonata was dull, and they were both ridiculously nervous. Nina should have played one of her flashy pieces to rouse an audience which was almost exclusively concerned with waiting until she had finished so that its own turn should come sooner. The important-looking lady, who was later addressed as Lady Gertrude, was most restless of all, her eyes continually turning to a fair young man with a pale tie, who smiled wanly at her each time he caught her glance.

Only one person in the room was apparently absorbed in the music. Boris Ivanovitch Petrov — a large, impressive figure occupying a small gold chair that seemed about to collapse. His heavy Slav face, with its deep sunk eyes and pointed brows, drew Nina's attention. That strange brooding face reminded her of Beethoven's death mask, and there was scarcely more life in it. She thought that here, at any rate, was someone who was listening to her playing. As a fact he was not. His gaze was fixed, but his mind was far away.

A stanza of his long poem was floating like a nebula in the dark profundity of his mind — his long poem in *terza rima* which was dedicated to Russia, the Russia that was no more, that he would never see again. His own life from his first moments was in that poem, and the first verse told how an uncle, bending over the newborn child, had been heard to say:

'Poor little ugly creature, why on earth were you born?'

Why indeed? he would ask himself now.

He was a singer because he had a splendid voice and it seemed to be his only saleable gift. He had worked tremendously hard with his training for three years, but he, too, had been driven to work that was beneath him, and had suffered humiliations which had sent him raging from the offices of cinema proprietors, restaurants, night clubs and the like. It was always the same story:

'We'll give you a trial, but you must get some more attractive stuff. These French and Russian songs are all very well, and the Volga Boat Song always goes down well. But get some of Guy Hardlot's things …'

'No, I cannot, I will not sing "Because"!' he would shout to the four walls of his small room. But he did, and heard with disgust the applause that greeted the opening chords of his most successful number, sung in a broken English which his audiences found quite attractive.

Fortunately his pride was consoled by the friendship of some of the exiled aristocrats of old Russia. They were ready to listen with rapture and tears to the songs of their lost country, and Boris spent many Sundays at an old country house which had survived in the outskirts of London, and where a hospitality that faintly recalled the glories of the past could be found. Those were comforting days for Boris, who moved large and serene, understood, approved, among people he could admire, pacing the old autumnal garden, acrid-scented on a golden afternoon, once (would he ever forget it?) by the side of a little woman for whom he had afterwards sung in the faded drawing-room. The still figures listening, reverently grouped round the little woman, seemed to fade and become infinitely remote in the creeping darkness.

A cheque had come to Boris a few days later.

'Please give a concert,' she wrote.

He had given it, of course, in one of the minor concert halls, and after his first song she had entered quietly with a companion, and taken her seat (which she had bought) in the front row. Boris had come down from the platform and bent over the hand of his royal benefactress, and received her sorrowful smile.

⁂

But the cheque had not been adequate, though it had almost emptied the purse of its donor. Boris lost over the concert and had to sing 'Because' for a week at a restaurant to make it up. The only tangible result of the concert was an introduction to Mrs Chalvey, and, though he had not the slightest hope that anything would come of it, he presented himself on the day appointed, and found himself seated on a gold chair while Joe and Nina played Beethoven.

As soon as they had done Mrs Chalvey rushed at them and thanked them with cold effusiveness. She did not, nor was she going to, ask them to play again. 'Duren must have been drunk,' she thought to herself, as she deposited them on two more gold chairs, and that, as far as she was concerned, was the end of them. The turn of the fair young man had come. He had a sweetly pretty tenor which he kept modestly in his throat, while Mrs Chalvey and Lady Gertrude exchanged delighted glances.

'What do you think of Peter?'

'Enchanting!' murmured Mrs Chalvey, who knew as well as anyone that voices should not be allowed to lurk in throats, but who found the person of the blonde Reter quite up to the standard of Lady Gertrude's numerous protégés. Besides, she saw in him another pupil for her own more than protégé.

'A few lessons with Victor. That's all he wants!' she cried when the audition was finished. Lady Gertrude was prepared for this; the principle of these two friends had always been mutually to live and let live, and, though Lady Gertrude allowed her fancy to rove more extensively than Mrs Chalvey, who had refused to wander beyond Victor for a surprising number of years, the freemasonry existing between them had never been disturbed.

As Lady Gertrude was about to leave, followed by Peter, Boris, with the rest, rose from his gold chair. The undoubling of this huge figure brought a faint gasp from Lady Gertrude who had been sitting with her back to the room when he had made his entrance, and had not seen him before.

'WHO IS THIS?' she flashed to Mrs Chalvey.

Quick as lightning her friend called to her, for she was already at the door:

'Won't you stay and hear Mr Petrov sing, my dear?'

Nodding graciously she sat down again near the door, and Boris, who felt that something must be done about that blonde young man and his pretensions, sang Prince Igor's Song for all he was worth.

'*Mais, c'est épatant!*' cried Lady Gertrude. In her moments of transport she always used French.

Boris was in the mood today, but he was not always in the mood, and that was the trouble. Emotion, deeply buried in the vast architecture of his personality, concealed as it were in a crypt, was not easily called forth. He should never have been a singer, for he had no facility of self-expression. Only on occasions could he get as much as he felt into his singing; this was one of them. Partly it was the challenge of the blonde young man and partly, yes, a great deal, the sympathetic interest already shown in him by the strange little Kosminski pair. They had all sat together while Peter performed and the glances they had exchanged brought them nearer than weeks of conversation.

'This is imbecile!' Boris was thinking. 'This is not singing. What is it? Who is this ridiculous young man who makes a fool of himself and us?'

It had been obvious that Joe and Nina agreed.

Then, for lack of an accompanist, Joe played for Boris, ecstatic and respectful.

Lady Gertrude called Boris to her as soon as he had finished, and meanwhile Mrs Chalvey had told as much of his history as she knew in what was scarcely a whisper. This was highly satisfactory to Lady Gertrude, for all her friend could tell her was that he had lately given a concert which had been royally attended and supported by all the important members of the Russian colony.

'You must come and see me,' said Lady Gertrude. 'I must run away now, but here is my card. Come next Wednesday at three o'clock.'

Peter, the fair young man, was uncertain at first whether to charm Boris or to sulk, but as it was immediately obvious that he could not coax a gleam from those eyes, which had already begun to look inwards again, he decided to sulk. Boris produced his own card, and Lady Gertrude took it tenderly and tucked it into her bag. Peter flung open the door, Lady Gertrude stared through Joe and Nina with an insolence that not even James the butler could have achieved, and, with bows and smiles for everyone else, swept out, Peter scowling at her heels.

The afternoon had fallen to pieces by this time, and such fragments as Joe and Nina were evidently expected to scatter. Boris went with them, as soon as he realised that they were not going to be asked to play again. They had become more forlorn as the afternoon advanced and the failure of their appearance was made manifest.

As soon as they were in the street Joe became almost tearful.

'That's the end of that. Nothing doing. She might have given us another chance.'

'The old bitch!' was all that Nina said, her eyes burning with the rage that had been so long suppressed.

'You must not notice these people,' said Boris soothingly. 'They are of no account at all. Dreadful vulgar people. Dreadful old woman.'

'That's no good. They're the people what get us on or not. We oughtn't ever to have gone, Nini. I won't have you insulted.' At this thought he actually did burst into tears. The whole afternoon had been designed to humiliate them, from the hateful arrogance of the butler James to the urgency with which they were frozen out of the studio.

'Perhaps you will come and practise with me?' suggested Boris, as soon as Joe's tears had been quenched by a few stern words from Nina. 'I need an accompanist every day, for I must study many new songs. I cannot pay much, you know.

Perhaps later —'

He wondered whether Lady Gertrude would be any use to him after all. Not much hope, he thought. Joe was consoled by his suggestion, and promised to come next day.

When Boris had disappeared into a tube station, Joe said to Nina:

'That's a very fine man. A very great gentleman, Nina my darling. The best man we have ever met, so we got something out of that old woman who insulted you after all. That old devil, she doesn't know and she wouldn't care, curse her. To think that you were never asked to play again —!'

'Oh, stop that, Joe. What does it matter? *I* didn't want to play again. Why d'you keep on?'

'Nini, let us get married! Let us have a wedding at once!'

'Whatever for?' asked the practical Nina. 'We're all right as we are, aren't we?'

'No, we're not. I shall go and get a licence tomorrow, and we'll have a proper wedding, with a cake and refreshments afterwards. I've got five pounds saved and shall spend it all on the wedding. You shall wear a white dress and everyone shall see you as a bride.'

'And who's everyone, I should like to know?'

'I shall send invites to all our relations. Your uncle Leon and my uncle Nathan and their families. Then there's the artists we know; they'd come. And perhaps our new friend Mr Petrov.'

Marrying Nina had suddenly become imperative, long though it had been delayed. To do Joe justice, she herself had been responsible for continual postponements. Now he would have no more nonsense; he must be able to say to such people as Mrs Chalvey: 'You dare to insult my wife!' Besides, this splendid new friend of theirs must be exhibited to all their relations and acquaintances.

Nina, amused and rather touched by Joe's enthusiasm,

consented to a registry office wedding and began to make herself a white frock. Her father, for all the romantic mystery that she had woven round him, had been in reality a small East End tailor, and one of the last garments he had made was the cape which Nina wore over her blue dress. She inherited a gift for cutting and her own taste was original. Joe bought some good material cheap, and she cut and stitched with the ardour of a craftsman who has found something worthwhile. Joe was certainly doing things well.

Every afternoon he turned up at Boris's rooms and played for an hour on the miniature piano which was so ridiculously out of proportion to the voice it accompanied. Boris was kind but remote; he felt sorry for this poor little Jew who was so anxious, but he did not want to get intimate.

Joe's happiest hours were spent in the little room, with its few books, which from much tender handling had each attained a personality, so that the shelf which held them seemed to radiate life, with its comfortable impression of good taste routing the commonness of furnished rooms. Perhaps he was conscious of the racial barrier, or perhaps his admiration for Boris came so near to hero worship that he was never quite at his ease with him. Whatever the reason might be, he could not bring himself to tell him about the wedding until a few days before the date.

'Will you do us the honour to come? It is on the eighth, and we have a reception in my rooms afterwards.'

'The eighth? That is too bad. Alas! I cannot come. I am singing at Lady Gertrude's At Home that afternoon.'

Joe's look of agonised disappointment startled Boris. But he could have no idea how bitter this moment was. It was impossible to alter the date; everything was inexorably fixed, but the guest of honour, whose presence was to awe both families into submission, would not be there. As well not be married at all!

'I'm awfully sorry,' said Boris, really moved by the sight of such dismay. 'But you understand I cannot give up the engagement however much I want to? Now let me make you some Russian tea, and you will tell me all about this wedding of which I knew nothing until this moment.'

While Boris was making the tea, Joe ventured to pick up a book, not so much to read it as to collect his distracted thoughts. He found one of Boris's cards in it, used as a marker, and this he examined attentively.

'Where do you get your visiting cards printed?' he asked. 'Excuse my saying it, but it's much better printed than mine. Look at the difference.' He produced one of his own.

'That is quite dreadful,' said Boris frankly. 'You must have a die made. Mine is not printed; it is copperplate. That is the way cards should be done. No other way.'

'Oh, I see. That's quite a thing to know. Can I take one of yours for a pattern? Better than trying to explain.'

'Of course,' said Boris, taking one out of his pocket book. 'I have my die at Asprey's, a shop in Bond Street.'

'Oh!' said Joe, in a hushed voice. He had looked in at the windows but had never known anyone who had ventured inside.

Boris had been invited several times by Lady Gertrude since keeping the appointment for three o'clock that Wednesday afternoon. He had dined, and sung afterwards to a few guests without a fee, and again he had dined and sung to her alone. She was going to introduce him to Covent Garden, where she had, it was said, great influence. Mrs Chalvey had gracefully resigned, so that Lady Gertrude had the field to herself. And Peter was having lessons with Victor.

On the eighth, the day of Joe's wedding and the At Home, Boris was asked to lunch with Lady Gertrude — very lightly, she said. He would have liked to refuse, as he never ate before singing, but, boring though he found her, he dared not risk offending her. There was no one else at lunch, and after coffee he suddenly apprehended Lady Gertrude. A film like a snail's track over the yellow old eyes — a clutching of withered acquisitive hands — and a nauseating scent enveloping him — there was nothing to do but to escape quickly. He left her without a word, opening the door quite quietly, shutting it gently behind him, and crept down the stairs into the hall, took his top hat and music case, and so into the street. He plunged along the pavement till, seeing a taxi, he hailed it as though it were a life-boat and he on a foundering ship. Then he sat back and wiped his forehead with his best silk handkerchief.

'That is the end of Lady Gertrude, and my career too, I suppose. But the limit is reached. Disgusting old woman! Someone should murder her; someone will … Blackmailers! They think we cannot refuse them and they insult us.' His thoughts turned to Nina and the cold insolence of Mrs Chalvey.

'Nina! And she is being married today; after all, I can go to her wedding.' A present had never occurred to him, and he had nothing in his pocket but his taxi fare. 'Perhaps they will welcome me even without a present.' He gave Joe's address to the driver.

The door was open and he went upstairs. He had been to Joe's rooms before and knew that 'rooms' meant a small bed-sitting room. There was no answer to his knock; he was too early.

'I shall wait and surprise them.'

He went in, with an 'Ah-h!' of amusement, for Joe had decorated his room like a Christmas tree; in the middle of a table of pies and confectionery the wedding-cake waited in frozen calm for the touch of the bride. He tiptoed in the silence of the small festive room that was now to be Nina's home, with a difference. He pictured her in her wedding frock; it would not become her dark skin, and the devilish glint in the deep eyes would mock the virginal whiteness.

So they had achieved some presents, he was glad to see. There were a few objects arranged on a small table with cards attached. A pair of hideous vases, which seemed familiar, dominated the rest. Beneath them he was surprised to find his own card, prominently displayed. He read:

To my dear friends Nina and Joe,

With best wishes for their future happiness.

Boris Ivanovitch Petrov

Of course, he remembered those vases; they came off the mantelpiece in this room. For the second time that day he must escape quickly and quietly, this time fearing to meet the wedding party, and confuse the bridegroom.

He would not see Nina with her wicked smile, wearing her white frock, after all.

7 The Writing Case

Anna's favourite retreat was the shrubbery of lauristinus that, within a high flint wall, enclosed the Grey estate, like an evergreen oasis in the chalk desert of the North Foreland. Shining dead leaves of lauristinus made a floor like tortoiseshell in this dark green world; the thin naked branches covered with pale green dust stretched up into the dense roof where birds nested. Fairies moved about in the fluttering silence, and Anna often saw them, but they were about their own business and never seemed to notice her.

There she stood, scraping the shiny floor with the little ash stick she had cut for herself; her father had brought her a new knife yesterday from the town. Walking into the town two miles away was rather an event, because nobody liked it much. It was a watering place, and now in August was full of what the Grey family considered dreadful people. Whenever Mr Grey went in he always brought something for Anna, and it was generally a knife because he knew she liked them better than anything. This one was large and smooth and brown with silver looking ends; not so manly as that rough horn one Phipps the gardener had given her, but at any rate not a girl's knife, because her brother John had borrowed it and had to be reminded to give it back. So that was all right.

She stood there, scraping up the pudding that lay under the tortoiseshell crust, and thinking of those presents up at the house. Mrs Grey was always trying to think of something new and original to amuse her large family. She was so bored herself, now that she had given birth to them all and brought them up quite beautifully and forgotten to make any friends for herself meanwhile, that she was at her wits' end to devise something that might mark the holidays as not too ordinary.

It was a long family. Mary and Laura were grown up and

used to spend the spring in Italy for Laura's health. They always brought back something for everybody — little jugs and mugs with *Bevi poco* and sometimes even *Bevi bene* on them, olive wood boxes with swallows flying over them, and, once, an enormous rosary for Anna, made of eucalyptus buds, which smelt strongly of cats. They stayed in Bordighera with a Scottish writer, whose imaginative tales were most fascinating of all when told by Mary on a walk.

Mary was small, brown and beautiful, like a little Spanish grandee. Her eyes shone with something that was more than intelligence. Everyone worshipped her, but to Laura, who had been guided from the moment she was born, through nursery and schoolroom, by those wonderful eyes, Mary was the whole world.

Two enormous brothers who were at Cambridge came after these two — so enormous that they scarcely belonged to Anna's life. Then Christine and Prue, who were fifteen and sixteen, wrapped up in their brothers and still fond of dressing dolls. Then John and Peter, and, after a gap of four years, Anna, who was eight. Booboo came after Anna, and attracted a lot of attention because he had curly Titian hair, red-brown eyes, and appealing ways. Anna had straight dark hair and a pale face; people seldom noticed her when Booboo was about, and, even if they did, she was silent and dull.

That was the family, so self-sufficient that it scarcely wanted a friend outside those flint walls; the family that Mrs Grey continually but quite unnecessarily, racked her brains to divert. She had a new idea in London just before the holidays. She amused herself by buying some really lovely and expensive presents to distribute. Then, to make it more exciting she had decided that lots should be drawn for these presents — that it should be a sort of raffle, only of course, there would be no money involved.

The presents were on view before the raffle, and it was the

sight of these that had driven Anna to her dusky retreat. She was going to ask the fairies, who seemed so indifferent to her existence, to intervene in the matter. The mere thought of that pig-skin writing-case sent her blood surging. It was a huge man's writing-case which folded in three, was full of capacious pockets, and was smartly confined in a belt as solid and effective as the belts John and Peter wore when they played games.

There was no reason, if the fairies were kind, why she should not become the owner of this case, though she knew that her mother was not thinking of her when she chose it. No, mother, alas! was still obstinately set on the idea that all little girls must like dolls, and Anna had shied as a pony might at something threatening when she saw a large wax baby doll in elaborate clothes, which lay with closed eyes between a set of Shakespeare and a terrestrial globe. She liked the look of the globe but did not dare to inspect it too closely because of the menacing proximity of that doll, and she passed with eyes averted. Then they lit on the writing-case and remained fixed, while her hands, trembling, explored the interior. Besides the vast pockets there was a book of blotting-paper bound in pig-skin and a yellow pen with a gold nib—a J. There were little pockets too, for stamps, and a pen-wiper. Anna could look no more and left the drawing-room in a yellow dream.

The menace of that doll! Why, why did mother try to make her like them? She had always tried to impress upon her that they were only useful for games like 'House', when they were put in chairs as visitors, or 'School', when they were set in rows. And a baby doll was more hopeless than anything. What could be done with a thing that lay with closed eyes in long embroidered clothes? Let Prue have that baby doll, or Christine. They would love dressing and undressing it and putting it to bed. Yes, even at their age. Anyway, she was not going to have it. If she drew it she would kill herself. Yes, kill herself, with that writing-case belonging to another. All she wanted in the world was the writing-case. She wanted it with passion. The smell of it still hung in her nostrils.

Pale and still she stood in that breathless shade, her small, fine hand clutching the ashen stick. No fairies stirred in the silence today, but peace stole over her as she stood, and she knew they had heard.

Everyone entered into the spirit of Mrs Grey's raffle. The elders realised how disappointed she would be if they were not excited, and the younger ones were excited. The lots were drawn out of Mr Grey's top-hat. Numbers were on the slips of paper, so that when Anna drew '5' she was no wiser.

It seemed hours before all the tickets were drawn. There was a great deal of chatter and laughter. Such a delicious idea of darling mother's in the middle of the summer holidays! But Anna sat tensely waiting. The presents were still on the table as she had seen them that morning.

'Mary, what's your number? Eldest first!' cried Mrs Grey. And, as Mary held it up, 'Why, you've got the baby doll. How absurd!'

Anna caught her breath with relief as the doll was given to Mary. Then Laura — the Shakespeare. How lovely! So pleased. The big brothers drew a horse and cart, intended for Booboo, and the terrestrial globe. Christine's ticket brought her a sketch of Taormina meant for Laura, Prue's a pair of masculine brushes in a morocco case. John drew Beethoven's Sonatas, meant for Christine, and Peter a fitted work-basket.

The writing-case was still unclaimed, with only Anna and Booboo left.

'Anna has the writing-case!"

It was put into her lap. She clasped it to her in silence. She did not open it. She knew every feature of it by heart already. Besides, she felt there was danger even now.

There were roars of laughter when Booboo was given a smoking cabinet.

'Here, Booboo, my dear, let's make an exchange.'

The big brother led the horse and cart over to Booboo, who gladly relinquished the smoking cabinet.

A general exchange of presents began. Anna sat there watching, in a fearful state of apprehension. Then the dreaded moment came.

Mary crossed the room with the doll and put it on Anna's lap.

'For you, my little Anna,' she said, and kissed her.

Under the doll lay the writing-case. Anna could not speak. Then she looked up and caught Laura's eye.

Laura was sitting on the arm of a chair glaring contemptuously at Anna. The writing-case creaked under the doll, which lay with an insipid smile and closed eyes. Anna's lap was terribly full.

'Well?' Laura's eyes were baleful.

'What?'

'Aren't you going to do anything?'

Mary's back was turned and she was admiring someone else's present as though to hide the fact that her own hands were empty. Anna knew that she had given her the doll because she wanted her to have it, not because she wanted the writing-case herself. She had turned away so quickly after putting the doll on Anna's lap. But even so — no one else had two presents —

Yet — she had drawn the writing-case. It was hers. The fairies had answered. No one would love it as she did. That doll! If Mary liked to give it to her, that was her affair. Of course she didn't want it herself, nor indeed, thought Anna, would she really want the writing-case, which wouldn't suit her a bit. Why should Anna sacrifice herself in this great moment — the very greatest moment she had ever known in her life?

'Mary, look at Anna. She's sticking to both. The greedy little beast. Can't *some*body do *some*thing?' Laura was exasperated.

Mary turned and smiled at Anna.

'Why shouldn't she? I gave her the doll.'

'Little beast, little beast!' There was hatred in Laura's eyes.

The doll slid to the floor. Anna held the writing-case against her heart. She didn't care what Laura or anyone thought.

It was her own beloved — manly, with an honest smell, her dear, dear possession.

8 With Custody of the Child

Guy opened the nursery door quietly. The long passage leading from his quarters to the rest of the house was very dark, and he had never been along it by himself. He had always clutched Marson's hand tightly when she took him along to his mother's room. Now he had to go alone, for, though he had told Marson that it was time for his visit, she had only turned her head from a whispered conversation with Jane, the under-nurse, and said:

''Ush, Master Guy. Your mother doesn't want you tonight.'

That was nonsense, of course. His mother would be as disappointed as he was on the nights when she didn't come and kiss him in bed. He tried to point this out to Marson, but she only waved her hand at him and went on talking to Jane.

His mother's room was always full of soft light, with a glowing fire and a polar bear skin stretched out in front of it. Her dressing-table was an Arabian Nights' store of enchanting things which he was allowed to admire but not to touch. Sitting on the white rug he could see, above the fire, his beautiful mother reflected in the round mirror, as she lay on her sofa smoking cigarettes, wearing bright pyjamas which made her look like a figure in a fairy tale. Sometimes he caught her eye in the glass, and, if she smiled then, he went to bed happy.

His visit in her rest hour had become a habit. Marson had brought him when he was a baby and a delightful new toy, and she had gone on bringing him ever since. At one time he used to tell his mother stories about the things he saw in the fire, but one night he looked up at the mirror and saw that she was reading, so he gave that up and would sit silently gazing, sometimes at the fire and sometimes at her in the mirror, making up his own stories, inspired by the warmth and glow of the room and her presence …

He shut the nursery door carefully. The passage was terribly dark, but he ran along it with his arms outstretched until he came with a thud against the baize door. It yielded, but only to a blacker darkness. There were no lights on the landing outside her room, and he stumbled across to the door and knocked.

Silence greeted him. The darkness was coiling round him like snakes, and terror seized him. With trembling hands he opened the door and went in. The great window, uncurtained, let in a cold grey light on the room that he had always seen bathed in warmth and colour. The grate was black; so were the corners of the room. The bed was faintly discernible but it was a horrible travesty of his mother's bed. A confusion of dresses and hats lay like tortured bodies heaped upon the counterpane. To Guy this dreadful scene meant death; his mother, he was sure, was dead. And then he saw a white face in the round mirror, just where hers used to be.

It was his own. He groped his way out of the room, his body shaking with uncontrollable sobs. Down in the hall far below there was now a light, and he clambered down the wide stairs towards it. At the bottom he found Shaddock, the parlour maid, watching him.

'Goodness gracious, Master Guy, you did give me a turn. I thought you was a ghost. Whatever's Mrs Marson doing, letting you wander round the house, tonight of all nights too. Why, what is the matter?' as Guy ran and hid his face in her skirts.

'My mummy! She's dead in her room. It's all dark; I saw her face —'

'What on earth are you talking about? Saw her face? Nonsense, child, your mother's gone out. Do stop howling and leave go my apron. O Lord, I shall start screaming myself if you don't be quiet.'

As she spoke, the latch-key turned in the lock of the front door.

'Hush, hush, here's master!' She tried to compose herself and the child as the tall, solemn man shut the front door and advanced frowning.

'What is all this noise?' he asked coldly.

Guy flung himself at his feet.

'Daddy, daddy, I've lost my mummy. She's dead in her room. I saw her face. Oh, light the lights and bring her back!'

'Get up, Guy, and control yourself. What is the meaning of all this, Shaddock?'

Shaddock bit her lip. 'I found Master Guy down here, sir, and was just taking him back to the nursery when you came in.'

'What was he doing down here?'

'I think he was looking for madame —'

'Well?'

'Madame is not here. She went away in a taxi this afternoon. There is a note in the drawing-room. I think.'

'Thank you, that will do.'

Shaddock moved away.

'She isn't dead, daddy? She will come back soon?'

The father stood frigidly looking down at his only child.

'Don't expect ever to see your mother again,' he said, and Guy shrieked. At the sound Shaddock turned.

'Take the child, Shaddock. Take him back to the nursery and don't let me see him again tonight. Run away, Guy. It's past your bed time.'

Guy was led up the wide stairs. Though he was generally afraid of Shaddock, he clung desperately to her cold hand. At the baize door she stopped; that was as far as she would take him, for even the events of today could not melt the reserve that existed between herself and Mrs Marson.

So he would have to travel that dark passage alone again. Shaddock should not see that he was frightened.

'There, are you all right now, Master Guy?'

'Yes, thank you, Shaddock. Good-night.'

The baize door boomed. He was alone in the dark, and he would never see his mother again. With a cry he ran down the passage and battered against the nursery door.

Mrs Marson, whose conversation with Jane had flowed on in placid half-tones during his absence, which she had not noticed, opened the door sharply, and he fell into her arms.

'You naughty little boy! Wherever have you been?'

'I went to see my mummy, but I've lost her. Daddy says I'll never see her again.'

Marson began putting him to bed with unusual zeal.

'Will she come back?' he asked, shivering in his pink pyjamas before the blazing fire.

'P'raps not, but there! you'll have your daddy to look after you.'

He threw himself on the floor.

'I don't know my daddy! I don't know him!'

9 Queer Lady

Virtue was five years old when they went to Dovercourt for the summer holidays. They stayed in one of a row of dull grey houses. The sea was always grey, the promenade was always grey and mother and the girls were dressed in grey, being in half-mourning for granny.

Virtue had given her cart and horse to the landlady's daughter on the first day of her visit, and had instantly regretted it, but her mother, though touched by an act of such reckless generosity — it was a favourite toy — had acquiesced, and there was no chance of getting it back. This loss blackened the already drab prospect. She definitely disliked Dovercourt. Mother was very sad; twice Virtue had found her crying, which had shocked her a good deal. Tears, she thought, were nursery things not indulged in by grown-ups. Her sisters were always quarrelling; her brothers were always out, only returning at dusk in a trail of sand and seaweed, carrying pails of languishing crustaceans — puzzling to Virtue and rather disgusting. Solemn boys they were, earnest even with shrimping-nets. Virtue would go out with her pail and spade and make dreary sand pies with the aid of Kate, whose rosy face was the only spot of colour in the dull day. They sold each other pies all the morning, and sometimes in the afternoon would build a castle. For a child of five she was as bored as it was possible to be.

One afternoon everybody except Virtue and Kate drove to a distant tea party. Virtue played on the balcony, leading a string up and down, trying to imagine that her lost horse and cart were attached to it. Suddenly on the next balcony appeared a wonderful being, all roseate, with bright gold hair. Virtue gazed. This was a fairy, of course, and even more beautiful than the fairy she saw in her dreams. It came to the rail which divided the two balconies. It held out its arms, and said:

'Hullo, you exquisite little thing. Come and talk to me.'

She was enfolded in those marvellous arms, her head was buried in a lace-filmed bosom that smelt of flowers. This was a dream! Or Fairyland. The room into which she was swiftly carried, seen through a veil of excitement, carried on the illusion, for it was not like any other room in the world. It was lighted mysteriously, and shimmered with gold stuffs, white fur rugs and silver ornaments. She was shown splendid things — was allowed to hold a silver pig and to set going a little musical box, from which sprang a bird that burst into song. Virtue, sure that it was alive, tried to stroke it, but as she touched it it disappeared with a snap and the box was silent. The lady laughed, a low, soft laugh rather like mother's, only somehow different.

'Poor birdie! He's frightened of such a big person. What's your name, little girl?'

'Virtoo.'

'*What?*'

'Virtoo.'

'Virtoo? Virtoo? Not Virtue?'

Virtue nodded.

The fairy laughed again and snatched her close.

'Oh, but that's too delicious! Too good to be true! Virtue! Virtue! With that face! You little love!'

She was hugged with rapture, and the fairy murmured 'Virtue' to herself several times, as though it were the funniest thing in the world.

'I must write and tell the prince that a little girl called Virtue paid me a visit. He won't believe it. Would you like to see the prince?'

A picture in a silver frame — a glorious creature in blue with a shiny hat and a sword. That settled it. Of course she was a fairy princess and this was the prince.

'Like him?'

Virtue nodded, gazing.

'Kiss him,' said the fairy, holding the picture close.

He was kissed.

'There, now, I can tell him he's been kissed by a young lady called Virtue. That will be something quite new for him.' She pressed the portrait to her own lips.

'That's not Virtue!' she laughed.

Virtue wondered why her name amused the fairy so much. She had been mildly teased about it by the boys, and her mother had told her that it was a name that demanded astonishing goodness from its possessor, which seemed a little bit unfair. She would much rather be plain Kate, and able to be as naughty as she liked. This she confided to her new friend.

'How would you like to be called Lilian and to be as naughty as you like all your life?'

'That's mother's name!' exclaimed Virtue. 'But she's not been naughty at all — not all her life.'

'It's my name too, and — well — I wasn't a very good little girl always. So your mother was never naughty. How do you know?'

'How could she be? Mothers are never naughty. Only their little girls are naughty. And their little boys —' she added hastily.

'Your mother's very pretty. I've seen her. She looks sad, though. Perhaps because she's so good. It doesn't do to be too good, my dear.'

Virtue thought of her mother's tears, and wondered if perhaps she had been naughty and that God had punished her — because she could not conceive of anyone less than

God punishing mother. She told about the tears.

'Poor mother! I believe she is sad. You must be kind to her,' was all the fairy said.

'I am,' said Virtue, and was lost once more among those perfumed laces.

'Little darling, little darling!' the fairy murmured to herself, half laughing. Then:

'Where's father?'

'Father's coming next week. He's aboard.'

'Aboard? I suppose you mean abroad. Where?'

After long discussion they decided that he must be in Germany, where Priscilla, a big sister, was studying the violin.

'That's where the prince lives. He is a German.'

If he were a German he couldn't be a fairy.

'Are you a fairy?'

'Ah, perhaps. Fairies never tell, you know.'

'But the prince? Can there be a German fairy?'

'Oh! Ha, ha! *He's* not a fairy, my dear. Solid flesh and blood and lots of it.'

This was puzzling, because Virtue was nearly sure that this lady must be a fairy. Nobody could have hands so transparently soft and white and covered with such glittering rings. So soft they were! Like the satin cushion on mother's dressing-table. Soft and sweet-scented as they caressed her face and ran through the straight, dark hair that Kate found so difficult to manage. Virtue was falling more and more under the spell of this wonderful being. She thought she would like to sit here for ever, scenting the perfume and touching the fragrant softness of her — never to go back even to dear Kate, whose hands were rough and tugged at her hair, or to mother, whose kiss was awaited every night with such ardour. No, this was different from mother's good-night kiss. She had thought that was the loveliest thing in the world until now —

'Please, may I stay with you always?'

'Virtue! If you only could. But what would mother say? And father in Germany? And all the little brothers and sisters? I hate to let you go, little love. I'd like to take you to Germany with me. I'm going there next month, when I leave this dull place.'

'Are you unhappy here?' Virtue asked hopefully.

'I am only here because I have been ill.'

'Are you ill?' Fairies could not be ill, surely.

'I was.' She smiled. 'Would you like to come to Germany?'

'And see the prince? Oh, please! Please take me to Germany.'

'We'll talk about that another day. Now you must go back. What will your nurse be doing, poor thing, with her Virtue gone?' She laughed again more than ever. 'Come again, little friend.'

She took her in her arms and carried her to the French window.

'Don't forget the bad fairy.'

'Let me come tomorrow,' said Virtue, clinging. 'I will come tomorrow for all day.'

'Yes, yes, tomorrow. I'll be looking out for you on the balcony. Good-bye, lovely, lovely baby!'

'Good-bye, good-bye! I shall come again tomorrow!'

When she entered the window she was seized roughly by Kate.

'Where have you been? Oh, my Lord, where have you been! I searched the house *and* the garden. Nothing but a piece of string on the balcony. Oh, you naughty girl, you've half killed me, and your mother out and all. Where have you been?'

'I've been with a fairy — over the balcony.'

Kate understood.

'A fairy!' she sneered. 'Yes, that's not a bad name. Whoever heard! What'll your mother say I don't like to think.'

Mother's good-night kiss was rather tame that night, for

already Virtue was dreaming of roses, pink lights, soft hands and lips warmly pressed to hers, and of a bird that sprang brilliantly from a tinkling box and settled on her shoulder singing so loud that she woke up screaming.

'A little fever.' Her mother was leaning over her again holding a glass of the medicine which smelt of night and which Kate called Nitre.

'Never mind,' murmured Virtue, turning over to sleep again. 'I shall see the fairy again tomorrow.'

But she never saw her again, except once, and that was far worse than never seeing her at all, for she appeared on the balcony a few days later, and, when Virtue rushed towards her, she vanished — as a fairy might.

10 The Poplar Avenue

There were twenty-two of them, planted ten feet from each other, in two solemn rows, by somebody who had conceived a great iron gate and an avenue to a square grey house. But of the conception only the poplars had materialised. They stood, straight and sleek, in a large paddock, their only companion a huge and ancient elm. A small black stream stemmed their advance at one end. Here they towered magnificent — in summer two hundred feet of glittering green, fed by the river. The farthest of the twenty-two were poor by comparison, as though a consciousness of futility had hindered their growth. For the iron gate was not there to justify them. They had grown with the others in their allotted places, obedient to the desire of the dreamer who had planted them, and they were all beautiful, straight and strong. But the two by the stream were kings among trees; they mounted to the sky each year more richly, always trim as though carefully brushed; no stray branches marred the perfect symmetry of their outline.

Instead of the solid bridge crossing the stream to the hypothetical house, there was a small wooden foot-bridge, and beyond it the white cottage with its jasmine covered terrace which Ebba Paule had bought because she wanted the poplar avenue. On sleepless nights she was soothed by the thought of these trees, their calm detachment from each other, their alliance, their indifference to the elements. They were never annoyed by blustering winds, tortured by roaring gales. They simply averted their well-groomed heads, as much as to say, 'When is this vulgar nonsense going to stop?'

Every night, when Lucile had cleared away the dinner from the green dining-room with its absurd little Gothic windows, Ebba would walk across the foot-bridge to her poplars. Here she would lean against one of the kings and stare down the avenue. The poplars, with their rhythmic serenity, their inevitability of line, made a kind of scaffolding round the shattered structure of her emotional life.

She had lived for more than a year in this cottage in the Rhône valley entirely remote from her world, with her maid as her only companion. She worked at the designing which had found such favour with Paris decorators that she was kept constantly busy. This was pleasant, anonymous work which did not involve meeting anyone, and it brought in enough to keep the household going without any strain on her small income. The house, the weekly bills, were all in Lucile's name, for Ebba was in hiding, a fugitive from love.

The limit of exasperation had driven her into the arms of a man whom she had already known slightly for two years as the rather underbred husband of an English friend. He was good-looking in the *Bel Ami* style: that they all had to admit. A barber's block, Ebba had decided, unheedful of the quiver of sensitive lips under the neat little moustache.

The great blue-green eyes set snakily below a rounded forehead were as inexpressive to her as bottle glass; the nostrils of the too classic nose had dilated in vain for her. Surely the glossy hair must be disgustingly clogged with pomade to cling so unalterably to his shapely head! Oh, yes, indeed, a barber's block, with no brains at all, as his wife was so constantly and publicly asserting. She was a fine, masterful woman, and considered herself a 'highbrow' because she read Freud and the critical weeklies. In order to explain Franco (his name was Francisco), she stressed his lack of intellect, and preferred to hint that theirs was a marriage of passion.

However that might be, Franco's passion was not all consumed at home. He was exceedingly popular among the many women friends of his wife who did not regard him merely as a barber's block. His English was first-rate, and his looks and his Latin ways did the rest. He moved in an aura of light-hearted gossip; his joyous attendance on his wife's attractive friends had become a diverting feature of the social landscape. No one, except occasionally the lady of the moment, took him seriously.

What did Mrs Franco really feel about it under her mask of good-humoured toleration? Realising that his faithlessness was inevitable, she sped him on his adventures with an encouraging smile, but she would, on the other hand, embarrass the lady of the moment by discussing his reactions in cold-blooded detail.

'I think Franco is really in love with you,' she would say cheerfully, fixing the lady with her handsome dark eyes. 'Your sex appeal, my dear! It's devastating. Don't be too hard on him' — here a disturbing gleam which penetrated direct to the 'I'm not' at the back of the victim's flickering lids. 'I don't believe in repressions, especially for people of Franco's temperament.'

Naturally no one knew what weapons she used at home, but the short duration of Franco's affairs was as much due to his wife's careful observation of them as to Franco's fickle nature. She never nipped in the bud; her method was a disintegrating blight.

Franco had remained a barber's block to Ebba until one night, when driving her home from a party to which she had gone alone, he had kissed her suddenly, as she fumbled for the key of her front door. There had been nothing to lead up to this. She had scarcely been conscious of him except as someone escorting her home, and their conversation had been negligible, of the party, and how dull it would have been if the champagne had been worse or less plentiful.

'Why on earth did you do that?' She was too surprised to pretend to be indignant.

'I've been wanting awfully to do it for two years.'

He did it again. A kiss that fluttered softly over her mouth for what seemed an age, before it settled and stayed. With one hand pressed to the round, snake forehead, and the other beating at his shirt-front, she fought the kiss which was like no other that she had ever known.

Such was the beginning of the Franco affair. A flimsy sheet of paper can start a dangerous fire if the ground is dry enough, and it was very dry just then for Ebba. Her husband, John, who at thirty-five, when she married him, had been amusing and attractive and passably good-looking, was now at forty-seven discoloured and ugly as a toad, and consequently more jealously possessive than ever. Dark misgivings clouded his mind as he saw her receding farther and farther from him, maturing as he withered. Her ash-blond hair had lost none of its colour in the twelve years of their marriage; the Grecian coil in the nape of her neck was no less heavy than it was on the night he had unwound it and clothed her in it, when she was his bride of eighteen. Her strange coloured eyes, like dark amber in shadow, had brightened with the years and her ivory skin was still unblemished. Resentment now routed admiration. Why could she not grow old with him? The playful malice of his early manner had turned to bitter sarcasm. His habit had always been to tease, but now he delighted to insult her in public, even at her own dinner-table, and watch her writhe. He had become quite intolerable.

He was an idle man, with plenty of money which he had not earned. She came from a different world. A rectory in Dorset, a miniature village of a dozen or so thatched cottages, bright patchwork hills, rich valleys sheltering prosperous farmsteads: this was the scene of her childhood. Her father, rector and scholar, had married a fair woman from Scandinavia, whose fame as a painter in her own country did not deter her from following the man she loved to a remote village, and it was in the barn which she had made into a studio that Ebba, their only child, learned the first principles of her mother's art.

She never went to school, but 'did lessons' in her father's study, rather vaguely-given lessons that were always delightful. Life was a beautiful and simple thing, ambling along like a green Dorset lane, till, when she was fifteen, sudden catastrophe wiped out at one stroke the careful design. Her parents were killed in a railway accident on one of their infrequent visits to the Continent, and the dazed child, snatched from all familiar scenes, took refuge with an aunt by marriage, who was the only relation in a position to receive her. Fortunately her mother had left her enough money to save her from being a financial burden on her guardian, and Aunt Agatha, who lived a superficially genial widowed life in Paris, was quite thrilled by her new responsibility. She was the last person the rector would have chosen for his child's guardian.

The complete change of aspect made Ebba's loss more bearable. She spent her days at an art school, and her evenings in Aunt Agatha's *salon*, not because she enjoyed it, but because her aunt liked to show her off to the crowd of cosmopolitans, thirsty men and defiant women, who flocked to her *soirées*. To one of these came John Paule, three years after the tragedy. By then Aunt Agatha had decided that, whatever happened, Ebba must be married as soon as possible. The novelty of having a charming niece had long ago worn thin, and Ebba had been aware for some time that her aunt was jealous of her. John Paule was much the most presentable man she had ever seen in her aunt's house, and, even if he had not seemed to promise everything, except youth, that one could hope from marriage, she would have accepted him to escape from the black cloud that she felt gathering round her.

A villa on the Riviera; a devoted husband who, he promised, would deny her nothing: here, it seemed, was a pleasant solution of the problem. The villa was not a disappointment. It was on one of the Caps between Cannes and Nice, off the beaten track, with a view of the Esterels and a shady garden. She was so delightfully ignorant of housekeeping that the long-established servants instantly adored her. The balance of such a perfectly run bachelor establishment should not, she felt, be disturbed. Lucile, daughter of the gardener, became her maid and her devoted slave.

As for the devoted husband, his only notion of marriage seemed to be possession, and Ebba did not want to be possessed. His point of view, crude and unimaginative, was quite conventional, but a little out of date. He could not see why she should want to work at her drawing after she became his wife, and resented, even tried to forbid, her making one of the garden rooms into a studio. It was soon obvious to him that in this studio her life was really lived, and he himself was shut out of a world he could not enter from lack of understanding. Compassionate at first, she had tried to draw him into it, but as he could not regard her work as anything but a childish diversion she indignantly locked him out, for she took herself and her art perhaps rather too seriously. She shirked no part of her duty as his wife, however boring she found it, and she was faithful to him, partly because she was fastidious and partly because she had never been tempted to be otherwise.

And now what alchemy had transformed the barber's block into a glowing, rapturous being whose desire for her brought warmth and happiness into her frozen heart?

She did not stop to ask. She was swept along on the spring tide of passion, and with a lover's eyes appraised Franco and found him a god.

He could draw, she found (but not nearly as well as she thought). He came to the studio and admired the right things. So intelligent after all! So much more intelligent than his wife, for all her Freudian jargon and pretentious culture! He, too, was disillusioned. Ah! they had so much to talk about when they were not kissing. That handsome wife was a perfect monster, and nagged the life out of him if he so much as looked at another woman.

'Good heavens, what a life you must lead, darling!' She reviewed in retrospect the long line of ladies he had so much more than looked at in the last two years.

'Franco, is she nagging you about me?'

'She has always nagged me about you. Always, because she has known that it has been only you all the time. I talk in my sleep, I think.'

'Has it always been me really, or am I one of the —'

He shut her mouth with a kiss. 'There must be none of that talk, please. I am too wildly in love to bear to think of all those others who meant nothing — nothing.'

'Poor souls,' she murmured, contentedly, stroking the head which she had been so glad to find did not after all depend for its sleekness on pomade.

Mrs Franco knew there was danger this time. She went cautiously with Ebba.

'Franco's not looking well. I think of taking him for a cure. After that he must really get a job of some kind. He ought to try to keep himself. It's undignified for a man of his age to be entirely dependent on his wife, don't you think, dear Ebba?'

Horrible woman, thought Ebba.

'Yes, very unpleasant for him,' was all she said.

Franco seemed irrevocably tied, and that was part of Mrs Franco's system. She had wrested him away from honest work when she married him, and any feeble effort to earn a living he might have made since had been sternly repressed, though she was always crying, 'Franco must get a job!'

But she kept him busy enough with the ordering of her villa, dealing with servants and tradesmen, arranging itineraries for the long, expensive tours which were essential to her health, and helping to entertain her many friends. He certainly earned his keep, but he was her servant, and, however he might flirt in his leisure moments, most damnably chained.

Now that he loved Ebba (and, yes, he really did love her), he must escape those chains, must he not? The obvious thing was to run away with her, but where to, and what would they live on? He knew that she was ready to go with him, but she hardly realised that if he left his wife he went penniless. There was the humiliating position, so neatly contrived for his enslavement.

It was, from every point of view, a desperate situation. Each day heaped up complexities. Everyone was talking, and everyone knew that this was not just one of Franco's little flirtations. There was no question of concealment; Ebba was a novice in intrigue, and Franco, after the first few weeks of transport, went about like a haunted man, his chains trailing dolefully. Mrs Franco, watching his discomfiture, decided on strong measures.

They were departing for America immediately, she announced.

'You go alone. I shall not come,' said Franco, rattling his chains defiantly.

'And what will you do?' with contempt.

'I shall get a job and live the life I want.'

She was disconcerted by a queer clutching pain at her heart.

'Don't be a damn fool. Get on to Cook's at once.'

Habit led him to the telephone.

✳

'I suppose this dago really is your lover, as they're all saying?' John asked Ebba, his bulged eyes and shaking hands belying the sarcastic indifference of his question.

'Yes, he really is.' His manner exasperated her, and she asked him in the same breath to divorce her.

He sneered. 'Perhaps you think he'll get that old harridan to divorce him, and that you'll live happily ever after? Don't believe it, my dear Ebba, whatever rubbish he may have been filling you up with. I suppose you know they're sailing for America in a fortnight?'

Ebba did not know. When she met Franco at their secret place of assignation she taxed him with it.

'Everything is booked,' he admitted. 'But I am not going. She does not know. I am finding a job, and I am coming away with you. Do not fear, my lovely Ebba. All will go right.'

He drew her to him and took her so gently that she was soothed and freed for the moment from misgivings. He was such an artist that his love-making was always in perfect tune.

But back in her room at the villa, where Lucile was waiting with the usual assurance that monsieur had not inquired for her, fearful doubts swept round her and kept her feverishly tossing. Franco, her darling, her enchanter — what was he really? Could he get a job, and could he keep it? What was to prevent his being carried off to America by his strong-minded wife? His will, if he had ever had much, was weakened by constant attrition, and she knew that he was afraid of himself. She had seen that tonight. Wouldn't it be better to let him go to America, than to stay and see him carried off by force? Stay — that was it! She must not stay. To leave John at any rate was urgently necessary. He had become so actively repulsive lately that to be in the same house with him was an affront to her senses.

Her senses were all that mattered now. A faint memory of her father a few months before he died suddenly came clearly to her consciousness.

'Love! Don't forget, Ebba darling,' he had said, 'that it begins and ends with the spirit. Anything else is no use, by itself.'

She must go. She simply could not go on. She must go and try to find herself again. Was it indeed herself, this fevered, intriguing creature, who only lived when she was in her lover's arms?

'I must get away!' she cried to the night. 'I can't bear this life any more.'

She did not waste time because she knew that she must not see Franco again. (Deep in her unconscious was the fear of an injury to her pride if Franco let his wife carry him off to America, but she was aware only of a moral revolt.)

Lucile, who thought her mistress was eloping with Franco, smuggled all the clothes she would want out of the house, enchanted to see a romantic climax to the affair. It was not until they were in the night train for Paris, when Ebba's fortitude, which had survived the preparations for departure, collapsed, and she fell into hopeless tears, that Lucile realised this was no elopement.

'But, madame! One cannot fly from love!' She was genuinely shocked, and Ebba was not in a state of mind to argue with her. She said:

'Only do not desert me, Lucile. I believe you are my one friend.'

'Where madame goes I go, without question.'

But she was bitterly disappointed.

Ebba had written to Franco:

Good-bye, dear lover. I can never explain, only please believe that what I have done is right for both of us. I hope you will go to America, and that you won't forget me, but that you will forgive me, and never try to find me. Ebba.

John, as soon as he was quite sure that Franco was not likely to join her, divorced her, and, when that was all settled, she found the poplars and retired to the cottage in the valley of the Rhône. Lucile was under a pledge of discretion, and only Ebba's bank and her lawyer were in the secret.

To stifle the pain, she would dwell on Franco's faults. She spread out his sketches which she had brought away with her own, and observed them critically.

'Why did I ever think he could draw?' No, that wasn't kind. She swept them away with a tear, remembering how he had looked while he was doing them. How weak he was! Of course he would have gone to America in any case. And if he had not, and they had gone away together, how hopeless it would have been. He would never have done any work, and they would both have been humiliated. Thus and thus she thought him out of her mind, belittling him, and ignoring (but for a lightning flash that sometimes would streak her memory) the ecstatic hours of their love. She found some tranquillity, dreaming under her poplars of the new life she was making, and how one day she would get entirely free from the past and begin all over again. But the distant past, the days of her childhood, she recalled more and more. Her mind dwelt on her parents' life, and the more she contemplated it, the more impossible seemed the existence which destiny had forced on her for the last fifteen years. She was thirty; could the two halves of a life be more utterly unrelated? That being so, why should she not obliterate the latter half as effectively as Fate, with one stroke, had obliterated the other?

It was one night in summer, after she had been in her retreat for more than a year, that she had a disquieting dream. The poplar avenue, which till now had soothed her sleeplessness, was on fire. Each tree became a torch of flame, and they burned and burned, stretching great orange flames to the sky with a roar and crackle, and she woke in tears.

'Lucile!' she cried when the faithful maid rushed in from her room next door, 'I dreamt the poplars were on fire!'

'On fire! *Ah, madame!*' was all Lucile said, but she made a *tisane*, which was her remedy for all occasions, and, after she had pulled aside the curtains and convinced her mistress that there was no fire in the paddock, she sat plumply in a chair until Ebba was asleep again. Then with a *clk* of her tongue she went back to bed and turned over with a sigh, her mind revolving many things.

✕

A summer gale was blowing from the west. All day great clouds had been bundling across the sky, and the flowers of late June, already swooning with midsummer heat, lay in voluptuous abandon along the borders. Ebba had rescued some of them, put them in bowls and given them aspirin. But the life had gone out of them; they were finished, before their time.

By the evening a full gale was tearing over the country. Torn clouds, fleeing the violence of the wind, raced high in the heavens over the full moon, at one moment leaving it clear in a luminous sapphire pool; at the next submerging it in an amber foam — the edge of a black obliteration.

'Madame is going out?' asked Lucile, as Ebba went to the garden door after dinner.

'Certainly. Why not?'

'It is — so rough. It is not fit.'

'Why, this is nothing. It's not even raining.'

'That is true; madame does, I know, go out in dreadful rain to visit her poplars. But I beg that madame will not go very far tonight.'

'Of course not. I never go farther than the poplars. Don't worry about me, Lucile, but get off to bed. Good-night.'

When Lucile had shut the glass door behind her mistress she stood and watched her cross the lawn with a curious but tender little smile. Then she went to the kitchen and opened the evening paper. She was not going to bed just yet.

Ebba crossed the trembling foot-bridge, under which even the black stream was agitated. Her head was bare, and she had put on a little dark jacket with silver buttons which she had bought two years ago in the Jardin des Fleurs.

There were the poplars! They swayed symmetrically, in perfect order, only at a new angle. The wind was playing a shrill shrieking tune in their close-knit branches. The clamour was tremendous, and Ebba thought of her dream of three weeks ago. But the splendid noise produced such a sense of exaltation as she had never known. This wild night was the justification of her philosophy. The steadfast poplars, so resolutely defying the elements, so faithfully guarding her, showing the way so clear, the exit so easy!

She leant her full length against one of the kings, as she always did on calmer nights. Against her body the great trunk vibrated, moving ever so slightly in the wind, and thrilling her with its resisting strength, like the play of strong muscles. She leaned back and watched the tempestuous sky and the harassed moon. How alive was the throbbing tree beneath her! She threw back her arms and clasped the trunk. They were her friends, these trees; they lived, they had hearts; the sap flowed as surely as the blood in her own veins. And there, at the end of the avenue, was the way out —

When, above the din she heard a step on the foot-bridge, she knew that Franco had found her.

She stayed leaning against the tree and could not speak. For a moment the moon was bright, and he stood before her silently, searching her, with eyes that shone darkly in his dead white face. The cleft in his small finely carved chin had deepened. She saw that he was thinner and looked ill. Yes, he looked wretched, and her heart was melting.

It was not possible to speak, but a faint gesture of her hands brought him nearer, and, as the tree stirred beneath her, his lips were fluttering over hers in the old way that she had tried to forget. The gleaming and blinking of her silver buttons attracted him.

'That little jacket!' He smiled. Then, shouting above the noise:

'Can we not go into the house, out of this horrible wind?'

'I am free, you know,' he said, when they were in the studio.

'Free?'

'She has died. Of heart. Oh, a long time ago, months ago, in America.'

'You went to America?'

'Of course! What could I do? You told me to go. Besides, you had disappeared. No one knew where. You made a fool of me before my wife and everyone. I do not understand these ways at all. There was no need to make yourself more desirable, because I was already too mad about you. How could you do it, Ebba? You have been horribly cruel to me, but I forgive you for I know that you are mine, however much you have tried to hide from me. You must have known I should find you some day, so why all this waste of time and emotion?'

'I wonder how you did find me.'

'Ah, a good friend helped me, but I must not tell. What does it matter now that I am here?'

Alas! She had to admit that it did not matter at all.

✖

Next morning the gale was gone. The garden lay in an exhausted sleep. In the east the tattered clouds of last night had gathered together and were moulded into a shining cumulus, rising from the plain like a fantastic mountain range carved in ivory. Delicate black pencilling outlined the static shapes.

Ebba stood at her window enchanted by that distant landscape from the storm. All wrought of vapour and light, it was more lovely than the earth, desirable as a landscape seen in a dream. She turned her eyes to the poplars. Motionless they pointed to the sky — not a breath disturbed them; but in the night the old elm had been blown down and lay across the avenue, blocking the 'way out'.

✕

Lucile, who had lunch for two simmering on the fire, was writing a letter home with a pen sharp as a needle, and chuckling every now and then.

11 The Unattainable

Wonderful Woolworth was opening a new shop. Mrs Heriot came to explore with the rest of the crowd. A pretty woman, and desperately sad-looking. She had never been in a Woolworth shop before, and was enchanted by the cleverness of it — the attractive way everything was arranged, and the ingenious play on the slogan '6d'. Everything sixpence, from a pepper pot to a baby's bonnet. Boot trees, sixpence. Aha! sixpence each — in other words a shilling. But wonderfully cheap at that. Oh, but astonishing!

'Marvellous, marvellous!' murmured Mrs Heriot, beginning to buy. She bought a block of writing paper for sixpence, an orange bathing cap for her bath, some bright little bead mats, 'to put under the teapot, madam', (Nannie would like these), a pair of scissors (sixpence the scissor), and a quantity of kitchen things.

It was a dense, but quiet, good-natured crowd. She was swept along with it, carrying her spoils. A counter of little soap figures attracted her. They were delightful and amusing. She had seen the same thing before, but, here at Woolworth's, ranged all together, they seemed little aristocrats of the soap world. She would buy two for the children; and she bought a pink baby and a Mickey Mouse. As they were being wrapped up, she noticed standing beside her a pale little girl whose chin just reached the level of the counter, who gazed with intense longing at the soapy wonders.

She was a poor little girl, and her mother beside her was puckering up her hard honest face over bars of household soap and such horrid necessities of life. She didn't look the kind of woman who would waste, or could afford to waste, a penny upon childish whims.

There didn't seem to be much chance of that little girl getting what she wanted. No, no chance at all.

Mrs Heriot took her parcel and walked away, but the child's face with its look of longing had arrested her. Had not she herself longed — oh! but how hopelessly — for the unattainable? What she longed for could never, never be hers. How ridiculous to think of that on the same day as a piece of soap! Never mind, it was all a question of degree. Here was a chance …

She turned, and found the girl still contemplating. She nudged her quietly.

'Here, my dear, this is for you.' The parcel changed hands in a moment. The child gasped, but Mrs Heriot did not give her time to speak, and disappeared into the crowd. The parcel was furtively opened. The very ones! She'd watched the lady buy them. Oh, Lordy! her own, her very own.

✖

'Come along — time we got home.'

The voice and horny hand of her mother brought her back to earth. Through the crowd they went. Oh, Gawd, supposing! —

She hid the parcel under her jacket.

'What's that you got there? What are you hiding? Speak up now! What is it? Come along, hand it over!'

The parcel was seized.

'Where you get this? Come along now. Out with it.'

'A lady give it me.'

'A lady! Yes, I should say so. You don't think you can come that over me again, do you? That's what you said when you stole the plums, or something like. "A lady give it me",' she mimicked. 'Yes, I shouldn't wonder. There's lots of ladies going round buying soap dollies to hand over to strange kids in the street. A likely tale, that, my handsome!'

'But it's true. A lady did give it me,' she repeated furiously, and knowing that it was no good. 'I tell you she did. I never took them. There's the parcel and the bill. If I'd took them there wouldn't be no parcel and no bill.'

'I'm not saying you took them off of the counter; you took them off of someone, and that's a sure thing. It wasn't enough that hiding your dad give you when you stole the plums? You can't stop your hands from picking and stealing, can't you? I'll soon show you. You think I'm going to have a thief in my family? Shaming your dad and me what have never had a breath against us? Not much, my girl, and if a hiding don't teach you I shall have to think of something else. Here goes for a start, anyway!'

She threw the parcel into the traffic. The pink baby was crushed instantly by a motor-bus, and the Mickey Mouse rolled out of sight.

The little girl's face tightened with rage, and tears of despair rolled down her cheeks.

She determined from that moment never to miss an opportunity of stealing.

Mrs Heriot, the same night, writing a letter to somewhere very far away, told the story of the little girl and the soap dolls.

'It was a wonderful moment for me, my dear, to know that I was helping someone to reach the Unattainable — though it probably seems trivial to you — (no, not to *you*). Such a heavenly surprise for her, and I love to think of that sad little person rejoicing tonight. She did want them so very much!'

12 Children of God

Mrs Penberthy was recovering from her tenth child, born on June the 3rd, 1904. On an average once in every eighteen months, four weeks comparative repose was forced upon her by the pains of childbirth. She would have made it three if she could, but, as each child brought her perilously near to the door of death, she was obliged to take the full measure of an inexpensive monthly nurse.

After her first confinement, and each one that followed, Doctor Boase had told the rector that it would not be safe for his wife to have another child, and each time the rector had said 'Quite so,' or words to that effect. But, as Mrs Penberthy's shy little sister Aunt Lizzie so delicately put it, 'Edwin always forgot.'

Edwin always forgot.

The fruits of Edwin's forgetfulness, gathered back into the Rectory fold from the friends' and relations' houses that had sheltered them during their mother's illness, were variously occupied about the house and garden. Two children had died as babies, so there were eight of them, counting the new boy, who slept in a perambulator under a tree. On what was more like a stale cake than a lawn, an incomplete croquet set with wide hoops and a bell in the middle straggled inconsequently. With its cracked mallets and balls it had been presented by Mr Burgess of The Hall, who had bought himself a new set of the latest pattern. Two bare-legged girls were playing a quarrelsome game. From the house came sounds of violent hammering, and a clatter of plates from the kitchen window, where the daily maid was trying to catch up with the lunch things, as it was just on tea time.

'Oh, cheat! Oh, cheat! I saw you move your ball! I did! I did!'

'Don't be such an ass. You know the blue ball has a chip out of it. I was only putting it on its right side. You can't play it when it's lying on the flat bit.'

'Oh, you rotten little outsider! I saw you push it in front of the hoop. Look at it! Plum in front! It wasn't there before. I shan't play with you. I can't play with cheats and liars.'

Maura flung her mallet in the direction of the cheat and flopped down beside her eldest sister who was mending an enormous hole in what remained of a dull grey sock.

'What is to be done with Ursula? She cheats at everything. I don't mind what she does at school. That doesn't matter. But I do think at games she might try to be straight. I don't understand it. Where on earth does she get it from?'

Elizabeth's tragic eyes glanced for a moment from the sock to her erring sister, who was finishing the game by herself with an air of bravado.

'Why worry? There's nothing to be done about it. She's a cheat, and there's an end of it. Don't play with her.'

'You're so beastly resigned, Betty. I want to reform her — try to convince her that decent people don't cheat or lie. Why are you so beastly resigned?'

'Because I know it's no use being anything else. Even if you could teach Ursula not to cheat, you would always know that she was a cheat by nature, and you couldn't ever do anything but distrust her. No one has taught her to cheat — unless she learnt it at the village school — so it must be just her nature, and the best thing is not to give her an opportunity.'

'You frighten me, Betty. I believe it's what Guy calls "cynical" — that way of looking at things.'

'Oh, well, if I am cynical, perhaps it's not surprising. Guy is too.' She stopped her darning for a moment and looked away towards the house.

'Guy's got something on his mind since he came back from the Mannings. He looks rotten — sort of haunted.'

'Guy's growing up. He's beginning to think — and understand things.'

'Oh, well, I'm glad I'm not beginning to grow up; if that's what it does to you. He looks miserable sometimes.'

'You're right, my dear. Keep young as long as you can.'

'Come and have a game with me.' Maura was rather frightened of Elizabeth in this sombre mood.

'My dear, no! Who's going to do all these socks and stockings? Malcolm and Ursula didn't have anything mended while they were away. They like my mending best. Very kind of them, I'm sure. There was nothing to do for Guy,' she added proudly.

'Guy can't bear your doing all this work. He was saying so this morning.'

'I know he can't. But he can't do much about it, poor boy.'

'Give me a sock to do.'

'Not now. It's enough for you to do your own mending in the holidays. Make the most of them while you've got them. When you leave school you don't get any, remember.'

A tremendous crash in the kitchen drew a faint cry from Mrs Penberthy who was lying on a dilapidated chaise longue, also presented by Mr Burgess, when it had become too shabby for his lawn. The seventh Penberthy, aged two, was solemnly turning over a rag picture book at her side.

'Maura, my dear!'

Maura ran to the mulberry tree and bent over her mother.

'I'm afraid Gladys has broken another plate, or perhaps something worse. It sounded like something more than a plate, but there's hardly anything left for her to break. Go and help her, there's a dear. Otherwise we shall never get tea.'

'All right, darling. Can you stand Malcolm's hammering? Shall I stop him?'

'Oh, no, please! I believe he's making something for me,

and wants to get it finished. So he told Elizabeth. A secret! Such a clever little carpenter!'

Maura, with a sceptical look, went towards the house, and as she did so the rector entered the gate at the bottom of the garden. Tall, sleek and well-cut, he looked at least ten years younger than his wife. In reality he was five years older. His slightly grizzled hair invaded his neck, not from carelessness, but because it was his manner. It gave him a sort of dignity, and at the same time enhanced the romance of his general appearance, especially when he wore the swinging cape he affected in the winter months. In the summer he wore his hair somewhat shorter, and today it only just dribbled over his collar.

'Well, and how is the invalid?' He patted his wife's hand with a kindly smile.

'Not an invalid any longer, father dear. I'm only lazy this afternoon. I had a walk this morning, you know.'

'To be sure. But you must be careful, my dear. *Piano, piano,* as they say in Italy. I have arranged for your churching on Saturday. You fainted last time, you remember, because you would have it too soon. By Saturday you should be strong enough.'

At this moment Maura's head appeared at the kitchen window.

'It was the last willow pattern vegetable dish, mother! It wasn't Gladys's fault. It jumped out of her hand.'

'What!' exclaimed the rector. 'Another breakage! Really this is insufferable. Two plates yesterday and the last vegetable dish today. I shall be glad, my dear Constance, when you are able to superintend the kitchen again. What are the girls doing? Where is Elizabeth?'

He was not greatly moved by the sight of his own grey sock which Elizabeth waved at him for answer.

'Well, well — there is a time for everything. Please

understand that we cannot afford to have all our china broken. We must eat off something. I assure you I cannot *afford* to invest in a new dinner service.'

The rector was annoyed, and retired towards the house. The hammering that had scarcely ceased all the afternoon stopped abruptly, and the rector's voice was heard, raised in angry expostulation. He reappeared almost immediately.

'Who gave leave for Malcolm to do his carpentering on the landing outside my study? What is the matter, I say, with the carpenter's shop? The whole place is in a disgusting mess, and stinks of glue, which he is apparently warming on my Primus stove.'

Malcolm at this moment slunk on to the lawn.

'There wasn't room in the carpenter's shop. I didn't mean to make a mess. I wanted to get it done quickly.'

'And what is this colossal piece of work, if I may ask?'

'A rabbit hutch, father. Jones is giving me a pair, and I haven't got anywhere to put them.'

Mrs Penberthy winced at this information, but she only said:

'I am afraid it is my fault that he worked in the house, as I gave him leave through Elizabeth. It was not good of you, Malcolm, to use your father's stove without permission.'

'I'm the only person that can make it work,' Malcolm growled.

The rector, painfully conscious of the truth of this remark, turned upon his son:

'Silence! Enough! Go and clear all the mess away at once. Where is tea? Surely it is more than time. I've had a thirsty walk. Many congratulations, my dear, on the new youngster. Everyone full of delight at another boy. Mrs Boger wanted to know how many pounds. I said eight. That's about it, isn't it,' with his hearty parochial laugh.

'Eight and a half to be quite correct, darling,' murmured his wife, with a note of heaviness in her voice.

'Ah, well — that's as near as makes no difference. A letter by this afternoon's post from Uncle George, by the way, my dear, approving my scheme for Guy in Canada. He says his neighbour, a worthy person of good family, takes farming pupils and will be glad to have Guy at the very lowest possible fee. I aired the question of Canada with the boy again yesterday, and he seemed unresponsive and not over-keen. However, this seems to be the course indicated for him. A most friendly note added by Aunt Emma — who, judging by her writing, I gather is somewhat failing — saying what a warm welcome her great-nephew will receive, and mentioning the cheery young society he will find out there. Yes, I am glad to think that the problem of Guy's future may be considered settled.'

Elizabeth, who had heard most of this conversation, rose very suddenly with a stocking on her hand and disappeared into the house ...

Malcolm at this moment emerged with his hutch and a bundle of shavings.

'Have you cleared up your horrible mess?' demanded the indignant rector.

'Maura's finishing it,' he mumbled.

'But Maura is to get tea!' the rector almost screamed, showing his beautiful white teeth much as a large dog might whose bone is being withheld. 'Good gracious! How long am I to wait for what should have been ready half an hour ago. Go back at once and send Maura to the kitchen and finish clearing up yourself.'

Malcolm, scowling, returned to the house, leaving his hutch in the middle of the lawn. Realising just in time that his tea would be again delayed if he complained of this, the rector turned his back on it. Malcolm passed through the dining-room window into the obscurity of the house.

In the dining-room hung the two family portraits that had been inherited by Edwin Penberthy. They were not of very great value, or they would have been sold long ago, but they were of a good school and period. John and Mary Penberthy, his great grandfather and grandmother, had been people of substance — courtiers — of the great world. They looked down proudly on the dingy poverty of the Rectory dining-room. These two handsome people had made a fine thing of life, going through it with dignity and decorum, and ending, as in those days all the best people ended, under a ponderous tomb whose laboured description of their virtues for once did not fall far short of the truth. There followed a reaction in their son Herbert, who scattered the carefully garnered fortune of his parents, loved too many women, and was too well loved by them, married a sad little lady for her fortune, spent it, and blew his brains out, leaving the sad little lady with nothing in the world but three small children. Of these the eldest was Edwin Penberthy's father, who had been put into the Church in order to occupy a family living. Edwin himself had gone as a scholar to Eton and Cambridge, scraping through on a meagre allowance, and going automatically into the Church, marrying the pretty rose-leaf daughter of his first vicar, and finally settling down in the parish of Mead, which was small as the Rectory was large, two wings having been added at various times by prolific incumbents.

Edwin Penberthy's inheritance amounted to a mere hundred pounds a year, and the living, including a few acres of glebe, brought in another hundred and fifty. There was room in the Rectory for the Penberthy family — lots of it — but it was as bare as a rabbit-warren. The scant furniture, faded and darned curtains and covers, dingy wall-papers and worn paint, testified to the forlorn poverty of the empty, echoing house.

Under the portraits of his ancestors sat Guy, the rector's eldest son, his hands buried in his fair hair, his mind absorbed by the book he was reading.

'Hullo, Guy,' said Malcolm. 'I didn't know you were here.'

'No, but I knew you were there. Hellish row you've been making.'

'Why didn't you sing out?'

'Well, I understood from Betty that you were doing something for mother. So I didn't interfere.'

Malcolm reddened slightly. 'I had to finish my hutch —'

'Oh, I see. Another illusion gone.' He rose and stretched his long grey-flannelled limbs. 'Someone will have to teach you not to be a public nuisance. The village school doesn't give you much of that, I know.'

'I'm coming to Burlingham next year, you know.'

'Worse and worse. You'll end as badly as I shall. Seedy masters, lousy boys, and a head's wife with the manners and smell of an under-housemaid. No hope of social reform there, I'm afraid.'

'Where's Manning at school?' asked Malcolm rather panderingly. He knew that the family of Guy's late host was somehow important to his brother, and he chose a good topic with which to change the subject, which threatened to become too personal.

'Manning's at Eton,' said Guy.

'I suppose his people are rich?'

'Not at all. His father is a parson with a small income and an unimportant living.'

'How can they do it, then?'

'Ah! now you're asking. Manning got a scholarship from a decent private school and there are only three Mannings, and there are eight Penberthys … Run along and wash your filthy hands for tea, little rabbit.'

'Rum chap, Guy,' thought Malcolm, plastering the walls with gluey scum as he sloped up to the bathroom. 'Why "rabbit" just because I'm making a hutch?' He poured some nutty rainwater into a cracked basin and picked up a wizened bit of soap.

✳

Tea appeared at last and a rush was made for Maura's scones, which were buttered on Sundays and jammed on week-days.

Elizabeth's eyes were red when she was fetched down from her room by Ursula. Maura poured out and Elizabeth sat silent and remote over her tea, refusing scones or cake.

'Hullo, Betsy, you look as if you'd been crying!' Malcolm exclaimed, taking his third scone. 'What's up?'

'Nothing's "up",' said Elizabeth disdainfully.

'Elizabeth's eyes are tired,' hastily interposed Mrs Penberthy, who had a lively sense of the situation. 'She has been darning all the afternoon.'

Mr Penberthy clucked and handed his cup. He was not going to have his grey socks flung in his face, as it were. That enormous hole, half filled, which his daughter had waved at him should have troubled his conscience. He had allowed it to spread until it became visible over the heel of his shoe; not till then did he discard those grey socks. He gave a little cough.

'You girls are lucky in your friends. I hear Mrs Burgess has sent another box of presents for you,' he said, helping himself to three lumps of sugar.

'Doris and Mona's cast-off clothing, you mean, I suppose,' said Guy.

'I've looked at them,' said. Elizabeth.

'Anything decent?' asked Maura.

'Nothing much. The blue hat which Doris wore in church all last year. Two blouses with all the buttons cut off, and a pair of shoes that ought to have buckles. Oh, and a dress for you, mother, all worn out under the arms.'

'Beastly!' said Guy, flushing.

The rector found this an opportune moment for rising from the tea table.

'Guy, a word with you in my study.' He led the way through the dining-room. Guy followed gloomily. When they were in the study the rector handed Guy his Uncle James's letter. Guy read it through and handed it back in silence, but it was not an empty silence.

'Well, my son, have you nothing to say?'

'I said all there was to say yesterday. You know I am not keen on the Colonies, but I am ready to go if you want me to.'

'My desire has always been that you and Malcolm should carve out your own careers in the Colonies. Have you any ideas for yourself?'

Guy's face seemed to catch fire, but the fire was instantly extinguished.

'No, father, none — that it's any use having.'

He added: 'I am ready to go and carve out a career, as you put it, in any colony you like. At any rate, though I shall hate the life, I shan't be under an obligation to anybody. I hope I shall be able to keep myself, and perhaps get Elizabeth to come out and keep house for me later on.' His eyes narrowed and he gave a strange, faunlike smile.

'Yes, yes, an excellent idea,' exclaimed the rector to ease the situation, and without any intention of losing Elizabeth's house-wifeliness. But, he was not altogether insensitive and was uncomfortably aware that all was not quite well with his eldest son.

'I have no doubt,' he went on with a trace of sarcasm, 'that you would prefer Cambridge to the Colonies. But you must understand, and I have explained over and over again, that our means do not admit of such a thing, either for you or

Malcolm. Facts must be faced, however unpleasant. We are now eight, and I am hard put to it to provide even the common necessities of life, much less the luxuries.'

The flame rose again in Guy's face, but this time it was not extinguished.

'You need not have had so many children.'

'What are you saying? It is God's will.'

'I don't think it's that —.' A blush stole to the roots of Guy's fair hair as he said this, slowly meeting his father's indignant eye with a look of such chilling comprehension that the indignant eye flinched. 'I think when a man's as poor as you are he ought to do without — luxuries. It isn't as though you had lost money. We should all be ready to sacrifice ourselves if you had, but you've always known exactly how much you had and you knew it was impossible to bring up a large family in any sort of decency. If you had ever thought of that — we shouldn't have had to do without necessities. I call it hypocritical to bring God into the argument at all. You just like to amuse yourself — that's all it is — and mother — and we all — suffer for it. We pay for your pleasures.'

Mr Penberthy gasped. He groped for his study table and began arranging books upon it with a hand that trembled when it was not grasping with exaggerated firmness the objects upon it. A sign of weakness. Guy went on:

'Don't imagine that our poverty has anything noble about it. It would be far more appropriate if we lived in a burrow than in this miserable barrack. It's indecent to be as poor as we are. Look at Malcolm and Ursula, picking up filthy ways at the village school, cheating and lying. What can you expect? We are despised and humiliated by rotten people who happen to have more money than we have. That common slut Mona Burgess and her cast-off clothing! No doubt she gloats over the sight of Elizabeth and Maura, both so much better-looking than her, wearing her old hats in church; patronising them when she ought to be making their beds and brushing their clothes. It's revolting. I don't know how you can bear it.'

By this time the rector had found his tongue, and with a trembling upper lip he reeled out a string of indignant platitudes, in which Divine Purpose and 'The Lord will provide', the sacred duties of marriage, played their usual part.

'Bosh!' Guy shouted at last. 'Call it self-indulgence and be honest for once. You know that mother's life has been in danger every time she's had a child, yet you go on —'

'Leave my room!' shouted the rector. 'Revolting! Disgusting! Depraved! What are we coming to, I should like to know? Out of my sight, you — you scoundrel!'

Guy, feeling much better after this outburst, went out, slamming the door of the study with such violence that the Rectory shivered.

So did the rector. That shattering and final impudence set him trembling again. He muttered under his breath several words that he had not used since he was an undergraduate, (and sparingly even then).

There was a small mirror in the corner of the study, to which he went unsteadily.

'Come, come, come, this will never do!'

Gazing at his disordered face, he smoothed his straggling hair, and finally gave himself a long-toothed smile, such a smile as he gave to his parishioners when they were troubled.

※

That night, by the light of two candles, Mrs Penberthy lay and watched her husband preparing for bed. He was brushing his sleek locks, standing there in his nightshirt that looked so like a surplice. They had already knelt together at the *prie dieu* which had been a wedding present.

'What was the matter with Guy tonight?' she asked. 'He seemed so queer and changed. Have you been having any trouble with him?'

'There was a little bother, but I was able to put things right.'

'What was it all about?'

'Oh, nothing that you would understand, my dear,' he answered in a tone that suggested 'for men only'. 'Nothing of any real consequence. Just a boyish difficulty that only a father can deal with,' he added, and slid into bed beside her.

13 Cushions

Roxy lazed in her deck chair. She had already been tucked up twice since dinner, and half a dozen times she had refused to go down and dance. The third and most interesting tuck-up would happen in about five minutes when Bruce Wynne would come along with his cigar. Tomorrow the great liner would be in dock, and she would meet her delightful lover, Gregory, whom she had not seen for six months. The marriage was all arranged, and she was to stay with his Aunt Marian, who would be the nearest thing to a mother-in-law, since Gregory Moore was as complete an orphan as herself. Roxy had been brought up by her Aunt Bud, who dealt very successfully in hats and gowns in Cape Town. She adored Roxy, who had never known what it was to be denied anything that it was possible for Aunt Bud to get. She was even allowed to have Gregory when she made it clear that she wanted him, though the marriage would mean no Roxy in Cape Town for Aunt Bud, and life a dreary waste of hats, gowns and clients. Gregory was a partner in a publishing firm, on holiday in South Africa. It was a chance meeting. They had no common friends. Gregory's sombre good looks, his dark untidy hair, his deep eyes and splendid stature, his unusualness, won Roxy, and made her other *beaux* look cheap. Gregory himself fell in love at once when he saw her one morning coming out of Aunt Bud's shop in a frock of bird's-egg blue. He haunted the neighbourhood till he saw that she belonged there, and then he went in and bought a hat, and made friends with Aunt Bud, who was quite unlike anything he had ever met. She was a stout, hard-bitten woman of the world, with a splendid record of lovers stretching well back into the eighties. Now her heart beat only for Roxy, who was naturally supposed to be her child. She might well have been, but, as a fact, was not. She was, however, a love child, daughter of Aunt Bud's niece, who died at the age of seventeen in giving birth to Roxy. And a very sad tale and a dreadful scandal in the family it was. But Aunt Bud took the baby, as no one seemed to want it, and adopted it legally so that all nonsense should be avoided. She had no patience with stuffy outlooks, she said. She never regretted the adoption, for every year added to the charm and beauty of her charge, till at eighteen she had every young man she met in thrall, and Aunt Bud had what she called a job to keep them off. She was almost mid-Victorian in her chaperonage.

Then came Gregory, spring days, picnics at Green Point and Table Bay, lunches and dinners at Aunt Bud's cosy little nest at Woodstock, where Gregory enjoyed the most unconventional parties he had ever known, and fell more deeply in love with Roxy every moment. And now here was Roxy on her way to get married.

And here was Bruce Wynne coming along with his cigar.

Bruce always appeared to be wearing new clothes, but never looked over-dressed. He seemed, too, to have just emerged from a Turkish bath, fresh, pink and exquisite, his naughty fair curls flattened down on his shapely head (no nonsense allowed from them or anybody else) — his tender blonde moustache caressing the red, faunlike mouth.

He was altogether delicious, Roxy thought; glossy like a buttercup, or a sovereign. She loved the way he laughed, with a 'khee-e-e-e' at the end of it, and a provoking habit of putting out, for a second, as a python might, a pointed little tongue. There was never any time to see whether it was forked or not. He came along now, his shirt-front glistening. Roxy knew, though she couldn't see in the dim light, how brightly his intense blue eyes were sparkling. They were almost luminous. Bother! Why was he so attractive?

'Ah! So you're here.' It sounded like 'A-sho-ya-hea,' because he ran his words into one another with a hushing of his s's which Roxy found delightful.

'Comfy?'

'Not at all. One foot's frozen.'

'Soon put that right.'

The tucking-up began all over again. The last beau had certainly made a poor business of it. The rug had to be taken off and the little feet stuffed again into their fur muff. When the rug was arranged perfectly and the cushions punched and pulled behind her head he threw himself into the chair beside her, and, after tucking himself up in his own neat rug, leant over her.

'Comfy now?'

'Lovely now.'

'Like a cosy little cat you are. Just like a little sleek kitten. Oh, by the way, I dreamt about you last night.'

'What?'

'You were curled up on my divan sound asleep. I came in and said "Hello, is this a kitten?" Then you opened one eye.'

'Only one?'

'Yes, don't interrupt. And then — well, anyway, that's all.'

'That all?'

'I expect I woke up then.'

'Rather dull. Did I look comfy?'

'Very.'

'That's right. Quite a good dream. What's your divan like?'

'Not bad. 'Sa matter of fact, it's black with gold and silver cushions, which sounds awfully banal, but the cushions are all tarnished, rather like copper. Good effect.'

'Um. Down cushions?'

'Good heavens, yes!'

'Jolly. I like lots and lots of cushions.'

'I thought you did.'

There was a pause, while they both gazed out at the black night. The swish and churn of the great vessel charging through the waves filled their ears.

'I say,' he said, 'this is our last night.'

'Yes. I know that.'

'Of course you do. But I mean — what's going to happen?'

'What about?'

'You know perfectly well. What am I going to do?'

The dark eager face of Gregory floated between them.

'Nothing can happen. You know I'm on my way to marry Gregory. You've known that all the time.'

'But I know you better now than I ever knew that.'

'Not so well as you think then. Nothing you or anybody can do will stop me from marrying Gregory.'

'You don't love him.'

'Oh, yes, I do. Indeed I do!'

His face was close to her now, and he looked more like a faun than ever.

'You don't.'

She shivered.

'You are conceited and rather impertinent. I shall go to bed.' She began to get out of her rug.

'Please don't go,' he took her hand gently and urged her back on to her cushions. 'I promise not to say any more if it bothers you. Only please take back that remark about my being impertinent. I am conceited, I agree without a tremor, but impertinent! Till you take that back I shan't tuck you up, and you've tumbled all your rugs again.'

They talked into the night. Bruce was 'sensible' most of the time, but did allude to the subject of further meetings.

'I don't see how it can be managed. You see, I am going to stay with Gregory's aunt and cousin till we're married, and shall be entirely in their hands. They probably wouldn't understand a strange young man about. Besides, I think

Gregory might object. But after I'm married —'

'Oh, I can see you then?'

'Why not? Once Gregory's got me he can't say anything.'

Bruce laughed.

'That's a great relief. Hurry up and get married.'

'It's all settled, you know. Six weeks today. Aunt Bud is going to arrive just in time for it. She can only leave the business for a minute, poor darling, but it will be a holiday for her.'

'Then what?'

'Then abroad for three weeks, and then — settle down.'

'Where? You never told me.'

'I don't know. Gregory has taken a house somewhere in the country not too far from London. He's very excited about it and is getting it furnished and things now.'

'So I can run down and see you sometimes?'

'Why not?'

'I shall live for that.'

'Don't exaggerate. It doesn't suit you.'

'At the risk of being called impertinent I assure you that I'm not exaggerating. I can prove it at great length but I know you would only interrupt me, so what's the good?'

'No good at all,' she agreed.

But when they said 'good-night' long after all the other passengers had gone to bed, and the deck was deserted, he kissed her long and fervently. She did not protest, for, after all, who does not kiss on the last night of a voyage? It is as inevitable as packing your suitcase.

Yet it tangled up her dreams a good deal.

※

Gregory held her in his arms. The sight of him had driven everything else from her mind. Wonderful he seemed, strong and beautiful, something one could adore! Regardless of the slow movement of the taxi as it traced its way through the traffic they embraced — almost publicly. A steely blue eye flashed an arrow from a car that shot past them, and Roxy through half-closed lids noted that the car was a smart one and that the blue eye belonged to Bruce. She clung closer to Gregory, and the taxi, taking advantage of a hiatus on the near side, bumped them together with a good-natured clumsiness.

'Roxy, loveliest thing in the world! Lovelier even than I thought.' He gazed at her demure rose-leaf face.

'Oh, I look like hell after the journey. I must have a good doing at the hairdresser's tomorrow. The man on the boat made a horrible mess of me.'

They arrived at Aunt Marion's house in Woburn Place. She was in the hall to greet them, and gave Roxy a musky kiss. Someone else shook hands, but did not kiss her — Cousin Ruth, clad in russet and beads, thin-lipped and drooping, with pretty hair. She took Roxy up to her room and watched her take her hat off.

'Did you have a good journey?'

'Very, thank you.'

'Were there any possible people on board?'

Roxy smiled.

'Yes, one or two — quite possible.'

'I suppose you haven't many friends in London, as you have never been here before?'

'I don't think I've got any — at least — well, perhaps one — or two.'

'We've got several quite amusing engagements for you, but of course we shall be very busy getting ready for the wedding, shan't we?'

'I expect so.'

'Your house is lovely. Gregory and I had such fun furnishing it — but I promised him I wouldn't tell you about it.'

'Why not?'

'I think he wants it to be a surprise. You're not to see it till you're married.'

'How quaint. I'm sure it's fascinating.'

'Of course. Gregory has the most perfect taste.' She paused and smiled: 'In wives too,' she added.

'Oh, how nice of you to say that!' Roxy was really grateful and kissed Ruth impulsively. Ruth blushed. It had been an effort, and Roxy knew it. Already she knew it. She appreciated this moment of unbending from what Aunt Bud would certainly have described as a 'stiff'.

Gregory and Roxy would sometimes escape and go out shopping or in the Park together.

'Did you enjoy the books I sent you?' he asked her one day.

'Oh, yes. Lovely books. Such lots of them too.'

'Which did you enjoy most?'

'*The Green Hat*, I think.'

'*The Green Hat*! But, my dearest, I never sent you that!'

'Didn't you? I know I read it. It must have been Aunt Bud's, then. Sorry, darling, I thought it was one of yours.'

After all, he thought, why try to improve her when she was perfect? Perhaps Ruth and Aunt Marion had been at the back of his mind when he had sent her all those books — he had a vague idea of guarding her against criticism. Aunt Marion and Ruth judged everyone almost entirely by his taste in literature and his cults, though in the latter they did not themselves see eye to eye. Aunt Marion was a Theosophist and Ruth a Mental Scientist.

'But surely, my dear Roxy,' exclaimed Ruth one day, 'you don't believe in a Personal God!'

'Personal? I don't know.' Roxy was bewildered.

She still said the little prayers that as a baby she had murmured into Aunt Bud's ear, kneeling on her lap with her arms round her neck, sweet and warm after her bath.

They were only a part of the process of going to bed, but were presumably addressed to a God, Personal or otherwise.

'Prayers? My dear child, CONCENTRATE! It's the same thing. God is in yourself. CONCENTRATE, and nothing is beyond you. That's the faith that can remove mountains. I believe firmly that I can achieve *anything* I want if I concentrate enough.'

'Oh!' said Roxy.

'I'm afraid our poor little Roxy has a very small mentality,' mourned Aunt Marion to Ruth after Roxy, among several other appalling howlers, had asked whether Madame Blavatsky was an opera singer. 'I am a *little* bit anxious about the future. Gregory, with his finely tuned mind —'

'Gregory is not in love with her mentality.'

'I suppose not. Still, I don't really understand, to be quite frank, and between ourselves —'

'Sex, my dear mother,' said Ruth in a tight throaty voice.

'Oh, ah, yes, to be sure. Probably.' Aunt Marion had been so long in intimate communion with the shades that she had almost passed beyond the consciousness of human contacts.

'The child oozes sex,' furthered Ruth.

'Unpleasant,' sighed Aunt Marion, turning with relief to *The Quest*. 'Still,' she added, before she settled down to her spiritual food, 'she is an unusually beautiful girl, and I'm sure has a very sweet nature.'

'Quite a dear,' said Ruth's throat.

They were kind and helpful all through the time of preparation, and Roxy, who had never been patronised, was quite unconscious of the dominant note in their behaviour. She was dreadfully bored by the 'engagements' which Ruth had said would be amusing. All Aunt Marion's friends were cranks of some kind, and her daughter's had only comparative youth to mitigate their dreariness. They did not dance — not even the younger ones, but after dinner everyone sat and talked, and their conversation was to Roxy complete nonsense. Aunt Marion's greatest friend, who was often at Woburn Place, was Miss Hyde. It was not enough for her that Aunt Marion was a vegetarian. She always brought her own food in a packet — her wheat symposia, as she called it: sickening looking stuff, Roxy thought it; and she drank chestnut shell tea for her rheumatism. Her slogan, which she was continually hurling across the table at Roxy, was 'DEEP BREATHING! That's PRAYER, my child!' Roxy began to wonder what prayer really was.

Gregory was apologetic about all these people. They bored him extremely, especially when his only idea was to be alone with Roxy. This he seldom was. Their walks together were his happiest times, because indoors Aunt Marion and Ruth were always coming into the room unexpectedly. There was no peace for the lovers.

The house in Woburn Place puzzled Roxy. It seemed to her almost completely empty. She wondered when she first arrived whether they were so poor that they had had to sell their furniture, but she came to the conclusion that, as they apparently had plenty of food, and books and servants, they must really like it best that way. Ruth's room was papered a dull buff, and the curtains over the good generous windows were of green serge. Roxy felt quite ill when she first went into it. By Ruth's bed was a very dark oak table which seemed to Roxy to be falling to pieces. When she remarked upon it, Ruth said:

'Jacobean, my dear! Genuine! Gregory found it for me. He's got a nose for that period.'

Why should Gregory cultivate a nose for these tumbledown old things that Aunt Bud wouldn't allow even in the housemaid's closet? Roxy was conscious that she would only be displaying her ignorance if she pursued the subject, so she dropped it with:

'*Isn't* he clever?'

There were several little *contretemps*, during these three weeks, which gave Roxy an insight into English life. One unfortunate incident was a visit to the kitchen at two in the morning, foraging for food. She was hungry because there had been Irish stew for dinner, and one thing she could not manage even for Aunt Marion's sake (who didn't eat it, by the way) was Irish stew.

'Would you like a tin of biscuits by your bed, my dear Roxy?' asked Ruth the morning after this visit. Her manner was rather stern.

'Oh, no, thank you very much, Ruth. I never eat biscuits, except with cheese.'

'I understand from cook that you went to the kitchen last night and ate bread and cheese.'

Woburn Place seemed to gape at the enormity of the misdemeanour.

'Yes, I was hungry, and found some delicious cheese.'

'Well, cook is rather annoyed about it. You know, dear, it would be better not to do that again. You can always have something by your bed at night. Only say what you want.'

'But why is cook annoyed? I didn't do anything except take bread and cheese, which I found quite easily. I'm so sorry. I had no idea —'

Aunt Bud's pretty house in Woodstock was beautifully run by two faithful maids who were Roxy's great friends, and the idea of Grace or Charlotte being annoyed because Roxy satisfied her hunger in their kitchen at two in the morning was ludicrous. She had been very friendly with cook, and Amy, the housemaid, who looked after her at Woburn Place, and it was a blow to her that cook should be annoyed. Cook ought to be glad that Roxy had found such delicious cheese. That seemed to Roxy the only view for cook to take. She hinted this gently to Ruth, who blushed and said it was difficult to explain, and in fact did not attempt to do so.

Gregory said all these little things were of no importance whatever. The only thing that mattered was Roxy, and she wasn't to bother about cook or what anybody thought or did. This was all so sweeping that it wasn't much comfort to Roxy, who really wanted to be nice and not upset anyone. She had a very difficult piece of diplomacy to pull off in the matter of the pillow. The pillows of her bed, covered though they were with really beautiful linen cases, were, in Roxy's view, too hard and unsympathetic for sleep. They filled out the fine linen cases so completely that they slithered, and were always slithering away in the night, slithering away right on to the floor. Roxy was too polite to say anything about this discomfort, but she did go out and buy herself a small ear pillow at the Maison de Blanc.

'Hullo, a little pillow!' exclaimed Ruth throatily, seeing the pillow, smugly arranged by Amy in a prominent position.

'Yes, I left my little ear pillow behind, so I had to buy a new one!' Roxy breathed heavily. That diplomatic reply came to her all in a moment.

'Do you always use one?'

'Oh, yes,' cried Roxy fervently. 'I'm never without one. I don't know *how* I've managed all these nights.'

'Funny child!' Ruth gave her gurgling laugh. 'Such an old lady affair.'

This annoyed Roxy so much that she nearly said, 'Your pillows are dam hard. That's why!' But for a spoilt child she had great self-control.

It must be admitted that Gregory was rather dreading the incursion of Aunt Bud into the Aunt Marion ménage, more on account of Aunt Bud than anything else. He was fond of the genial lady who had brought Roxy up, and, though they had nothing whatever in common except Roxy, his

heart went out to her whenever he thought of her. Aunt Bud
fortunately insisted upon staying at an hotel during her visit,
which would last only a short ten days. She was bringing
with her the wedding gown which her girls had been
working at with devotion, so her arrival was of the utmost
importance. When she did arrive Gregory and Roxy met her.
She was tremendously smart in the right travelling clothes,
and her luggage was of the best and latest but not glaringly
new. Anyone would be proud to meet such a well turned
out lady, but Gregory's misgivings were not allayed, and he
responded to her resounding kiss with a sinking heart. He
was never really quite sure how graciously unpleasant his
own aunt might be.

Roxy lunched with Aunt Bud at her hotel. Ruth had chosen
a perfectly respectable and comfortable temperance hotel in
their own neighbourhood. As soon as lunch was over Aunt
Bud announced that she was moving to the Savoy, as she was
not going to spend her holiday drinking lemonade. This was
at once effected, and they passed the afternoon unpacking
in a luxurious room much more suited to her taste than the
dingily commodious apartment chosen by Ruth.

'Look here, my darling, why did they put me in that place?
Are they that kind?'

'Temperance? Well, Aunt Marion is. She's a vegetarian too,
and eats the most dreadful food, but Gregory drinks beer,
and I have a glass of white wine at dinner if I want it.'

'Hum. Beer. White wine. Well, we shall see. As long as
you're happy, my pet. Are you?'

'Oh, I adore Gregory.'

There was a slight reservation, and Aunt Bud felt it, but
she said nothing more. The wedding dress was now revealed.

'Aunt Bud! Oh, Buddie! how perfect. Do let me try it on.'

Aunt Bud nearly fainted.

'Try it on! My lamb! Not till your wedding morning.'

'Superstitious old Bud!'

'I should hope so. Sorry I haven't a family veil to lend you. I never had one myself, nor did your poor little mother, so I found you this.' She produced a film of Brussels lace which she laid on the wedding dress.

'And you don't try that on either.'

The wedding things were packed and taken in Aunt Bud's hired car to Woburn Place, where she was to dine with the family. An exhibition of the clothes eased the first bad quarter of an hour, and Aunt Marion and Ruth were able to be genuinely enthusiastic over the perfect taste of the gown and the beauty of the lace veil. Indeed, throughout dinner everyone was on tenterhooks of good behaviour. Aunt Bud was quiet and dignified, chiefly because the house depressed her almost to tears. She wore a well-cut black dress with some good jewellery. She had plenty of that. The general atmosphere of mutual toleration at all costs carried the evening to a successful conclusion.

Only in the hired car on the way to her hotel Aunt Bud indulged in a few tears. She grasped the situation in a moment. Those flat-footed women were patronising Roxy — and there was something else behind it. She had an idea what it was. But there was Gregory, he was all right. As much in love as anyone would wish. After all, Roxy was marrying *him*. And no one once in love with Roxy could ever be anything else, so there was no reason why Roxy shouldn't have a very good time, if she managed to keep those two Thin-lips at a respectful distance.

Aunt Bud very wisely did not impose herself too often upon Woburn Place. It was not so much wisdom, perhaps, as dislike of the atmosphere, which she found stifling and quite unlike anything she had ever had to endure before. She had had a short way with her parents who were stuffy in quite another manner. There had never been any question of staying in her own home a moment longer than was absolutely necessary, and since then she had lived the freelance existence which had made her what she was — a woman of the world with a sensitive heart still beating, and a keen, almost psychic, understanding of situations.

Two days before the wedding Aunt Bud and Roxy were walking in Bond Street, when a very strange thing happened. Roxy was gazing into Asprey's window, and her eyes were torn from the contemplation of a dressing-case that she would have preferred to the one Gregory was giving her, to encounter a blue flame — the eyes of Bruce Wynne.

There had been no communication between them since they landed. Roxy had asked this, and Bruce, with her promise to see him after her marriage, had respected her wish. But here he was, with his strange blue eyes, his high colour mounting, and his primrose hair, as he took off his hat, sleeker than ever under London discipline.

Roxy introduced Aunt Bud, and he turned and walked a little way with them. It was impossible to stand and talk at Asprey's corner. They went up Grafton Street and stood outside the Medici shop. Here some kind of conversation went on, but Roxy was not sure what they talked about. She gazed vaguely into the Medici window. Aunt Bud was being voluble, and all three of them seemed to be feverish. To Roxy it was like a dream; she wandered about in it letting the others talk. He asked them to lunch, and then she woke up and said No, they were lunching at home. Aunt Bud was evidently disappointed at this decision of Roxy's and questioned it.

'Oh, yes, Aunt Bud, we must go back. We must go back!' She took Aunt Bud's arm and dismissed Bruce with a sweet smile, watching him walk away with a strange, helpless emotion.

Aunt Bud hailed a taxi and they sat there holding hands.

'Goodness gracious!' Aunt Bud kept murmuring. 'Good gracious! What on earth? Good Lord!'

Then, as they settled down into a block, she said:

'Who is this? Why didn't you tell me about him?'

'Why should I, darling? I just met him on the boat and haven't seen him since.'

'Come now, you can't get away with that. He's in love with you, and you know it.'

'Well, why not? You must know what it is to have two people in love with you at once, don't you?'

'I certainly do.' Aunt Bud sent a pleasant backward glance into the past. 'But this — good Lord!'

'Now you're good-lording again. What's the matter?'

Aunt Bud turned and looked searchingly into Roxy's eyes.

'Don't you tell me —' was all she said. But she thought a great deal more. She hadn't lived all these years for nothing nor lived with all those different — well, had lots of experience anyway. If ever two people had flamed up — but she didn't dare to say it. After all, the wedding was the day after tomorrow, and it would be Roxy's business to — but of course it was too late. Damn it all, what was the girl thinking of?

The truth was that Aunt Bud had taken a violent fancy to Bruce. He was a type after her own heart — just what she would have chosen herself for Roxy — just the type she had loved in her young days. She was fond of Gregory, but she had always deplored his lack of smartness, and now she deplored his relations as well. She thought them terrible, as depressing as wet trees, and she didn't know how Roxy was going to bear it. After all, she couldn't spend *all* her time in Gregory's arms. When novelty wears off —

'Look here, Roxina,' she said when they were back at the Savoy. 'Tell me truthfully now and for ever. Do you really love Gregory enough to stand his people? There's still time — at least there isn't really, but it's a life and death question. Think, child! Don't just think of Gregory in bed. You can't be all your time there, you know. The Thin-lips will gather round you when the honeymoon's over.'

'Vulgar Bud!'

'Yes, vulgar Bud. But I'm a realist. You don't know what that is, and I'm not sure that I do. But someone once told me that I was one, and he was always right. I see you walking into what I should describe as a nest of vipers, and it's my duty to warn you. If you want to cry off this wedding now and marry that boy, I will work the whole thing for you. You're in love with him. Don't you tell me —'

'But I do tell you. I want Gregory. Honestly, Aunt Bud, I want Gregory.'

'That's your last word?'

'My last word, Bud, now and for ever.'

'Well, it saves a lot of trouble certainly. I shan't have to deal with those Thin-lips or disappoint poor old Gregory, who *is* in love with you, there's no doubt.'

'Of course. I couldn't let him down now, even if I wanted to. The house is all ready for me too.'

'Yes, this house! Where is it and why haven't I been taken to see it?'

'No one's to see it till we're married. Ruth's going to get it all fixed up finally while we're in Italy.'

'The devil she is ...'

Roxy, fond as she was of Aunt Bud, never obeyed her unless it was perfectly convenient. That night, when everyone had gone to bed, she tried on her wedding dress and veil, and practised the long train which was going to be carried by two weedy little nephews of Aunt Marion's. She was not superstitious.

'Silly Aunt Bud! As if this train didn't take hours to learn,' and she swept up and down her room for half an hour, with

Gregory and Bruce doing a seesaw in her mind all the time. She rather wished that Bruce might see her in this dress, which was really divine, but of course he wouldn't. She didn't know Aunt Bud had asked him to come to the church.

He was there. She spied him when it was all over and she went down the aisle on Gregory's arm, but she only got a keen shaft from his glinting eyes — he did not come to the house, nor did he even speak to Aunt Bud, who had given her away weeping and clad in exquisite *bois de rose*. She was tremendously well-dressed, as usual, but emotionally what she called a horrid mess. Who that had loved and cherished Roxy all these eighteen years could look unmoved upon her now, pale and elfin in her wedding garments? Not Aunt Bud. Besides, she was worried to death about the whole thing. The wrong man, she felt, was taking her Roxy from her. She could have smacked Bruce for his want of enterprise. She was in half a mind to cancel her sailing next week, and see how things shaped after the honeymoon. Perhaps better not interfere too much. Besides, there was the business, which was being run entirely in order that Roxy should have a good legacy when Bud popped off. There was no one really looking after it while she was in England …

Getting away was a terrible business, and even Roxy was glad when the pulp that was Aunt Bud was left derelict upon the platform at Victoria. It was so unkind to poor Gregory to cry, but it was really awful parting from Aunt Bud, specially as she was so upset.

They went straight through to Florence, and Roxy was delighted with the suite of rooms Gregory had engaged at the hotel. This was a very good beginning. They had a terrace of their own, where they were able to lunch in the fragrant spring sunshine, Roxy with her new squirrel wrap round her shoulders, as the April air was still fresh. Life was lovely. Florence was lovely. She wrote to Aunt Bud:

Darling Aunt Bud:

Florence is lovely. The hotel is so comfy. We drove up to Feazoly yesterday, quite a good car but the roads are rather bad. We spend the mornings looking at pictures (oils). Gregory is very keen on them. The Pity gallery is enormous, I don't think it ever comes to an end. I send you a card of one that Gregory says is like me. Do you think so? You will see her name is *Giovanna Tornabuoni*. What a name, poor thing! But mine is

Roxy Moore.

When Gregory took Roxy to see the Botticelli room at the Medici gallery he made her sit in front of the *Primavera*.

'Look, Roxy. There's a picture you must love. Look at the daybreak light! No one but Botticelli has ever got that mystic dawn light so perfectly. And that's Flora, wreathed in flowers on the right. She's rather like you, I think.'

Roxy was gazing at the picture, but she was not seeing the dawn light. Something queer was happening. She did not see Flora either, for suddenly Bruce appeared in her mind and hammered on her consciousness. Why suddenly did she think of Bruce? Gregory was delighted to see her so entranced.

'I knew you'd love this. I shall get you a Medici print of it.'

Medici! That was it. This was the picture she had been looking at that day, when Bruce and Aunt Bud were talking outside the Medici shop. Unconsciously she had noticed almost every detail, and how it had burnt itself into her mind!

'I don't like it, dear. I don't want a Medici print of it.'

'Don't like it! Roxy! Don't even whisper that. It's — it's almost blasphemous.'

'Sorry, Gregory darling. I've got very bad taste, I know.'

He was appeased when she admired everything else he wanted her to admire, which she made a point of doing.

These tiring mornings in the galleries bored her extremely, but she looked forward to the evenings, which had many compensations. She taught Gregory to dance, and he was as ready to learn as she was to go round the galleries with him. They were full of mutual accommodation, the main thing being that they were for present purposes a well-matched couple.

As the honeymoon faded away they went by easy stages through France, which Roxy did not enjoy so much. Some of the hotels were quite second-rate, with wretched bathrooms and hard pillows. The roads were good, however, and they had some splendid motoring, which involved the exploration of various cathedrals that Gregory simply had to see. When at last they arrived in London, Roxy was quite glad to get back to Woburn Place, where they stayed two nights before going to their new home in Essex.

Ruth was there finishing off. How devoted of Ruth! 'Dear Ruth, she has so enjoyed getting it all ready for you,' said Aunt Marion as they sat at dinner.

'It's very sweet of her,' agreed Roxy. 'I'm so excited about it and longing to see it.'

'Tomorrow I shall take you home,' said Gregory rather sententiously.

An air of finality about that.

They motored down in Gregory's new two-seater, a wedding present from Aunt Marion and Ruth. It was not frightfully comfortable — still, it was a car. Ruth had arrived at Woburn Place in the morning. She had installed the household and ordered dinner at Dove's End. Roxy had interviewed the servants before she was married, but Ruth had engaged them. There were only two maids besides the gardener-chauffeur, and she hoped they would be like Grace and Charlotte.

They were only an hour from London, and arrived at Dove's End in the afternoon. Roxy cried out when she saw the house, which was two cottages, half-timbered and gabled. Thatched porches sheltered the two front doors, and a sun-dial, flanked by a crazy pavement, stood in the middle of the prim little garden. A huge elm tree towered on one side of the house, half concealing an old barn converted into a garage.

'Oh, Gregory! What a pet! And a front door each.'

She did not object in the least when Gregory took her up in his arms and carried her over the threshold of her new home, though the two maids were waiting in the hall to greet them and it must have looked rather silly. The hall was a big room, and tea was ready for them there, shining silver on a dark oak table.

'Will you have tea first, or shall I show you round?'

He was so evidently dying to show her round first that she said tea could wait, though she was tired and thirsty. The hall turned out to be the principal living-room. There was a small dining-room looking out on the back, which was a formal garden ending in railings with a field beyond — 'their field'. The dining-room was dark and furnished with oak. A black dresser was covered with pewter. The chairs were Windsor chairs. The room was exactly like one of the rooms they had looked at in the South Kensington Museum. (Oh, yes, Gregory had taken her all round the museums.)

'It's all absolutely the period,' breathed Gregory.

'What period?'

'Jacobean, of course.'

'Oh, of course.' Who was this Jacob?

Upstairs was a beautiful bedroom with a high roof and crooked beams, rather like an old church.

'Only the bed is baroque,' Gregory said, apologetically almost.

'Baroque! What fun!' It was a high four-poster with spiral posts, like dark barley sugar, Roxy thought, and a fine old embroidered tester and curtains. Quickly, when Gregory's back was turned, she punched the pillows. Not bad, but she'd known softer. She had feared that perhaps Jacob was responsible for the springs too, but they were evidently modern.

'And this Court cupboard has been tinkered up a bit and converted to hang your dresses.'

A dear old thing, but of course no long glass and as inconvenient as possible.

'And this hutch is more Gothic than Jacobean.'

'Hutch!'

'For your hats, I thought.'

'Oh, I see, very quaint.'

Downstairs in the hall she looked round more particularly, and concluded that the furnishing of it was not finished. Tentatively she said:

'And the hall? All ready for us?'

'Yes, everything but the spinning-wheel. This is your daybed. I had a wonderful bit of luck finding that.'

It was oak and leather, and lay under a window, stark and cushionless. Then her mind woke up. Where were the easy chairs? Oak, oak, oak everywhere, and not a cushion to be seen. Well, she would alter all that in time. Meanwhile, here was tea which would be very welcome. It was good, and there were some delicious home-made cakes. Come, this was not so bad.

The May evenings were cool and a log fire had been lit in the old brick fireplace. After tea they sat in the chimney corner and life seemed quite worthwhile again, though they *were* sitting on what Gregory called a 'settle', which Roxy thought a very bad name for such a hard seat.

When she went up to dress for dinner she found instead of her gold teagown an unknown and voluminous garment of pale powder blue laid out for her.

'Do you mind, darling, wearing this? I had it copied for you from an old seventeenth century picture. It is simply made for you, and you will look so wonderful sitting there in the candlelight.'

Candlelight! Is it possible there is no electric light? Well, if Gregory wanted fancy dress she didn't mind, as long as it wasn't too unbecoming. The old style with its full sleeves and trim bodice, from which her neck and shoulders emerged as white as the broad lace of its collar, was not unbecoming at all, she had to admit to herself, as she put on the little pink slippers with their shoe-roses. But still, what about putting on a record and having a foxtrot after dinner? But was there a gramophone? She didn't remember seeing one.

There wasn't one. Gregory promised to get a Jacobean model when he saw how disappointed she was. So Jacob did make gramophones after all.

Gregory began going up to town for his publishing, and drove Roxy up one day. She went to Marshall and Snelgrove and bought three glorious cushions for the daybed and one long one to put in front of the fire. They arrived next morning and when Gregory came home they were all set out, brightening up the hall considerably, she thought. Gregory's 'Oh, my dear!' was involuntary, but he checked himself and said cheerfully, 'Where did these come from?'

Then on Sunday Ruth came down to lunch. Roxy was upstairs when she arrived, and as she got to the stair-head she heard Ruth exclaim:

'Greg, my dear! What are these frightful cushions doing here? Oh, no, my dear boy, no, *no*, NO!'

Gregory replied self-consciously and in a low voice:

'They're Roxy's purchase. I think she finds the day-bed rather hard.'

'Heavens! Darling Roxy, of course it's very natural. What handsome cushions too. We might cover them with some dark linen and they would scream a little bit less.'

Roxy turned and went back to her room. She did not want to embarrass them by appearing too soon. She was unhappy about those cushions being so wrong, because they were the joy of her life — the only sympathetic things in the whole of that carefully furnished house.

'I must be wrong,' she mused, regarding herself in the mirror with a frown. 'And yet Gregory doesn't seem to mind.' She cheered up and went downstairs. Ruth and Gregory were poring over a book, some new publication of Gregory's, and Ruth was talking jargon about formats and founts. They went on talking about them after Roxy had kissed Ruth, and they sat down to lunch talking about them, which Roxy thought was rather rude. Gregory did try to change the subject, but Ruth always went back to it. There was a distinct air of superiority about Ruth today, which Roxy had never noticed before. She supposed it was the cushions.

'Well, little Roxy,' said Ruth when they were alone after lunch. 'Of course you like your little house.'

'Of course. Look, the spinning-wheel arrived yesterday. It just fills up that bare corner.'

'You don't like bare corners, do you?'

Roxy shot a quick glance at her.

'Not too many of them. How do you know?'

'I guessed,' laughed Ruth in her throat.

There was something rather unpleasant about Ruth today. Roxy wished she would go. Those cushions were becoming more challenging every moment. They almost hurled themselves at Ruth, and Roxy began to feel that there was nothing else in the room. But Ruth said nothing about them. There was a glint, however, in her eye when she waved at Roxy as Gregory drove her off to the station.

'I'm not sure that I care very much for Ruth after all,' she thought, as she waited in the sad twilight for Gregory's return.

Dora came in to light the fire, and Roxy was glad to see her cheerful rosy face. The maids were a great success, and were devoted to Roxy from the first. She was not at all a usual mistress, though she had a natural gift for keeping house, which did not involve interference or prying. Her friendliness was almost disarming at first, till they got used to it. She was dreadfully afraid they must be bored in that remote place, so far from pictures or theatres, and without wireless to colour the long evenings. Gregory was firm on this subject. Nothing would induce him to accept wireless in his Jacobean house. The gramophone was as far as he would go, and that was against his principles. Roxy, lonely on days when he went to town, would teach Maud and Dora to foxtrot, and when she found that they were both 'walking out' she suggested to Gregory that they should have a little dance for them every now and then in the evening. Gregory only said:

'Please, darling! Our sacred evenings!'

So she asked them on a Saturday afternoon when Gregory was playing golf with his partner, Mr Moule. The young gardener and his wife came too, and they all danced till nearly seven, when Gregory came in with Mr Moule, and the servants retired embarrassed to the kitchen. Roxy was flushed but not embarrassed. She had thoroughly enjoyed the afternoon. The young men were extremely nice, and they knew how to dance, and she was pleased that Maud and Dora had obviously been happy. So it was rather depressing to find Gregory really angry for the first time since their marriage.

'Supposing visitors had come while it was going on!'

Visitors had begun to come with disturbing frequency — mostly long-toothed women in dun clothes accompanied by dogs.

'Yes, that would have been a bore. I should have had to see them.'

It would certainly have been difficult for Dora to say 'not at home' under the circumstances.

'That's not what I mean. I mean, what on earth would they have thought?'

'That we were all enjoying ourselves very much, I should hope.'

But Gregory was seriously annoyed, chiefly, Roxy thought, because Mr Moule had been a witness of the distressing scene.

'Besides, I don't like these young men in the house. You never know —'

'But they're most respectable young men. One's a postman and the other's in Roberts' Stores.'

'That isn't quite the point. If they begin coming here when they like, where will it end?'

'Well, of course, if you don't let me entertain them, I don't know where it *will* end. They must meet somehow, and I should have thought that this would be the best place.'

'Why *must* they meet?'

'Because they're engaged, of course. Only I hope they won't get married yet, because they are both such darlings.'

'Hardly darlings, but very nice girls. But as for their being engaged, what they call walking out is hardly being engaged.'

'Well, darling Gregory, if you must know the truth, it amuses me to have them in to dance. I love dancing, and I haven't had much of it since we were married.'

'I'm afraid you are dreadfully bored,' he said in a boring voice. 'Here we are married only four months, and already you're bored. You ought to see more people. Why don't you get to know some of the people round here?'

'I haven't seen anyone that might amuse me. By the way, there was a man on board called Bruce Wynne who would like to see this place. Shall I ask him down?' - What nonchalance!

Gregory, alarmed by her evident depression, jumped at the idea.

'Do! Ask him to lunch on Sunday. Is he interested in old things?'

'Tremendously!'

'Splendid. I shall enjoy showing him round.'

Bruce came to lunch on Sunday, and cleverly brought his sister, Mrs Stretton, who was like him and very pretty. Roxy was delighted to find that Bruce really was interested in old things, and showed such a knowledge of Jacobean furniture that Gregory was won. He admired all the right things, and was specially enthusiastic about the daybed. Roxy caught an impish glance as he turned over the Marshall cushions and examined the leather underneath them.

'Not a trace of restoration. 'S the best I've ever seen. Just the right thing for you, Mrs Moore.'

What a little devil! He knew quite well it wasn't.

Mrs Stretton was much the nicest woman Roxy had met since she came to England, and when they left they invited Gregory to bring Roxy to lunch at Claridge's next week. Gregory was not very keen on Claridge's, but with Roxy's new phase in mind he gladly accepted.

The lunch was only the beginning of a series, which brightened Roxy's life, but soon bored Gregory, whom nobody missed when he pleaded pressure of work. And one day Mrs Stretton had a headache, and Roxy and Bruce lunched alone.

'You see what patience will do,' he said. 'Three weeks since we came down to Dove's End, and I haven't been alone with you for a second. Is your marriage happy?'

This before the cocktails were taken away!

'Very!'

'Good. Now, what shall we eat?'

She knew he wasn't in the least impressed by her emphatic 'Very.' Patience! Yes, he had patience. She herself had none. Ruth — she didn't want to think about Ruth. Ruth, she felt, was concentrating rather hard.

Bruce was much too wise to allude to anything personal

after Roxy's 'Very,' and so general did their conversation become that she had no hesitation in going to see his flat in Chelsea after lunch. It looked over the river to Battersea and was on the top floor as all good flats should be. An enchanting room with a huge bow-window — a lived-in room with nothing but beautiful things in it and no atmosphere of the South Kensington Museum. And there was the divan, black and tarnished gold and silver. 'I love your room!'

'So glad. It's fairly successful. Rather empty.'

'It's very full compared to Dove's End.'

'I think Dove's End is very full."

Such a funny, detached way of making love — looking out coldly at the river all the time. They had some tea, and he put Roxy in a taxi when it was time for her to go and pick up Gregory at the office. She knew quite well how much Bruce wanted to make love to her, and she admired his originality in not creating an ordinary situation out of her visit to his flat. Only as he put her in the taxi he said:

'You know I'm always here if you want me. Always.'

As Gregory asked no questions about lunch she didn't tell him she had been alone with Bruce. Ruth joined them at the office with a suitcase. She was coming for a visit and Aunt Marion was arriving tomorrow. Roxy was rather nervous about it.

They all three bunched into the two-seater.

'How are your smart friends?' asked Ruth.

'Which?'

'The well-groomed young man and his sister. I forget their names.'

Ruth had met them in the office, and until now had not alluded to them.

'Oh, all right. Such dears!'

'What sort are they? I couldn't make out.'

'What sort? Oh, good sort.'

'I mean socially. What set are they in? They evidently have plenty of money, but I couldn't place them. Are they —?'

'Oh, yes,' cried Roxy, who had no idea what Ruth meant except that she meant to sneer.

'They're related to half the peerage,' said Gregory with cold emphasis. 'I looked them up.'

So Gregory looked up people too. He was always saying, 'I'll look it up,' and rushing to a bookshelf.

Aunt Marion had not been down to Dove's End since the marriage and she was full of enthusiasm.

'What taste Gregory has, hasn't he Roxy! You must be proud of your perfect little house. What a lovely daybed! I *think*, though, that I personally should prefer it *without* the cushions. Not quite in the period, are they? I think he's made a mistake there.'

Put up to that by Ruth, thought Roxy, who said aloud:

'Personally I prefer it *with*. I expect you would too, if it was the only more or less comfortable thing you had to sit on.'

Aunt Marion's eyebrows went up. Wasn't Roxy becoming a tiny bit aggressive? Mildly and sweetly she said:

'Of course, dear, I understand. You like to be comfortable, I know.'

Aunt Marion never lost her temper or her poise. It was part of her religion, and most trying for other people. Roxy underwent a really bad crisis during this visit. The two Thin-lips and Gregory seemed to merge into the atmosphere of the house. It had been a hostile atmosphere from the first, and now these people were all drawn into it. The house belonged to them. They were all angular, uncomfortable people. There wasn't a bit of padding to their minds: they were as polished and glossy as the chairs. And Gregory seemed changed. She was tempted to tell Aunt Bud about the Thin-lips, but her aunt's letters were already so full of ill-concealed anxiety that she refrained from upsetting her any more. Gregory really was changed. He was taking things for granted — recovering from the ecstatic wonder of their love. Only in the night was he sometimes the Gregory she had fallen in love with, but even the nights were losing their glamour for her. Really she had reached the end of his mystery. Bed was becoming as commonplace as breakfast.

'I don't think you love me any more,' she said one morning when he was starting late for town and gave her rather a hurried kiss.

'My darling Roxy, what nonsense! I adore you, you know quite well. But we can't always be honeymooning. I must get some work done. I've neglected everything since we were married.'

But Roxy wanted to be always honeymooning. She did not see what was the good of being married otherwise.

Gregory was over-serious, Aunt Marion over-polite, and Ruth was becoming more sarcastic every day. She hardly troubled to conceal her contempt for Roxy, and when Gregory was not there she was occasionally offensive.

At last Roxy complained to Gregory.

'If Ruth can't hide the fact that she hates me, it would be much better for her to go back to Woburn Place, wouldn't it?'

'My dear child! Hate you? Ruth is devoted to you. She has a queer way sometimes, I know, but that means nothing.'

'Then you say she is to stay however rude she is to me?'

'Of course she must stay as long as she likes. You must get that idea out of your head. You are really full of fancies nowadays. Nothing is farther from Ruth's mind than to be rude to you. I know her too well not to be sure of that.'

'You do know her well, there's no doubt about that. But perhaps you don't really know her as well as I do. She's changed completely to me since we were married. She was never really nice to me, but now she's perfectly horrid, and I wish, if she's going to stay, you'd ask her to pretend to like me, at any rate while she's a guest in my house.'

Roxy cried. Gregory was concerned, and decided to speak to Ruth, though he was sure she had not meant to be unkind. Poor little Roxy was in a queer state. Perhaps —

He ventured his supposition.

'No, I'm *not* going to have a baby, thank goodness, and it's not my imagination about Ruth. Please tell her to go or behave herself.'

This was extremely awkward. He went to Ruth's room and told her exactly what had happened.

'Silly child,' she exclaimed, blushing scarlet all the same. 'She must know I am devoted to her. I am so sorry, Greg dear. I'll make a point of being specially nice to her. Of course, I'd no idea she had got such a fantastic notion in her head. You can imagine that the last thing I would wish to do is to hurt her feelings.'

Gregory was completely satisfied with this. He was so sure of Ruth, with whom he had lived all his life without ever finding her out. Ruth was more polite with Roxy as a result of this interview, but there was a sneer behind her politeness that Roxy could not endure.

'Look here,' she said again to Gregory two days later. 'Will you ask Aunt Marion to go back to Woburn Place tomorrow? Ruth is just as bad as ever, though she's not so rude. Will you send them away?'

'But my darling Roxy, I can't do that. Aunt Marion is like my mother, and Ruth —'

'Your sister, I suppose.'

'Yes, that is what I was going to say.'

'Then you won't send them away?'

'I really can't send them away. Perhaps they will go back next week. I'll try to arrange that. You must try to be patient —'

'Patient! Everybody's much too patient! Very well,' she said. 'Do as you like.'

There was such a change in her tone that Gregory looked up.

'What's the matter?'

'Oh, nothing. Let them stay.'

'That's right. I'm glad you're going to be sensible about it. Wise Roxy.'

'Yes, I'm getting quite wise.'

✳

She ran away. The next day she ran away.

She left a note for Gregory:

Gregory Dear:

I can't be Jacobean. I think I am bamboo or something that doesn't go with your period.

I'm not coming back, but I know you'll be all right. I can see your life all mapped out for you, and you'll be much happier with the right person, which isn't

Roxy.

He found this when he came back from town with Ruth. Aunt Marion had been out all day with Miss Hyde, and was not coming back till the evening. He gave the note to Ruth, and went without a word to his room and locked himself in.

Ruth read the note, the blood rushing from her heart to her head, and from her head to her heart. He had looked at her as he went upstairs, and she knew that he hated her. A great sickness came over her. 'The faith that removes mountains.' The god in her suddenly shrivelled and she felt feebly mortal. Roxy had been too clever. She had run away much, much too soon, before Gregory had begun to get tired of her.

Aunt Marion came back and found an apparently empty house. Ruth and Gregory were locked in separate solitudes, and Roxy had disappeared. 'Very strange.'

But Aunt Marion alone took a bright view of the situation. She was sure, though she did not say so immediately, that all was for the best, and she kissed Ruth's tear-stained face with optimistic fervour.

✳

When Bruce came home to his Chelsea flat that evening he found Roxy asleep on the black divan with tarnished gold and silver cushions.

'Ah! Sh — hya — ya at last,' he said, as he kissed her awake.

Notes on *Tatting* and *Mandolinata*

BY KATE MACDONALD

Tatting

Chapter One

interesting condition: a coy Victorian euphemism for being pregnant.

Cremorne: the old nineteenth-century Cremorne pleasure gardens, that lay between Chelsea Harbour and the King's Road.

baked letters: letters from scarlet fever patients were baked in a low oven before being sent, to avoid spreading infection.

cotta: a short white surplice, worn over everyday clothes by choristers.

Lancer's uniform: a striking black and red military uniform.

ADC: Amateur Dramatic Club, a Cambridge University student society, founded in 1855.

been eating dinners: part of the process of reading for the Bar and becoming a barrister at one of the Inns of Court.

St Mary Magdalene, Paddington: a late nineteenth-century Anglican church in north-west London, with a strong Anglo-Catholic or High Anglican history.

St Alban's, Holborn: another nineteenth-century London parish church, with possibly even Higher leanings than St Mary Magdalene. The first Perpetual Curate of St Alban's introduced elaborate Anglo-Catholic liturgical ritual and the hearing of confessions, as well as a strong programme of social work and poverty relief in the neighbouring slums.

Little Church Around the Corner: a nineteenth-century Episcopal church in New York City, strongly Anglo-Catholic in its ritual and service to the poor.

'A bone in me leg': a traditional English folk saying, often used in mockery of someone trying to avoid a task or effort.

shieling: in this context the Scots name for a shepherd's hut in the hills, usually little more than one room and a fireplace.

frowst: a thick atmosphere contributed to by smoke from the fire, pipe smoke (shag) and humidity from drying garments and wet dogs.

Windsor chair: a cushionless wooden chair designed for sitting upright in at a table, rather than reclining in in comfort.

Chapter Two

notorious: the Reverend Sandys Wason, on whom Father St John was based, had gained a reputation in the church for his notoriously single-minded Anglo-Catholic practices in an otherwise Low Church parish.

Eights Week: four days of boat races between the colleges of Oxford University, that always take place in the fifth week of Trinity term, in May.

hideous gargoyle: John's rooms at Oxford were undoubtedly in an older part of his college where the gargoyles were less decorative than preventative.

Chapter Three

Asperges: the ritual act of sprinkling with holy water.

half-ripe blackberry: a flushed deep red.

do it on purpose to annoy: quotation from *Alice in Wonderland*.

'Up guards and at 'em': an old saying associated with a command made by the Duke of Wellington at the Battle of Waterloo in 1815, but is likely to have been in use before that.

LSD: abbreviation for pounds, shillings and pence (pre-decimal pennies were abbreviated to 'd').

towans: a Cornish term for sand dunes, but used more on the north coast than the south coast where Gunwalloe and Cury are.

redding up: dialect for cleaning and setting a room to rights.

mesembryanthemum: a desert-loving succulent with a brightly coloured, many-petalled daisy-like flower.

other cure: Father St John is responsible for two parishes.

rubber: Father St John and his dummy hand have won both games of bridge to win the rubber.

Chapter Four

Band of Mercy, Band of Hope: the Band of Mercy was an early animal welfare organisation, whereas the Band of Hope was and still is a Christian charity working to end alcohol and drug abuse by young people.

The Duchy: the royal Duchy of Cornwall is the possession of the eldest child of the reigning monarch, with its own rights and legal privileges.

the jingle: the small open carriage driven by Miss Want.

Chapter Six

Winsor and Newton: manufacturers and purveyors of fine art supplies for nearly two hundred years.

Chapter Seven

a fly: a covered carriage.

Bromo: a type of lavatory paper.

Chapter Nine

knocked her up: knocked at her door loud enough to wake her.

logorrhea: uncontrollable loquacity, of indifferent quality.

a budget: a large number of letters.

Mandolinata

1 The Angle of Error

Spiaggia: An invented Italian seaside resort called 'Beach', probably based on the author's life in Capri.

cicale: Italian, cicadas.

jalousies: louvred windows, where the panes can be tilted to admit air.

giovannott': Italian, young man.

buttarmi via: Italian, throw me away, cast me out.

figlio mio: Italian, my son.

Per Bene: Italian, For Good.

inglese pazzi: Italian, crazy English.

Vicin' 'o mare: the opening lines of the refrain to *Vicin' 'o mare*, 'Near the sea', a traditional Neapolitan song.

gente per bene: Italian, good people.

antipatico: Italian, unfriendly.

Dio mio: Italian, my god.

Ebbene: Italian, well.

2 Mandolinata

maresciallo: Italian, marshal or officer.

Lungo-lungo: Italian, Long-long.

Carin' assai! Com' ha fatto bene il Signorin' Suicidio!: Italian, So lovely! How well Signor Suicide has done.

modo signorile: Italian, gentlemanly manner.

3 La Bonne Mine

Oui, c'est moi – tel comme l'autre: French, Yes, that's me. They say I was handsome at that age. That's my sister – we were very alike.

Ma proprio un amore: Italian, Really, a darling.

Un ragazzo per bene: Italian, A good boy.

accanitamente: Italian, fiercely.

Ma, pero, fui contenta – del primo ordine: Italian, But I was happy about this, because he started to bore me, very, very much. Really annoying.

mortificata assai assai: Italian, Really, really mortified.

corteggiante: Italian, he who had been courting her.

brutta figura: Italian, a bad figure.

simpaticone: Italian, Appealing, a friendly guy.

E molto scrupuloso: Italian, And very scrupulous.

Un ragazzo molto fino: Italian, A very fine boy.

Ci piace assai: Italian, We like him a lot.

Magna Graecia: the Imperial Roman name for the Greek-speaking colonies in southern Italy, which included Calabria.

Il faut avoir toujours la bonne mine: French, You should always put a good face upon things.

Com' é simpatico, quell' signorin': Italian, How nice he is, that gentleman.

Pardon pour hier soir: French, Apologies for yesterday evening.

4.1 Miss Mabel Ebony

casetta: Italian, cottage.

buona passeggiata: Italian, Have a good walk.

Ecco la signorina inglese: Italian, That's the English lady.

marinaio: Italian, boatman.

Vieni sul mar! … tuo marinar!: refrain of an Italian song first recorded by Enrico Caruso in 1905, 'Come to the sea! Come for a row. Feel the intoxication of your sailor!'.

Two Lovely Black Eyes: Edwardian music-hall song.

4.2 Lillie in Rome

Favorisca, signora!: Italian, Your favour, Madam.

salotta: Italian, the living-room.

5 The Suit

Che bellezza: Italian, How beautiful.

Evviva il nostro caro Signorin'!: Italian, Long life to our dear Signor'.

Facciamo la festa del pov' Angelo: Italian, Let's celebrate poor Angelo.

Boje moy: Russian, My god.

6 The Wedding Present

terza rima: a complex form of verse in which the first and third lines of each three-line stanza rhyme, and the same rhyme travels to the next stanza in a different position.

Guy Hardlot: Guy d'Hardelot was the pen-name of Helen Guy, a French pianist and composer. Her then most famous song was 'Because', which had been recorded by Enrico Caruso in 1912 and released as a record in 1913.

Mais, c'est épatant!: French, But, it's amazing!

9 Queer Lady

fairy: a Victorian name for a showgirl or a prostitute.

12 Children of God

Piano, piano: Italian, very quietly.

13 Cushions

tucked up: Roxy is lying in a deckchair on board an ocean liner, wrapped up warmly in rugs against the breeze.

The Green Hat: a celebrated bestseller of the 1920s by Michael Arlen.

Madame Blavatsky: a Russian-American mystic who co-founded the Theosophical Society in 1975, and was revered by her followers.

ear pillow: a soft pillow with a hole in the centre, like a doughnut, to allow sleep without putting pressure on the ear.

Feazoly, Pity: Fiesole and the Pitti, one of the great Florentine art museums of the Renaissance.

Latchkey Ladies

Marjorie Grant

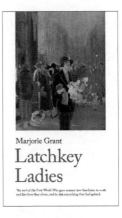

Marjorie Grant
Latchkey
Ladies

The end of the First World War gave women new freedom, to work and live they chose, and to risk everything they had gained.

Maquita Gilroy is a Government clerk with a lively sense of self-preservation.

Anne Carey is drifting between jobs, bored of her fiancé, and longing for something to give her life meaning. Then she meets Philip Dampier, a married man whose plays she admires.

Petunia Garry, a beautiful teenage chorus girl with no background and dubious morals, is swept up by an idealistic soldier, who is determined to mould her into what he wants his wife to be.

Gertrude Denby, an Admiral's daughter and an endlessly patient companion to an irritating employer, is so very tired of living out her life in hired rooms.

These latchkey ladies live in London at the end of the First World War. They are determined to use their new freedoms, but they tread a fine line between independence and disaster.

> 'Fear woke her in the defenceless hour of dawn. She sat up in bed and faced it at last, shivering so that her teeth chattered, but valiant. She was certain that she was going to have a child.'

With an Introduction by Sarah LeFanu, author of *Rose Macaulay* (2003), and *Dreaming of Rose* (2021), *Latchkey Ladies* is a powerful and moving novel from 1921, about the lives and choices of single women. Marjorie Grant was a Canadian novelist and reviewer, and a close friend of Rose Macaulay. *Latchkey Ladies* was her first novel.

The Outcast and The Rite

Stories of Landscape and Fear, 1925–38

Helen de Guerry Simpson

The long forgotten Australian author Helen de Guerry Simpson (1897-1940) was a prize-winning historical novelist, and wrote uncanny terror like a scalpel applied lightly to the nerves. She published many supernatural short stories before her untimely death in 1940 in London. This new edition selects the best of her unsettling writing. Featured stories about historic structures with intentions of their own include:

- 'Young Magic', in which Viola's secret invisible childhood friend gives her terrifying supernatural powers.
- 'As Much More Land', in which an Oxford undergraduate challenges a haunted bedroom to scare him.
- 'Teigne', in which a house with a curse is stripped of all its fittings.
- 'Disturbing Experience of an Elderly Lady', in which a new-made widow buys the house she has always longed for.

The Introduction is by Melissa Edmundson, senior lecturer at Clemson University, South Carolina, a leading scholar of women's Weird fiction and supernatural writing from the early twentieth century.